BOOKS BY J. C. MCKENZIE

The Lark Morgan Series

Death Stealer *(prequel)*

Death Maker

Death Raiser

Death Taker

Isle and Eyrie Series

Cormorant Run

Heir of the Eyrie

House of Moon and Stars

The Night House

House of Chaos

Crawford Investigations

Conspiracy of Ravens

Nevermore

Queen of Corvids

The Call of Corvids

From the Shadows

Into the Fire

Dark Legacy

Embrace the Flame

The Carus Series

Shifter (Shift Happens)

Beast (Beast Coast)

Demonic (Carpe Demon)

Cursed (Shift Work)

Carus (Beast of All)

Obsidian Flame

Dangerous Dreams

Dangerous Liaisons

Dangerous Decisions

That Old Black Magic

The Good Griffin

Standalones

Immortal Throne (with Harper A. Brooks)

Call of the Deep (The Shucker's Booktique)

Stormbound (Be My Love)

MARKED

J. C. McKenzie

COPYRIGHT INFORMATION

Marked

Contact Information: jcmckenzie@jcmckenzie.ca

Cover Art: Hannah Sternjakob

Character Art: Koti Komori

Publishing History:

First JCM Publications Edition, 2024

ISBN: 978-1990143-48-9 (print)

ISBN: 978-1990143-49-6 (ebook)

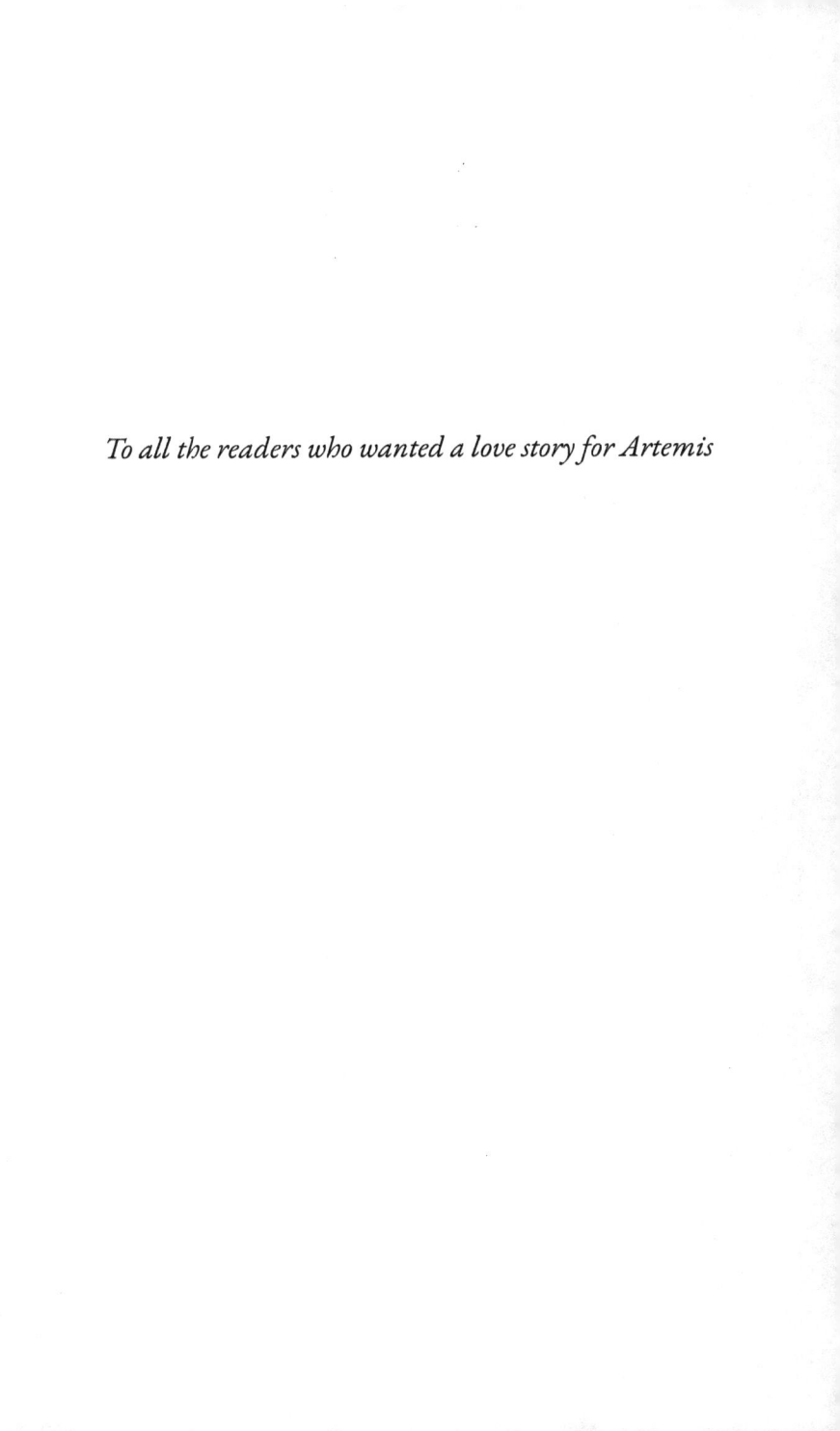

To all the readers who wanted a love story for Artemis

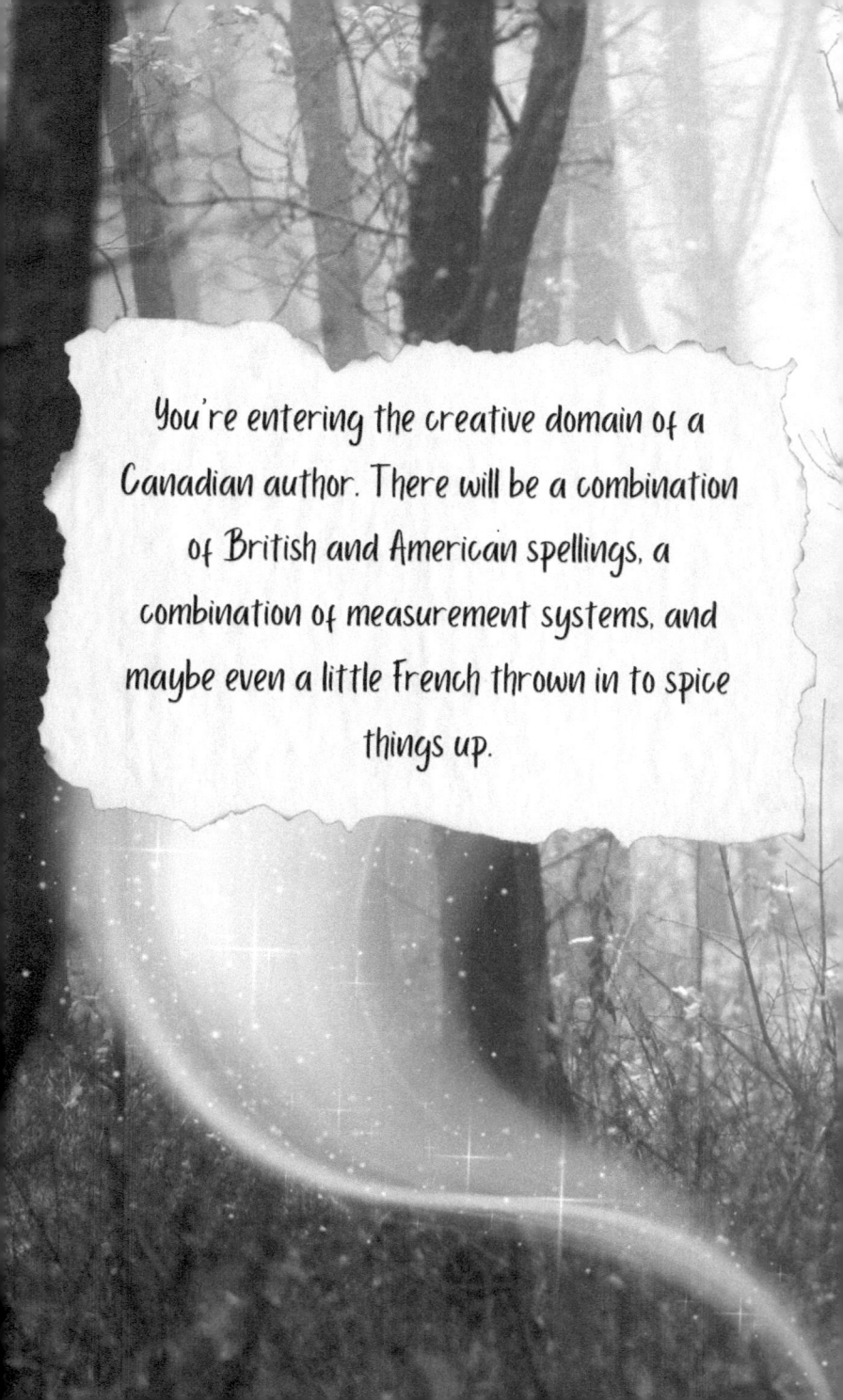

You're entering the creative domain of a Canadian author. There will be a combination of British and American spellings, a combination of measurement systems, and maybe even a little French thrown in to spice things up.

This book contains explicit language, death, violence, mention of child abuse and neglect (occurs in the past, off page), general assholery, and animal harm, injury and death (hunting for food).

Please read with care.

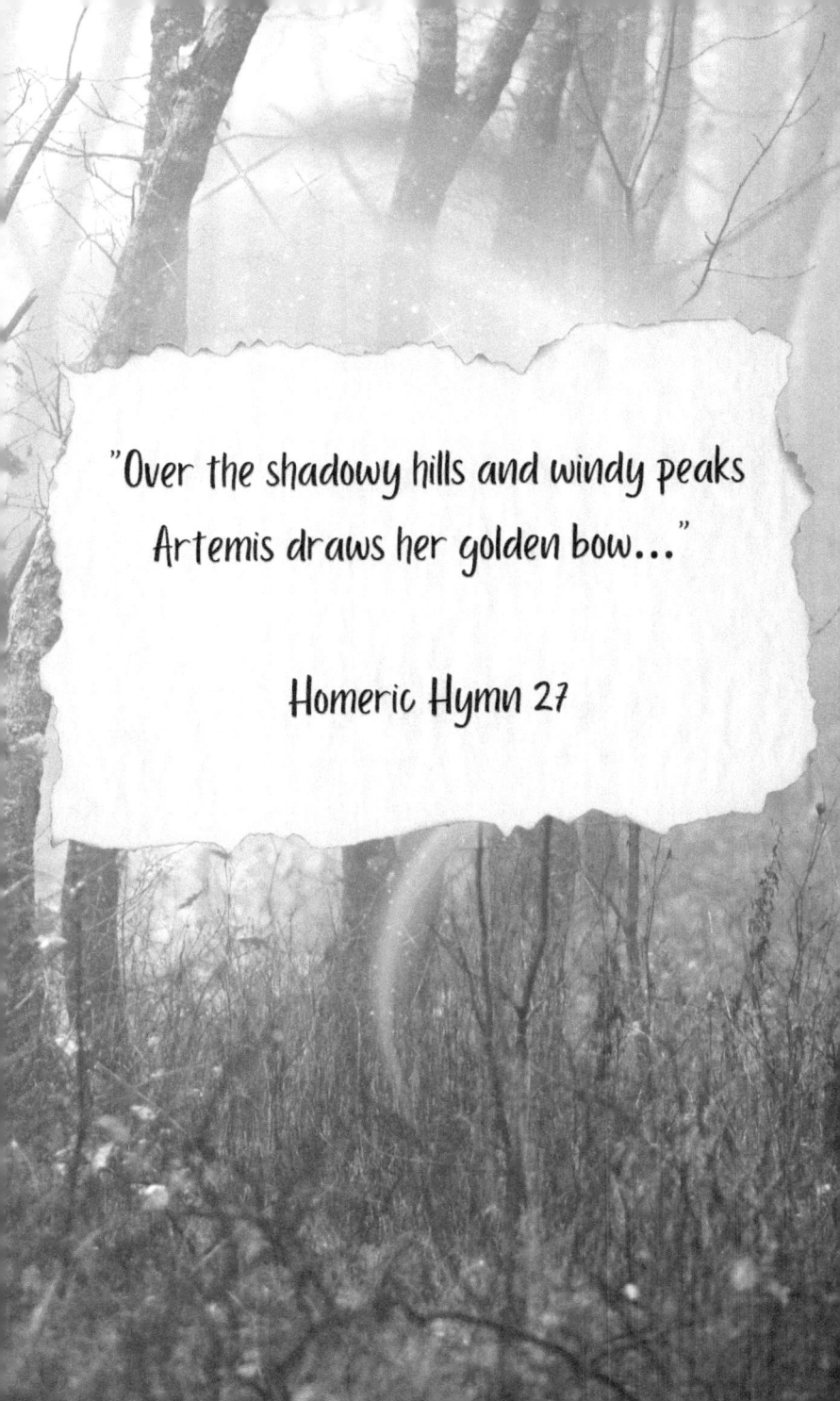

"Over the shadowy hills and windy peaks
Artemis draws her golden bow…"

Homeric Hymn 27

I

All that crap could've been summarized in a single message. This entire trip was a waste of my phaaning time.

Rain splattered on my head and dripped down my face as I stomped through the forest bordering the nymph-infested river of Danu. I always left the city of Wast feeling dirty.

The broken buildings of the once thriving metropolis cast a long shadow over the river and surrounding forest as a reminder of the days before the phaanon and galeon war.

Though most of the city had been reclaimed, no one ventured into the ruins on the eastern side of the city. Not after so many went in, and so few returned. That section of Wast was left alone, a constant blemish on the growing city and a reminder of how a world full of technology and culture was so easily destroyed.

As one of the last phaanon strongholds during their

ultimately unsuccessful war with the galeons hundreds of years ago, the ancient city had been decimated. Over time, a bustling community reclaimed the area despite crumbling buildings and cracked streets. Now, pick-pockets milled in the crowded marketplaces and deadly thieves lurked in the shadows.

The phaanons were long gone now, as were most of the pureblood galeons, but the echoes of their existence remained.

Visiting a city built on death, ruins and poverty wasn't why I felt dirty, though. No, it was meeting with Queen Titania, the leader of the forest hunters. The queen wasn't much of a hunter so much as a politician, yet she'd maneuvered herself into a position where she could dictate the actions of everyone else.

Including me.

As one of the few galeons bonded to a familiar, I wasn't just gifted with an ever-lasting lifespan but also an indestructible one. The queen of hunters had named me, Artemis, Guardian of the Forbidden Forest.

There wasn't exactly a lot of competition for the role, and given the high level of danger, having an unkillable hunter in place made sense to everyone, including myself.

I protected the familiars who lived in the forbidden forest surrounding Wast—another remnant of the phaanons—but it also meant I had to attend the queen's monthly meetings.

Despite my success as her one and only guardian, Queen Titania always spoke to me as though I were still the twelve-year-old child she'd pulled from the streets. It wasn't that I was ungrateful for her intervention or the turn of events that granted me a better life. But she would never let me forget it, nor forget that I served her and always would.

Anger welled up inside of me. Saving twelve-year-old twins shouldn't require a lifetime of indentured service as payment.

Not that I wanted to do anything else.

I'd never trade my familiar for anything in the world and protecting unbonded ones gave me purpose and validation. I wasn't a victim of abuse from a rundown orphanage. I wasn't a good for nothing street rat.

I was a protector.

An image of Nala's panting face with her tongue lolling out the side of her snout surfaced.

I missed her.

I'd left her at home because she didn't like the city, or the queen anymore than I did. But now I wished I was already walking through my cabin's door instead of looking at an hour-long hike through the forest to reach home.

Maybe this rain would wash away all the city filth before I made it to the cabin.

The City of Wast...

I always thought an "e" had been purposefully dropped from the name in an attempt to rebrand the city as something less disastrous.

I preferred the forest to the crowded streets of that city any day.

A growl rose from the surrounding trees. I straightened and turned toward the sound.

Nala? I leaned forward.

The sound of a sharp whistle pierced my ear. The unmistakable hiss of an arrow cutting through the air was a sound I knew all too well from training. The arrow narrowly missed me and struck the base of a tree to my right. Someone had just tried to end my life.

Without hesitation, I dove to the ground, the cold, hard earth meeting my palms as I rolled into a defensive crouch.

With a steady hand, I unsheathed my dagger and faced my attacker, the magic coursing through my veins calling for blood. But instead of a faceless enemy, I saw a man with rugged features and intense light brown eyes. He held his bow steady, aiming directly at me.

All that mattered now was survival. He was close, too close for the bow to be an effective weapon, but if he tried to drop it now and draw the dagger strapped to his thigh, I would gain the advantage.

He had one shot. One more attempt to take my life, and I'd be damned if I gave him an easy target. I clutched my dagger and leaned forward, ready to strike.

Before I could attack, a dark, furry figure leapt from the bushes and smashed into the hunter, clamping jaws into the man with a loud snap.

This wolf wasn't Nala.

I straightened from my crouch as the wild animal tore out the man's throat. Blood sprayed the damp path and my leather boots.

A wave of conflicting emotions slammed into me—relief, confusion and gratitude. My heart continued to race as adrenaline rushed through my veins. The danger had passed, but my body hadn't received the message yet.

The wolf paused over the body, breathing heavy, before turning to me. Its yellow gaze flashed under the moonlight. I didn't recognize this wolf. Granted, I didn't know all the ones in the area, but I would've remembered seeing this one—all black, with blazing yellow eyes. I took several deep breaths and tried to shake away the urge to run.

"Thank you," I said.

Maybe I should've notched an arrow to protect myself from the wolf.

Maybe I shouldn't listen to my gut which told me this wolf wasn't dangerous. At least not to me.

Maybe I should talk to someone about my inner dialogue during dangerous situations.

The wolf huffed at me before springing forward. Its large fuzzy body brushed past my legs before it crashed into the bushes and disappeared into the forest.

I let out a long breath and my magic faded away, unused and angry. My gut served me well in situations like these and I couldn't explain why. It wasn't like I actually communicated with familiars. My brother claimed I was part wolf myself. Others in the town of Perga called me feral behind my back.

I didn't care what others thought of me.

All I cared about was protecting the unbonded familiars in the forest and today, it seemed, one decided to return the favour.

2

Blake sighed and pocketed the message I'd scribbled for the queen. "You certainly keep me busy, Emi."

"It's all about the job security." I winked.

Tall and lean, Blake had striking blue eyes and a mischievous smile. As the queen's messenger, he travelled back and forth between Perga and Wast. Magic might've replaced the technology from a time prior to the phaanon and galeon war, but not instant messaging. No vehicles, either. Phones and cars only remained in story books that had crumbled with age long ago.

Now, the queen and king relied on messengers like Blake to distribute information and disseminate orders.

Blake's gaze snagged on my blood-spattered boots and his grin faltered. "Good...hunting?"

I flashed him a closed-mouthed smile. Technically, it was good hunting for the wolf, but I didn't want to get into details with Blake. The attack needed to be reported to the queen first—I'd rather she heard the information from me than from gossip.

"Did you just get back?" A familiar husky voice called out from behind me.

Blake stiffened at the sound of my best friend's voice. He pulled his bag over his shoulders and turned to leave.

I spun to find Lesley sauntering over from the street that led to the center of town. She had a curvy, hourglass figure that made men and women drool. Coils of deep brown hair surrounded her heart-shaped face. With her full lips, large round eyes, cute button nose and slightly flushed cheeks, she always appeared as if she'd just been caught doing something incredibly naughty. She might look like sex personified, and she might joke around about casual liaisons, but my friend was more reserved than me when it came to relationships.

"Hey, Sley." I waved.

Sley flashed me a wide smile, but she quickly narrowed her eyes as her gaze slid to something over my shoulder. Blake had slipped into the shadows of the forest.

"Hey, Emi," she said. "Was that Blake?"

"Couldn't tell from the red tips of his ears?"

"I don't know why he's avoiding me." She frowned at the forest.

"Don't you?" I raised both eyebrows. "He went to your place with a bouquet of flowers to profess his undying love and was greeted by Graham...and Graham's cock."

"I still can't believe that idiot answered the door

without his pants on," Sley grumbled. Okay, she might be more reserved than me, but she wasn't celibate. She'd had an arrangement with Graham for months, despite not liking him much. Perga had limited romantic options, unless we were willing to commute or take a chance on one of the transient hunters.

"Sley," I said.

"What?"

"That's not the point. The point is you know perfectly well why Blake is avoiding you. Graham made sure he told everyone and anyone who'd listen in an attempt to further humiliate him and to also keep your options limited. I can't believe you let that jerk in your bed."

"Me neither," Sley huffed. "I dumped him, too. Blake didn't deserve any of that, but we weren't in a relationship. I didn't do anything wrong. I've been trying to apologize for how he was greeted at my home, but how am I to make things right when he won't even look at me?"

I grimaced. I was currently avoiding someone myself and didn't have any answers for my friend. "Come on. You can have a drink at my place, and I'll tell you how I got attacked coming back from Wast."

"What?" Sley swatted my arm. "Tell me everything."

So, I did.

I told her the story as we made our way down the forest path that led to my cabin.

My small home sat on the outskirts of the village near the tail end of the brook. I had long put out the fire from last night to stave off the cold, but the smell of smoke still clung to the air along with the sharp tang of pine.

As I stepped through the entrance, I hung my bow and quiver on hooks by the door. When I turned around, a wolf flew through the air, barrelling into me. The force of the impact knocked me over. My back slammed into the floor and the large animal smothered me with its fluffy body.

"Gah!" I attempted to fend off the tongue slathering my face. "Nala!"

My familiar yipped and backed up. She sat on her haunches beside me and opened her mouth to pant, her tongue lolled out the side.

"I wasn't even gone a full day," I said.

She slurped her tongue and continued to pant.

"I missed you." I reached out and ran my hands through her fur. She ducked her head so I could scratch behind her ears.

"You two set a high standard for relationships," Sley said as she stepped into the cabin behind me.

I scrambled off the floor and wiped my face. "You want to be slobbered all over?"

"Well...I wouldn't say no..." She shrugged.

I laughed and shook my head. Before I could respond with something witty, Nala bumped into my legs before slipping out of the cabin.

"Let me guess." Sley closed the door behind my familiar. "Workshop?"

I smiled and some of the tension from the meeting

and attack eased away. My friend knew me well. "Grab the wine?"

"Of course."

Sley sauntered off to my kitchen to grab the beverages while I made my way through the cabin to the back room that housed my workshop.

A large wooden table sat in the centre of the room with an assortment of arrow-making tools spread across its worn surface. A large fireplace lined one wall while a small table with two chairs were pushed against the other. A door on the far side of the workshop led to the outside and had a custom trapdoor built into the bottom portion for Nala to enter and exit as she pleased.

"I have something for you, too." Sley walked into the workshop and set the bottle of wine and two glasses down on the side table. We spent a lot of time in this room—I made arrows while Sley sat in one of the chairs to the side and unloaded all the town's latest gossip.

Sley pulled the strap for her shoulder bag over her head and slung the bag over the corner of her favourite chair. Flipping the top flap back, she dug into the leather bag to pull out a roll of twine. "For you."

"Thank you." I reached out and took the roll of twine from her and placed it beside my other supplies on the workbench. "But now I'm afraid to ask what it will cost me. I'm not into slobber."

She giggled and flopped into her seat. "I think a bottle of wine sounds pretty good to me."

"You also need to eat, Sley. And half a bottle of wine is not enough payment for this twine."

"Oh...not this bottle." She reached forward and uncorked the bottle. "I'll take another one before I leave. You always bring back the best stuff from Wast."

"Not this time."

"Did you get anything?" She poured generous servings into both glasses before shoving the cork back into the bottle. "Gossip? Food?"

"Just a headache."

Sley sighed and picked up a glass to hand to me.

I shook my head and glanced at the workbench. "Not yet. I want to get some arrows made before I crash."

"And I want to drink while I watch you turn Gavin's wood, Graham's arrowheads and my twine into your fancy famous arrows."

I turned toward the work awaiting me. "Just promise me this will be the only time we ever talk about Gavin's wood."

Sley giggled and sipped her wine.

Though we had currency in the form of gales, most commerce in Perga ran on trade. I paid Gavin three rabbits for a pile of wood lathed into arrow shafts and Graham a whole deer for a bucket of his finest arrowheads.

I reached for the mortar and added a concoction of flour, water and pale pink blossoms from a late-blooming flower found on the outskirts of the Danu Forest. I let my magic flow over me and the ingredients while I used the pestle to mix the materials into a sticky paste. I still didn't know everything about my own powers—I didn't know if adding my magic made a difference at all. My aim was perfect with or without my special arrows. But it felt right.

The paste shimmered, echoing my magic's touch as I continued to smash and mix the paste to create a potent glue that I would use to bind wood and metal. Raindrops pattered along the roof while I worked and Sley drank.

I loved evenings like this.

Sley had moved to stand beside me, her glass in hand, her gaze sparkling with amusement. "You've made enough to supply an army."

"I find it calming to make them," I said. "Besides, I never know when I'm going to need more or when I'll have another chance to make them. Better to be over prepared than face an empty quiver."

Sley hummed in agreement before plucking one of my finished arrows from a basket beside the bench. She ran the tip of her finger along the edge of the fletching. "I wish we knew where these feathers came from. No one's ever brought a bird back that matches them, but it must be spectacular."

At first glance, the feathers appeared ordinary and white, like those found on winter geese or swans, but on closer inspection, these feathers weren't just different, they were extraordinary. They glowed and sparkled under the moonlight and gave off whisps of magic that felt both familiar and foreign. Under sunlight, they shimmered with metallic colours of the rainbow.

"Me, too," I said. "Since I find them in the Danu Forest, I like to think they're a gift from one of the familiars I protect." Like the wolf who protected me earlier tonight. "Does that sound weird?"

She shook her head. "You could never be anything other than awesome."

"I'm sure some of the others in town would disagree with that statement." I shrugged as if it didn't bother me and for the most part, it didn't. I had a job to do, and I did it well. I nodded at the twine Sley had brought. "The twine looks really nice. Thank you."

Sley's smile spread across her whole face. "It's the strongest I've made to date and since I made it specifically with you in mind, I like to think the forest spirits knew and helped me."

I swallowed and reached out to touch the twine. A faint ebb of magic slipped off the surface.

"So, no," Sley continued. "I don't think you're weird. Like I said, I think you're pretty phaaning awesome."

I had the best of best friends. "I'm still not slobbering on you."

Sley shrugged. "Nala will do it."

She would, too. Instead of commenting, I reached for the first piece of Gavin's wood and cut a small notch in the shaft, about a quarter of the total length.

"For someone who doesn't like to talk about it, you're certainly good at handling Gavin's wood," Sley noted.

I continued to cut. "Gross."

"Still not interested?" She peered at me over the rim of her glass.

"Not in this lifetime. He might be big and beefy now,

but I can't forget how he treated me when we were younger. He was such an asshole."

"You guys were five."

"Twelve. I was twelve when I moved to Perga with my brother, and Gavin was a relentless jerk. Some people are irredeemable. He called us the orphans." It was more than that, but I hadn't told Sley about my life on the streets nor the time before that—the time when I had lived in an orphanage and, aside from the love I had for my brother, knew only sadness and pain.

"Didn't Gavin call everyone that?" Sley asked.

"No. Just me, Paul and another guy, who was also an absolute jerk, but that's another story." I continued to cut notches into the wooden shafts and ignored the pang in my chest. Though no one in town would truly understand how traumatic the nickname was for me, that didn't take away the pain, or the anger.

"The thing is, Gavin wasn't wrong," I said. "The three of us were orphans, but we didn't need it spat at us every day." Placing my knife on the bench, I picked up one of the prepped shafts and dipped the cut end into the glue. "He also used to drip tree sap in my hair."

Sley sucked in a breath. "No."

"Yeah. One time it was so bad Paul had to sheer my hair off because we couldn't get the sap out." I took a deep breath. "Gavin only started being nice to me when I grew boobs."

Sley grunted and took another sip of wine while I reached for one of the arrowheads. Holding the dipped shaft in one hand and holding the arrowhead in the other, I jammed the sharp metal into the cut, careful not to slice my hand open. "You weren't here but trust me when I say Gavin and Graham were the town bullies. I'd give my business to anyone else if I could."

Sadly, Perga was a small town. That meant options were limited for romance and business alike.

I slathered more of the magical glue around the contact area before wrapping Sley's twine around the notch and base of the arrowhead. The twine tingled in my hands as I tied it off and coated the area with more glue.

I repeated the process until I had an arrowhead tied into the notch of each shaft. While I worked, Sley made a fire in the nearby hearth and hummed a song I didn't recognize. She walked around my workshop, poking at things and peering at arrows in various stages of production before returning to my side.

"I feel like there's a dirty joke somewhere in this whole process." Sley waved her hand at my workbench before taking another sip of wine.

I picked up the baby arrows and blinked at Sley. "I don't know what you're talking about. I'm innocently working here, slathering the slits of hard wooden shafts with my magical glue paste and you have to make it sound dirty."

Sley choked on her wine. She coughed and laughed at the same time, spraying wine back into her glass. She coughed again and shook her head. "I deserved that."

Leaving the arrows strategically placed near the hearth, I paused to watch the play of light and shadow along the metal from the fire. After they dried, I could move on to cutting the back of the shaft to create the notch that would fit my bowstring. I'd also add the fletching from the mystery bird's feathers.

If I wanted to, I could work on them some more in about an hour after they'd dried. That wouldn't happen, though. In about an hour, I'd be happily wine-drunk with my best friend, probably deep in a conversation about town gossip or the last book I read.

With that happy thought in my head, I moved to the recently finished batch of arrows. They'd finished drying and if I tested a few now, I'd have more arrows to shoot tomorrow.

I picked up the top arrow from the pile and flexed it between my two hands. The colourful shimmer of the feathers caught the light from the fire, their magic whispering along my skin.

"You know," Sley mused. "They say phaanons had the ability to change shapes."

Phaanons? The mythical beings cursed about in the ancient Galeon tales? Why would Sley bring them up now? An unexpected snap shattered the silence, and I stared down at the broken arrow in my hands.

"Oops." I shot Sley a sheepish grin. "Why are you thinking about phaanons?"

"I wasn't. At least not at first. I was thinking about how you were attacked." Sley handed me a full glass of wine.

I placed the ruined arrow in the discard bin and plucked the glass from her hand.

"Which led me to think of one of the stories I heard growing up," Sley continued.

"That phaanons could change shape?" I took a sip and let the heady taste of red wine flow over my tongue. Mmmm. That was good. "What kind of shape? Like...a ball?"

"Like a mountain lion or bear." She widened her eyes. "Maybe it wasn't a familiar who came to your aid. Maybe it was a phaanon."

I frowned into my wine. "Phaanons were eradicated years ago. And even if they weren't, why would one come to my aid?"

Nala whined outside the front door, and I jerked my head in that direction. We walked out of the workshop and paused our conversation to let Nala in. My familiar could've easily used the trap door in the shop, but she had a habit of doing this when I'd been gone for awhile—like she needed me to open the door to know I still cared. Which was silly, because she could sense my emotions better than I could detect hers. If she needed the validation, though, I'd gladly give it to her instead of making a fuss.

Nala shook her coat right beside me, spraying me with rainwater. She padded her way into the workshop where she'd plop down in front of the fire like she did every night.

Instead of following my familiar, I joined Sley on the couch in the small living room. I wanted to continue our conversation. "Phaanons despised the very existence of galeons. If phaanons still existed, it's much more likely that the man trying to exterminate me was one, not the wolf."

"Did he have pointy ears?" Her gaze drifted to the top of mine, which were blunt and definitely not pointy.

"Of course not," I said.

"Did he try to kill you with his blood?" she asked next.

"What? No." I frowned at her. "Why would you even ask that?"

She shrugged before leaning back into the couch cushion. "I heard somewhere that's how phaanons killed galeons during the war."

"We've all heard a lot of stories about phaanons over the years. I heard they sung galeons to their deaths like sirens from those old stories. I hate to disagree with you but think you're wrong about the phaanons."

"Traitor." She stared into her wine as she swirled her glass.

"They're just rumours," I reminded her. "And they're baseless—stories told at night to keep young galeons in line."

"If you say so." She continued to examine her drink. "But I'm holding onto my dream of being rescued by a gorgeous phaanon warrior with a nine-inch schlong and you can't change my mind."

I threw up my hands in mock surrender. "Who am I to crush your dreams?" I paused and studied my friend's grinning face. "Rescue you from what?"

Nala chose that moment to jump up on the couch between us, her body still damp. She flopped down on the cushion and curled up, tucking her long nose behind her legs. This was why I couldn't have nice things. Instead, I had a thick blanket covering the couch for moments like this.

I wouldn't change a thing.

I reached out and gave Nala a few pets before turning my attention back to Sley.

"From this mundane life," she said, answering my earlier question. "Where the biggest excitement and mystery in my life is who raided Perga's food stores. Again."

I straightened from petting Nala. "Someone's stealing?"

"Don't look so excited."

"But nothing happens in Perga," I said. "Except bed hopping."

"Well...now one of us is a thief."

Everyone in town provided food to a collective bank in lieu of paying a tithe or tax. One of Sley's roles in town was to collect, maintain and distribute the food in times of need. Right now, our stores should be at a healthy level. During winter, that often changed.

"So?" I nudged my friend. "Who's stealing?"

Sley shrugged. "No idea. That's partly why I was looking for you earlier. I just got distracted by wine, watching you work and listening to you bitch about what a shitty human Gavin is. I'm here for all of that. But I also need help tracking down the thief."

And who better to catch a thief than a retired one?

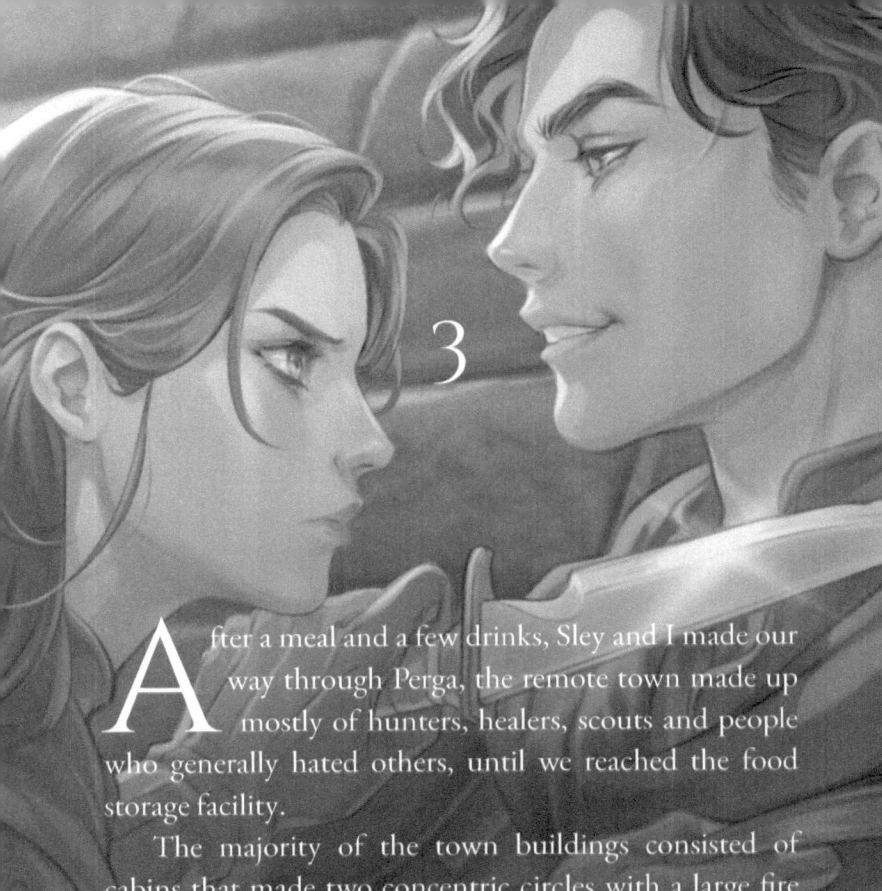

3

After a meal and a few drinks, Sley and I made our way through Perga, the remote town made up mostly of hunters, healers, scouts and people who generally hated others, until we reached the food storage facility.

The majority of the town buildings consisted of cabins that made two concentric circles with a large fire pit in the centre for social gatherings. The main road from Wast split the circle in half. My cabin was situated beyond the outer circle on the far side of town and sat mostly in the forest. I liked it that way. More privacy.

Most of the queen's hunters lived in Perga. We didn't have much time for cultivating gardens or managing livestock aside from chickens. Instead, we fished in the nearby river or hunted for our food in the field or the neighbouring forest. The money the queen paid us went toward buying or bartering for other staples and supplies like vegetables and flour.

Most of the hunters stuck to themselves. We weren't braiding each other's hair by the firepit each night, but I was certain most of them would drag me from a burning building.

Even Gavin.

Though he'd probably try to grope me in the process.

The storage house loomed ahead like a forgotten tomb, its once sturdy walls now worn and weathered under the weight of time and the harsh elements. We'd have to rebuild it sooner than later, but it had at least one more winter in it.

Sley let out a heavy breath beside me, her gaze scanning the exterior while her mouth twisted down.

"How much did they take?" I asked. How could anyone steal from the community?

"Not enough to ruin us," Sley replied, her expression pinched as she pulled open the door. "At least not yet. But they've taken enough to cause a noticeable strain if it's a harsh winter. They must've been siphoning off our dry stock bit by bit over a long period of time. I have no idea when it started."

"Jerks."

"I have stronger words," she said.

So did I. Following Sley inside, I paused at the entrance long enough to let my vision adjust. Slowly, the images of barrels, crates and boxes took shape and crystallized. Stale air with hints of grain, dust and leather floated by me.

It looked exactly like it had the last time I'd visited. "How did you figure out something was stolen?"

Sley pointed to the corner of the room where a number of grain barrels lined the wall. "Those used to be full, but now they're only half-full."

"I'm more of a half-empty kind of girl, myself," I said as I walked over to the barrels.

"That doesn't surprise me at all," Sley said.

The seals on the barrels were broken, but that wouldn't have been enough to give me pause. Most of the seals in here had been broken. We reused containers whenever possible. I wouldn't have taken a second look at these barrels if Sley hadn't pointed them out. Leaning closer, I inspected the broken seal. "They dusted off the lids."

"That's what caught my eye," Sley admitted. "The absence of dust. Isn't that sad? It was only when I looked closer that I noticed the broken seal and looked inside."

"Smart. I'm not sure I would've caught the change at all." I waved at the dust in the air. Something red in the corner of my vision snagged my attention and I turned toward it. A vibrant red scarf lay next to a barrel of grain in the corner of the room.

"This looks familiar." I picked up the fabric for closer examination.

"Oh, it does." She reached forward and ran her fingers along the silky fabric, her brow furrowed. "I can't remember where I've seen it, though."

"Could be a clue." I shoved the scarf into my pocket.

"It could also be a coincidence." Sley shrugged. "A lot of people have access to this place, including you and me."

Someone cleared their throat behind us.

Sley jumped and let out a high-pitched squeak while I pulled my dagger from its sheath and spun around.

Blake stood at the entrance, the fading sunlight behind him casting sinister shadows over his face while dust motes danced in the air.

Sley stiffened and narrowed her eyes. "We're in the middle of an investigation. What are you doing here?"

"I heard about the thefts," he said.

"Who told you?"

He grimaced. "Everyone?"

Sley scowled at the messenger. "Is petty crime what it takes to get you to talk to me?"

He blushed and looked down at the ground before producing a letter from his bag and extending it toward me. "Sorry to cut your investigation short. I have a message for Emi."

I recognized the queen's seal from a distance and swallowed a groan. Stepping forward, I took the letter from Blake and broke the seal. "That was fast."

"She insisted I run," he said.

"Is it bad?" Sley peered over my shoulder.

I shook my head, though my stomach sunk as I quickly scanned the writing, the slant of the letters a familiar sight. "Just new orders."

4

Nala tilted her head at me and blinked, a question clear in her gaze. Yeah, I questioned my life choices all the time, too. I'd ended up drinking even more wine with Sley last night and though I'd managed to walk off most of the sluggishness and clear my mind, my stomach still occasionally twisted and rolled.

"Come on, Nala, just a little farther." I slipped past my familiar and continued down the path. Little more than a deer trail, the wet moss squished, and small twigs snapped under my boots. Dew drops fractured the light as the sun snuck over the tree canopy above. The heat of the day staved off the chill in the air. As winter approached, the sunlight would grow weaker, and I'd have to wear furs along with my dark leather hunting gear and cloak to stay warm.

Nala whined and I reached down to run my hand through her thick fur. Even in Autumn before her winter coat came in, she managed to get mats. I'd spend a good chunk of this evening brushing them out.

"Not much longer," I promised her.

The queen had sent me on a fool's errand. At least it felt that way. The man who'd attacked me was already dead, but after I'd reported my attack, Queen Titania assumed that meant illegal hunters had infiltrated the forbidden forest. As in plural. Apparently, there had been other reports of an unknown hunter in the Danu Forest, but the queen had no proof this meant more than one man was involved and with the body of my assailant rotting alongside the path to Wast my trip out to the forest was futile.

Chilly wind brushed through the leaves and birds chirped merrily as they flittered from branch to branch overhead. Birds of all kinds had a habit of following me through the forest and I'd grown accustomed to their company over the years.

Nala had come from these woods, as had most of the familiars bound to galeons. This was their home, and to protect the future familiars, we needed to protect this forest.

Times were rough, the citizens of Wast grew more desperate as winter approached, but they would never venture into the Dannu Forest when there were other less dangerous locations to search for food. Stepping into the Danu Forest without permission meant certain death.

I was the judge, jury and executioner. The guardian of the forest.

The trees glistened under the sun but revealed nothing. The secrets of the woods remained hidden in the shadows.

I sighed and kicked a rock along the path. I hadn't seen any signs of another hunter, let alone a whole party of them. Either the other witnesses were flat out wrong, or they'd intentionally lied on their report to the queen.

And why?

To waste my phaaning time.

This was almost as bad as being pulled into another meeting to hear the monthly reports.

The path led to the Danu River and followed along the bank until it converged with another river, marking the end of the Danu Forest. I always enjoyed this section of the path as the river was a beautiful sight at anytime of year.

Today, it felt different, though.

Magic danced over the surface of the water, making it shimmer. Soft laughter floated in the air along with the pull of magic.

A naiad.

Water nymphs were long-lived, but not immortal. They had remained neutral during the phaanon-galeon war, choosing not to get involved and it paid off. They survived, while others like the brownies and fairies did not.

Where any of the magical creatures had come from before the war still remained a mystery. At one time, this had been a world of technology and science, and the next, the phaanon-galeon war had spilled into the streets from an unknown land, killed all technology and left a scar on society that still festered, along with magical remnants like naiads, familiars, and immortal descendants.

"Stay here, Nala."

My familiar whined and flopped down on the ground. Even though I told her to stay, I knew without a doubt that she'd rush to my side if I needed her.

Naiads weren't typically violent and were solitary in nature. I had no reason to fear seeking one out. Maybe this naiad had seen something that would help my investigation. Plus, I just wanted to meet her. I rarely saw water nymphs. Though the Danu River was infested with them farther to the east toward Vitor, they rarely travelled this far west. The last one who'd ventured into this territory had been kindly asked to leave after she kept luring lusty men into the icy depths of the water during winter.

So, some naiads could be violent, but...the men in such cases deserved it.

It's not like the naiad had taken over their freewill like a siren. Those men had chosen to enter the water because they wanted to take something that wasn't freely offered. Did the naiad encourage them? Of course. But not with any magical compulsion. If the men had any respect for magical creatures, solid morals, or common sense, they would've and could've stayed out of the river.

I walked closer to the water's edge and crouched down.

The singing stopped.

"I'm not here to harm you," I said, dipping my

28

fingers into the river. The icy water flowed over my skin, leaving me chilled as I released my power slowly. Letting my magical signature act as an introduction, I held my breath and waited to see if it worked.

The naiad rose from the water a few feet away. Sunlight reflected off her pale, mother-of-pearl skin. She'd woven river flowers and grass through her long hair which was tinted the same blue and green of the water.

Though delicate and fragile in appearance, her large blue-green eyes flashed with irritation. "What do you want, Child of Mab?"

"Who's Mab?" I leaned closer. "Do you know who my parents are? Were?"

The naiad snarled as if she'd ingested something foul. "I know what you are and that's enough."

Ah. So, the term was in reference to galeons. Awesome.

"The air is foul on my skin. You knocked on my door with your power. What do you want?"

Well, this naiad certainly wasn't trying to seduce me into entering the frigid waters to die of hypothermia.

A win?

"I live in the nearby town of Perga where a bunch of supplies were stolen. Do you know anything about that?"

The water creature recoiled, swiftly pushing away from the bank. "You dare suggest I am a thief?" she hissed angrily, her eyes shifting from bright blue to intense green.

"No, wait. Come back," I called out. "That wasn't what I was suggesting."

The naiad paused, poised to dive under the water and disappear from sight.

"I'd hoped you saw something," I explained.

The naiad straightened and blinked at me. "Like what?"

"Like strange, unfamiliar hunters carrying supplies away from town?" I bit my lip. Was it too much to ask for a break in this case?

"You are the first hunter I've seen," the naiad said. "One too many, if you ask me. But even if I'd seen others, you all look unfamiliar to me. I don't normally come this way."

Drat. That would've made things so much easier. "What brings you here?"

The naiad cocked her head and blinked at me again. After an uncomfortably silent minute, she spoke. "I, too, am searching for something I've lost."

"Oh." I straightened from my crouch and shook some feeling back into my legs. "What are you looking for? Maybe I can help?"

The naiad scoffed, spraying water in front of her. "I doubt that."

"Then may I know your name?" I asked. "I'm Artemis, the guardian of this forest."

The naiad's unimpressed expression remained unchanged. If anything, her lips curled down farther. "Names have power, and I will give you none over me."

Before I could respond, the naiad dove under the water, the magic in the air fading away.

Well, that was insulting. I was the guardian of the

forbidden forest, the protector of familiars and other magical creatures, and this one wanted nothing to do with me.

The rejection stung a little.

True, I'd given her no reason to trust me, but neither had I given her a reason to fear me.

I shook off the sting and walked back to where Nala waited, her tail thumping on the damp moss. She stood when I approached and bumped her furry body into mine.

I scratched her head behind the ears. "Let's continue, girl."

She yipped in agreement and followed me as I continued along the path that ran parallel to the river. Nala kept pace, an easy lope to stay by my side. I was running out of forest to find this mysterious hunter or pack of hunters, and with each step I became increasingly annoyed. My thoughts had come full circle.

This really was a useless waste of time.

Nala growled and her ears pinned back. As my familiar, she sensed my emotions and her reaction to my strong irritation was a good reminder to temper myself. Taking a deep breath, I forced my shoulders to relax, pushing them down on the exhale. Stomping around the forest wouldn't make the scouting mission finish any faster and huffing about lying witnesses wouldn't change my current assignment. This negative emotion only succeeded in draining my energy, and possibly diverting my focus from the objective.

I ran my hands along Nala's back again.

She stopped growling and her ears pinged forward. She wagged her tail hesitantly. When I continued to pat her, the wagging increased. Wolves weren't supposed to wag their tails like dogs, but Nala wasn't an ordinary wolf.

She was mine—my soul bonded familiar.

As descendants of pureblood galeons, immortals carried an eternal life essence—the ability to extend their lifespans for centuries—but without a bonded familiar, immortals could still be killed. They were still vulnerable. With a bonded familiar, galeon descendants couldn't be killed, at least not anymore.

There weren't many of us.

And aside from King Oberon and Queen Titania of Wast, there weren't any pureblood galeons at all. The war with the phaanons had been brutal.

I scratched Nala behind the ears. "You're the bestest."

She leaned into the touch, her weight pressing into my legs and almost knocking me over.

I ruffled her fur. If I stopped now, we could return to the cabin by nightfall and snuggle by the fire.

But that wasn't going to happen.

Even if I was one-hundred percent confident the wolf killed the only hunter, I needed to make sure. I needed to either eliminate the possibility more hunters roamed these woods or track them down.

One report had mentioned spotting a hunter by the slow babbling brook running through the southeastern corner of the forest, not far from where I'd been attacked.

We'd walked along the bank all morning and I hadn't spotted a single track.

Nala had senses far superior to mine and she hadn't detected anything yet, either, and the forest hadn't sent its warm band of wind as a warning.

The magic of the forbidden forest didn't always reach out to me, but I'd learned a long time ago to never ignore the magic when it appeared. In the winter, the forest's magic came to me as a warm wind, and in the summer, it brought a chill in the air.

Today, the forest remained neutral.

Now nearing the edge of the outer perimeter, where the trees gave way to a meadow of tall grass and wildflowers and the brook converged with the Danu, the larger faster flowing river, I was ready to go home.

The sound of a snapping branch shattered the peaceful ambiance of the forest and froze me and Nala in our tracks. Instincts kicked in immediately as I recognized the threat.

Hunters.

A warm band of wind teased my hair and magic danced over me, beckoning me to play along. The unexpected magical heat kissed my chilled skin.

"Run," I commanded. I lunged to the side and used the nearby tree as cover, as an arrow whistled through the air where I'd just stood. My heart raced as I cursed under my breath. That arrowhead had come too close to piercing my skin.

That was the second arrow in two days to narrowly miss my face.

Two too many.

Anger boiled within me. This was a brazen and reckless attack. Why? Because they recognized me as the guardian, or because I was unlucky enough to cross their path?

Nala growled—a ferocious deep rumble—before taking off into the underbrush, but even her impressive skills would not protect her from arrows.

In one fluid motion, I drew an arrow from my quiver and notched it in my bow before spinning around to face the attackers. With the magic of perfect accuracy running through my veins, I released the arrow. It found its mark, sinking deep into the chest of a burly man wearing a tan leather vest and pants. He grunted, his weathered face twisting in pain, before he toppled to the ground.

Shifting my aim, I fired off two more arrows into the moving bushes to the right of where the first man had fallen. One man cried out and another gurgled. I quickly ducked behind cover again as another round of arrows flew past me.

There were more hunters than the three I'd just taken out and they were getting bolder. Instead of retreating or regrouping, they emerged from the shadows and tried to skewer my head with their inferior skills.

Guess the reports weren't full of shit after all. I shouldn't have dismissed them so readily. I should've been more prepared.

More arrows flew past me as I remained behind cover. I took a deep breath and waited. My heart thundered in my chest, threatening to burst through bone and consume my hearing. The hunters would have to move if they wanted a clear shot.

Leaning into the rough bark of the tree, I clutched my bow in my sweaty fist. I had four more arrows in my quiver, and though I was immortal, getting shot wasn't a fun experience or something I quickly healed from. If they hit me well enough, they could incapacitate me, leaving me vulnerable.

But I refused to let fear overtake me. I was the guardian of this forest, and I would not back down. I would make them pay for their insolence.

Taking another deep breath, I squeezed my eyes shut and focused on slowing my breathing. I needed to find that place of stillness, the calm centre within me where I could access powers unique to my lineage.

A sense of serenity washed over me.

Time slowed.

The warm band of magical wind wrapped around me. My focus narrowed to the sounds of the forest surrounding me. Branches and dried pine needles snapped behind me. The gentle fall wind teased the leaves of thick underbrush. The hunters breathed heavy and spread out to surround me, getting closer.

Now.

With swift motion, I spun away from the tree and let my arrows fly in rapid succession. One. Two. Three.

They each found their marks with deadly accuracy.

Three more hunters fell to the ground in tandem, blurs of green wool and tan leather. One. Two. Three.

I had one arrow left.

Tightening my sweaty grip on the bow, I notched my last arrow.

I was the guardian of the forest.

And I did not fail.

Turning, I found myself facing another hunter, his bow already raised, and the arrow notched. Before he could release it, a dark blur launched from the bushes.

Nala clamped her powerful jaws onto the man's face, knocking him to the ground with a blood-curdling scream. She snarled viciously as she tore into his throat, her coat getting splattered with his blood and staining the nearby tree trunk. It was an unsettlingly familiar sight, reminiscent of my previous encounter with a hunter.

As adrenaline coursed through my body, I took stock of the aftermath. This wouldn't be the last time Nala and I faced danger in these woods, but we would always survive—because we were fierce, and we were unstoppable.

Nala was okay. I was okay. Everything was—

Eerie dread spread over my skin, raising each individual hair along my neck and the magical band of air tightened around me in warning again.

Even as Nala straightened, ears pinned back, I was spinning around with an arrow notched. Time slowed to a standstill. I released the shaft. My arrow flew true, striking another hunter about twenty feet away. Unlike his arrow that flew wide, mine hit him straight in the chest, slicing through his green wool sweater to puncture his heart. Death was instantaneous.

The man fell to the ground, but not before I saw his

expression. He didn't appear shocked, or surprised. Not even horror or pain spread across his expression. Instead, the unknown man died with a smile on his face.

Pain shot through my stomach.

I looked down seeing no injury. I patted my flat belly and found no wound from where the pain radiated.

No.

I spun around.

Nala.

My familiar lay on her side, an arrow protruding from her abdomen.

"Nala!" I ran to her side, throwing myself on the ground to kneel beside her. She lifted her head and whined before dropping back to rest on the forest floor. Her chest rose and fell, but a rattling made each breath sound painful, the same pain that echoed in my own body.

I swung my bow over my shoulder and reached for my familiar.

"It's okay, girl," I told her, carefully scooping her off the ground. Wet dirt and blood caked her fur.

My muscles screamed in protest.

Nala might be on the small side for a wolf, but she was still heavy. We were at least an hour from Perga. I'd have to throw her over my shoulders to make it there quickly. The trip would cause more damage, but we couldn't stay here.

Decision already made, I moved her in my arms. She yipped in pain.

"Sorry, Nala."

The next part was tricky. I had to keep the arrow in to prevent blood loss, but I also didn't want to agitate the wound even more. As gently as I could, I lifted and draped her over my shoulders so her injured side faced up.

She sagged into my body as I stood up.

"It's going to be okay," I said again, more to myself, then to Nala. "Everything is going to be okay."

It had to be.

She was my everything.

5

I kicked open the door and stepped inside Orion's cabin. The door swung back so hard it hit the wall with a loud bang and shook the building.

Nala had gone limp over twenty minutes ago and her blood had run down my body the entire way back to Perga. My clothes were now saturated with sweat and blood.

"What the phaan?" Orion stepped from the hallway that led to more rooms in the back. He held a cloth and used it to wipe his hands before tossing it to the side. His gaze snagged on me. "Emi?"

Concern streaked his expression as his gaze scanned me from head to toe before settling on Nala.

"Nala?"

"Help her." My lungs burned. My eyes stung. I had run the last half of the trip, not sure it was enough and cursing myself for not being stronger, faster, better. "Please."

I kept replaying the battle in my head, wondering what I could've done differently. But nothing would change the current situation. None of those negative thoughts would heal my best friend. Nothing could rewind time.

She was supposed to be unkillable like me, heal like me, but something was wrong. Different. I felt it in my gut with the pain that echoed from her injury.

"Follow me." Orion spun on his heel and walked down the hallway he'd just left. I trailed after him to a small treatment room—one of the many in his cabin—and he stepped to the side so I could gently lay Nala on the examination table.

I hadn't been back here in months. Not since I woke up naked beside Orion after a wild night of drinking.

Nala had cut her foot chasing bandits to the forest, and after Orion patched her up, he'd offered me a drink. That night started out like a million other nights before, but something had changed, Orion was determined.

He finally made his move, and I went with it.

I shook the memories of tangled naked limbs from my mind and ran my hand along Nala's blood-matted fur before moving out of the way. With shaky legs, I made it to the single chair in the corner of the room before collapsing.

Orion had already approached Nala to inspect the wound.

"Any other injuries?" he asked.

I tried to speak, but my voice came out like a croak.

Swallowing, I cleared my throat and tried again. "Just the arrow."

Nala was still breathing, though more laboured than before, and she hadn't voluntarily moved or whined when I placed her on the table.

Magic stirred in the air as Orion reached for his gift. He was the best healer in Perga. He should've been working in the palace, but for some reason, the royals hadn't called for him once. Their loss, our gain. And once the town realized how talented Orion was, they kept him very busy. That's why he had stopped hunting with me. That and I preferred to work alone.

If anyone could heal Nala, he could.

"Will she be okay?" I whispered. I dreaded the answer, yet I also needed to hear it.

"Galeon familiars are just as invincible as their bonded immortals. It will be okay." His words were meant to soothe me, but they had the opposite effect. "She will be okay."

"She isn't healing, though," I said. "She should've healed by now."

"Shush." His magic flowed over my familiar's body. Not gifted with healing, I couldn't see or follow exactly what he did with his power, but my skin always tingled when he used it.

A memory of him using his powers on my naked body surged up, and my body heated. This was not the time to think about our night together. Especially when it would never happen again.

Tall with wide shoulders and bulky muscles, Orion

was a specimen of a man. We'd hunted together for years without crossing that line. But Nala's previous injury, booze and a little suggestion, it had been easy falling in bed with him. Even easier to enjoy my time there. When we'd woken up together the next morning, though, and he told me he loved me, I panicked.

I didn't feel the same way and I never could.

I'd avoided Orion ever since because, apparently, despite being twenty-five years old, I still insisted on acting like a child. And I hated myself for it. I was the feared guardian and an honest conversation with someone I cared for scared me more than a band of poachers.

In my defense, I didn't have a lot of experience with relationships.

I might be a monumental asshole, but Orion wasn't. He was everything good in the world, and despite my poor handling of the situation, I knew without a doubt that he wouldn't make Nala pay for any hurt feelings he might have because of me.

He'd help Nala.

And hopefully, he'd save her.

I tore my gaze away from monitoring the rise and fall of Nala's chest to risk a glance at Orion. He was generally easy to read unless he wore his healer face—an expressionless mask to hide the seriousness of the situation. He rarely had cause to use it around me—Nala's last injury would've killed a normal wolf but had mostly healed by the time I'd reached him. When he did use his healer face, though, it sent prickles along my spine.

Right now, his brow was furrowed, and his blonde hair fell over his face as he bent over my familiar to focus on her wound. The cabin filled with his magic as he worked, his hands moving over Nala's body. With a step to his left, he blocked my view of Nala and his face.

"Orion?" I asked, too exhausted to move from my seat. I craned my neck to catch a glimpse of my familiar.

He didn't bother replying. Instead, he stepped to the right so I could see my girl again. Her breathing didn't seem as labored as before, but maybe that was wishful thinking.

Orion pushed his blonde hair away from his face before placing one hand on the wound. He reached forward with the other, gripped the arrow shaft, and pulled. I lurched out of my seat. A wave of nausea flooded my senses and my vision wavered. My ass hit the chair and then everything went black.

"E mi?" A familiar deep voice teased my senses. "Emi?"

My eyelids fluttered open, and I found Orion crouched in front of me. Concern etched his brow. One of his hands cradled my face and the other rested on my knee. With him so close, nestled between my thighs, memories of our night together flared up and sent heat rushing to my face.

"You passed out." He dropped his hand from my face, and then, as if he, too, realized the intimate position, lurched to his feet. Taking a step back, he ran a hand through his hair.

"What happened?" he asked.

"The queen sent me to follow up on some reports about a hunter in the Danu. The queen suspected there were more than one and it turned out she was right. I walked into an ambush."

Orion's expression darkened. He stilled as if he feared

44

he'd lose control of his anger if he moved. "The queen never should've sent you on your own like that. She treats you like you're disposable."

"She treats me like I'm capable and unkillable...which I am. Besides, I wasn't alone. I had Nala."

Orion shook his head and snapped his mouth shut on whatever he'd planned to say next.

"Did you run all the way here with her over your shoulders?" he finally asked, breaking the silence.

"Of course not," I said.

He crossed his arms over his chest.

"Only about half the way." He didn't know where I'd been, so there was no point arguing or lying, but I did anyway.

Again, childish. My brother sometimes accused me of purposefully acting out in an attempt to reclaim something I never truly got to experience—a childhood.

And then I'd prove him right by telling him to phaan off or that I didn't need a therapist, thank you very much.

Which was a total lie. After what we went through as children in that orphanage, I definitely needed a therapist.

If only I could trust one with my secrets.

The heat in the room increased and I pulled at the neckline of my shirt. I needed to check on Nala and then I needed to get out of here. I pushed off the chair to stand, only to have Orion place his hand on my shoulder.

He gently applied pressure, knocking me back in the seat. "You need to sit. I can't have you passing out again."

"How is she?" I leaned to the side to find Nala still on the table. Her chest expanded and deflated at a regular rate, and her paws twitched as if she dreamed of chasing rabbits. A bandage had been wrapped around her torso, the padding over the wound already stained red.

How long had I been out?

"She's going to be fine," Orion said. "I told you. Galeon familiars are tough."

I let out a long pent-up breath. "Really?"

He nodded. "Really. She has a little nerve damage to her hind leg that will take some time to heal. She's not mending as quickly as she usually does, so I don't have a time frame for you. And I don't know why this injury has affected her differently. You're lucky you got her here as quickly as you did, any further delay would've been catastrophic to her recovery time and may have led to more nerve damage."

He hesitated, and I tore my gaze away from Nala to study my former hunting partner. "But?"

"But I fear the injury may have strained the bond that exists between the two of you. You passed out from her pain and when I used my magic to assess you for injuries, the bond didn't feel as strong as it used to."

"What does that mean?"

"You're vulnerable."

"I've never been vulnerable." I bit my lip. That was also a lie. I had been vulnerable as a child, and I'd paid for that with pain.

"Yet, you just passed out. Death isn't always the worst fate, Emi. You might be immortal, you might not be killable, but you can still be hurt. Damaged. You need to rest. Nala needs to heal."

Unease swirled in my gut. Orion assumed like everyone else my immortality was tied to Nala, and maybe it was now. But it hadn't always been that way. I'd had enough run-ins with death before meeting my companion to question everything I'd been told about galeon descendants. But how did I question the information without revealing my secrets?

"Let the bond grow strong again." Orion's words ripped me away from my thoughts. "You shouldn't go hunting with her right now and I don't think you should go hunting without her either. Maybe take it easy. Stay in Perga until she's healed."

"Take it easy?" I smiled at Orion's comment. "I'm not familiar with that term."

Orion pressed his lips together and took a deep breath. "I'm aware. But for Nala's sake, you better find a way."

"She really will be fine?" I whispered.

Orion expression softened. "Yes. I don't suppose you'd let her stay here for a few days?"

I glanced at Nala, her coat matted with dried blood. "No. I think it's best I take her home and make her comfortable."

As if she heard her name, Nala stirred, her body twitching. She thumped her tail on the table. But her eyes stayed shut. She must be exhausted. Normally, she'd bounce awake and bowl me over.

I stood from the uncomfortable chair and staggered

past Orion to make my way to her. My vision swam, my head grew light. I fell forward but caught myself on the operating table.

Nala's eyes popped open, and she whined. She scrambled on the smooth surface to sit up.

Orion groaned somewhere behind me and mumbled something about peas and pods.

A wet tongue slapped my cheek.

My eyes stung, and I reached forward to grab the scruff of her neck.

My familiar.

My heart.

My companion for life. The one thing that promised to stay with me when everyone else left.

I rested my head against hers and closed my eyes, inhaling the nutty scent of her fur.

Nala whined again and began to pant. The foulness of her breath hit me, and I recoiled.

"Ugh, girl. You need a mint."

Her tail thumped harder on the tabletop as if she understood what I said and found it hilarious.

"Come on." Orion stepped forward and ran his hand down Nala's back. "I'll help you get her home."

7

Orion followed close behind me with Nala in his arms, as I made my way along the rocky path leading up to the front door of my cabin. His leather boots made a soft scuffing sound along the dirt, but he hadn't spoken since we left his place.

With a quick flick of the wrist, I unlocked the door and swung it wide to make room for Orion and Nala. Fading light shone through the window to illuminate the interior.

Home.

When Orion stepped inside, the place grew smaller. He'd been over countless of times before, hanging out and sharing food until the sun started to lighten the sky. That all stopped when we'd slept together.

I followed them inside and closed the door behind me.

Part of me wanted to ask Orion to stay, to use his strong arms and wicked tongue to help me unwind and

49

forget how close I'd come to losing my familiar. To forget if she'd been anything other than a bonded animal, she would've died today.

Instead, I remained silent and watched as Orion gently set Nala down on the couch. He straightened and looked over at me expectantly.

"Thank you for all your help," I said.

He nodded, his Adam's apple bobbing as he swallowed. "Of course. I'd do anything to help Nala."

He would do anything to help me, too. And the thought warmed my heart.

Then I remembered how I'd left things between us and that I was a giant asshole. My legs itched to run. I locked my knees instead and pulled my shoulders back. No more running. I was better than this. Stronger.

"Look, Rye—" I started.

"Emi," Orion said.

We paused and exchanged a look.

Orion waved his hand in my direction. "Ladies first."

"I..." I pulled my bow free and hung it on the hook by the door.

He pressed lips together. "You've been avoiding me."

I didn't bother denying it.

"I am not an idiot, Emi. I realize our night together meant more to me than it did to you."

"It's not that." Well, it was. It totally was. I liked him, but I could never love him. How could I let anything develop between us when I held on to so many secrets? I'd accepted long ago that I'd live a long and lonely life.

Even if I could trust Orion with the truth, or

somehow stomach a big fat lie existing between us, I couldn't hold love in my heart.

I'd tried that once. It ended with heartbreak and a hard life lesson.

I'd never find love again, and I didn't want to. Love deserved complete honesty and trust, and that wasn't something I could give. Nor something I could afford emotionally.

Orion narrowed his eyes, but then another thought must've crossed his mind because his expression softened. "Did you... Did you not enjoy our time together?"

"No." I winced. "No. That's definitely not it." The man had a way with his hips and tongue. "Definitely not that."

He rocked back on his heels as his eyebrows slashed down in a severe frown. "Then it's what I said in the morning."

I sighed, unsure whether to reach out and touch him, but that felt like such a condescending thing to do. "I like you, Rye."

"Just not like that."

"Not like that," I admitted. I liked him as a friend and occasional hunting partner. I respected him. I liked who he was, but I wasn't in love with him.

"Well, shit, Emi. You should've just said something." He crossed arms over his chest. "I thought I meant enough to you to at least warrant an honest conversation."

"Your penis was literally resting on my thigh. Excuse

me if I didn't feel like breaking your heart in that moment."

His lips lifted at the corners, not enough to be a whole smile, but enough to tell me I'd amused him. "It takes a little more than that to break my heart."

"Noted."

"So, explain what happened next? I told you I loved you and then we had one last round before you ran away. What was that? A pity phaan or an attempt to distract me from how you didn't return my sentiments?"

"No."

He waited.

"Maybe a little of a distraction, but that wasn't the only reason."

"You just wanted to take me for another ride?"

"Maybe." Yes. Definitely yes.

I really was a horrible person.

His mouth twisted into a wide smile. "You're fine with sleeping with me even though you don't love me."

"I'm sorry. You didn't deserve that. I should've told you I wasn't looking for anything serious. I'm a terrible person."

Maybe I should take my brother's advice and talk to someone about all the feelings twisting me up inside. But I couldn't risk telling a therapist all my problems, all the things holding me back, so what was the point?

Orion shook his head and stepped in close. "No, you're not. But you are confusing. So what if you don't love me? That's obviously not a requirement for what we did together. And guess what? Nothing bad happened.

I'm okay with you not returning my feelings. What I'm not okay with is you ignoring me instead of coming to my bed and screaming my name."

"But—"

He reached out, grabbed the strap of my quiver, and pulled. I staggered forward into the heat of his body.

"Let me phaan you senseless, Emi."

"What about that heart of yours?"

"Like I said, it doesn't break that easily."

"But—"

"Let me worry about my own heart." He let go of the strap, releasing me. "But stop avoiding me."

"Okay."

He glanced over at Nala before turning toward the door. "You know where to find me."

He left me standing there, mouth gaped open with thoughts and memories swirling around in my head. Heat spread through my body. It wasn't as though I avoided casual relationships. I avoided relationships, altogether. Which meant I went for prolonged periods of time without any physical or emotional companionship. But I'd found myself getting more and more lonely.

Why shouldn't I pursue something physical with Orion? He made me feel safe. He was a great person. And he certainly knew how to take care of my needs.

I shook my head and grabbed a book from the nearby bookshelf. I didn't have to decide anything right now and I wanted to rest with Nala before I contacted the queen. Eventually, I needed to report what had happened at the forest's edge, but I had an hour to settle my thoughts and relax my mind and body before I dealt with that stress.

I curled up on the couch beside Nala and opened my book. I'd left the story where the main character just met the love interest, but she didn't know he's a prince in disguise, and currently thought he was an ass.

I sunk into the couch a little more, my lips curling up, and read the banter between the characters while I gave Nala some pets with my free hand. She might be sleeping, but I liked to believe somewhere in her subconscious she still knew I was right beside her.

The door to my cabin burst open, a cold gust of air blowing in from the outside.

I jerked upright so fast the book flew from my hands and fell to the floor with a clatter.

Nala snapped awake and lurched up, only to tense, and yelp in pain.

I turned toward the door in time to watch my brother stroll into my cabin with one of his friends as though he owned the place.

I scowled at my brother. I didn't recognize his friend. He'd turned away as soon as he'd walked through the door to study the wall with bookshelves and framed drawings.

"Have you ever heard of knocking?" I kissed Nala's head and inhaled her nutty scent before reaching down to retrieve my book. Several of the pages had bent in the fall and I'd lost my place.

If he wasn't my brother, I would've killed him.

Phaan, I might kill him anyway.

"Come on, Emi. Is that any way to greet your favourite brother?" He held his arms wide, and a grin spreading across his face.

"You're my only brother." I unbent the damaged pages of my book before closing the cover and setting it down on the cushion beside me. With a deep breath and a silent prayer for patience, I pulled myself off the couch to face my twin.

So much for relaxing.

Paul had a smile that got him in and out of trouble. His tall frame took up most of the entranceway and his personality could fill the whole cabin on its own. With the same brown hair, hazel eyes, fair skin, and straight nose, most people figured out we were siblings, but not everyone guessed we were twins.

Though we didn't know who got here first, Paul had arrived in this messed up world on the same day as me and got all the charisma. He thrived in the spotlight and always knew how to say the right thing to put people at ease. Looking at him was like looking at pure sunshine. If you stared too long or got too close, you'd burn yourself, but that didn't stop everyone from wanting to enter his orbit.

If Paul was the sun, then I was his shadow, existing in the dark, operating in stealth. My only redeeming qualities were Nala and my ability to protect the forest animals.

That was why I was a guardian of the forest. The only guardian of the forest. And my brother worked for the queen at the castle in Wast as a politician of sorts. He represented Perga and negotiated trade deals.

"I *am* your only brother." Paul's smile grew. "Which is all the more reason for you to indulge me."

"I'm not going to indulge your complete lack of manners. You can't just barge in here with your random friends." I waved at the other guy, who still hadn't said a thing. He hadn't even bothered to look my way, his back still turned to me as he studied my bookshelves. He was probably some city snob, and his manners were more appalling than my brother's, which said a lot.

"What if I was naked? What if I had someone over?"

Paul snorted. "We both know you're too much of a harpy to entertain anyone, and this is—"

"I don't give a phaan who he is. Get out."

Maybe I should get Orion to come back so I could properly scandalize my brother, and then he'd think twice about barging in.

"You really should," Paul said.

I shut my mouth and frowned. I really should what?

I glanced at the back of the tall stranger. In slow motion, he turned around to face me. He was attractive in that dark, brooding, "I have issues" way. Olive skin tone, straight nose with a slight upturn at the end, full lips pulled up at the corners as if he found this amusing. A wave of dread crashed through my body as the man's gaze lifted to meet mine. There was no mistaking that devastating face, nor the familiar hatred flashing in his dark gaze.

"Hello, Mouse."

8

I stared at the man in front of me at a loss for words. I hadn't seen Ace in years. What was it now? Five years? I had been twenty when he'd left and hopelessly in love. Frankly, I could go another five years before I faced Ace again. The infatuation had long fled, replaced with low simmering anger and hatred.

I turned to Paul. "You can't be serious."

"I thought you'd be happy," Paul said. "You were in love with this guy. Practically obsessed."

I ignored the heat travelling across my cheeks and jabbed my finger in the air at my brother. "I was not."

"Don't be shy, Mouse. Everyone knew you had a thing for me." Ace had a beautifully seductive voice. Crap. I forgot how much I liked how his voice sounded.

"Just another reason why I hate people and work alone." I scowled. "They talk too much about shit that doesn't involve them."

Ace smirked.

"I was a twenty-year-old girl with a crush at best." I lifted my chin, despite the half-truth. I was twenty when he'd broken my heart, but I'd known Ace since I was twelve, and he was fourteen. I'd had a crush on him for eight years before he saw me as anything other than my brother's sister and even that was short lived. His affection only lasted long enough to get my hopes up. "I would've swooned over anyone with a heartbeat who smiled in my direction."

"Funny. I don't remember smiling at you at all." Ace rubbed the stubble on his chin.

Well, he certainly had a selective memory. My problem was that I didn't suffer from the same affliction. I remembered everything.

Everything.

Every word, every gesture, every stolen moment and my heart had broken into a million pieces because of it.

"Okay, I'll bite." I folded my arms over my chest. "Why is he here? And why should I care?" And why wasn't Paul angrier? He had just as much cause to hate Ace. Had he forgiven him so easily?

This guy had left both of us without a word. Just thinking about those first days when we realized he was gone brought up a whole well of emotions—sadness, grief, pain. I settled on anger and held it close.

Meanwhile, Ace kept his expression passive, his large, toned body relaxed, his brown gaze locked on mine.

Paul let out a long, exasperated breath before jerking his thumb in Ace's direction. "He's—" Paul's gaze landed on Nala. "Shit, Emi. What happened?"

"Witnesses claimed to see a hunter at the edge of the Danu Forest and filed reports with the palace," I explained. "The queen sent me out to have a look."

"And you found him?" Ace's gaze widened.

He really shouldn't have been so surprised. This was my job, after all, and I was good at it. He probably still thought of me as the naïve twenty-year-old I'd been when he left.

"I found *them*," I said. "Turns out there was more than one. They shot Nala, but I made sure they paid for it."

"They're all dead?" he asked.

"Yes."

"How can you be sure?" Ace asked.

I winced. At one point in my life, I more than liked a lot about this man. But right now, I just wanted to smack him.

"I shot them all." I raised my eyebrow. "None of them got away, if that's what you're asking."

"Did you inspect their tracks to ensure they didn't have a spotter who took off once the fight broke out?" Ace asked.

"No." Dammit. That was a good point. "I was too busy looking after my familiar. I planned to go back after I got some rest and made my report to Queen Titania."

"The spotter will be long gone by then."

"If there was a spotter, they were already long gone as soon as the fight broke out. My familiar will always be my priority."

Ace pressed his lips together and nodded in a short jerk. "Of course."

"Why is he here?" I jabbed the air with my finger and pointed at the man who'd broken my heart.

My brother sighed. "He's your new partner."

My brain misfired and I sat in silence while I tried to process that statement.

"My new partner?" I rocked back on my heels and stared at Ace, taking in his eerie silence, and deep brown eyes that almost appeared black. He was taller than my brother, which put him around six foot five, and he had a strong build and centred way of moving.

He was nice to look at.

He'd always been nice to look at. But the years that he had been gone had turned him from a young man to something much more devastating.

His attitude still sucked, though.

"I don't need a partner," I snapped. From what I remembered of Ace's hunting skills, he was average at best anyway. "I have Nala."

"The queen disagrees." Amusement pulled at Paul's lips. He always found humour in situations where all I ever found was irritation.

"For better or worse, Ace is your new partner." Paul's grin grew and I seriously debated reaching for my bow and arrows. They were sadly out of reach. Without a doubt, whatever came out of his mouth next would—

"Try not to sleep with this one," Paul said.

I sputtered.

"Besides..." Paul continued, unfazed by the murder

in my gaze. "Is this anyway to greet an old friend of ours?" My brother obviously woke up this morning and chose violence. He was determined to put his life in danger today.

I ignored his question and stuck to his statement about Queen Titania. "When did the queen make this decision and why didn't she say anything to me during our meeting yesterday morning or when she gave me my order last night?"

"She assigned Ace as your partner this morning," Paul said. "But it was after Blake left with the queen's other letters. She felt you'd receive this information better in person anyway."

I glared at my brother. I normally loved him so much but right now he was being a jerk. I wish he hadn't said that part about sleeping with my last partner in front of Ace. I didn't want Ace knowing anything about me besides the bare minimum.

Orion and I had always worked well together, and it had made sense to team up to go after larger poaching groups in the past, but he'd never been assigned as my partner. The queen had never dictated how I got the job done as long as I got it done. At least not until now. "Queen Titania can't have a problem with my work."

I was the best, dammit. I was the only one with a familiar who was allowed in the sacred forest and my shooting accuracy surpassed even Paul's. He might be her favorite, but I was her best.

My brother shrugged. "Ace is new. The queen wants you to show him around."

I narrowed my eyes. Ace was new? He grew up in Perga with us. He might not have been a hunter for the queen, but he wasn't exactly unfamiliar with this area or the town.

"Still going by Ace, huh?" I asked. His full name was Actaeon, but he always claimed it was a mouthful and that he preferred his nickname.

He shrugged. "Normally, the ladies love it."

His expression didn't change. He said those words with a serious deadpan, and a flat tone.

"First time for everything, I guess," I said before turning back to Paul. "If Queen Titania wants a tour guide, why aren't you doing it?"

"I don't make the rules," my twin said.

"I'm not any more pleased about this than you, Mouse," Ace said.

I always hated his nickname for me. "I have a name."

"Would you prefer princess? You're certainly acting like one. And I certainly don't need an immature spit of a girl leading me around the forest. I will do well enough on my own without your..." He waved his hand in the air. "Drama."

"My drama?"

"Everyone's heard of the youngest galeon descendent to bond a familiar with a questionable respect for author-ity." His gaze finally dropped to rake my body from head to toe. "I see not much has changed. I'd hoped you'd matured over these last few years, but you're the same snarky little brat. Can't say I'm impressed, and I certainly can't say I want any part of whatever shit-fest you're getting yourself into."

I sucked in a breath and glared at my brother. "Absolutely not."

"I knew you would say that." Paul sighed and reached inside his jacket to pull out a folded piece of paper with a coffee stain on the corner. He held out the paper and waved it in front of me. "From the queen."

"Did you use it as a napkin?" I snatched the letter from his hand and quickly unfolded it. Scanning the words, my mind struggled to make sense of this idiocy. "She's threatening my job. I am the only guardian of the Danu Forest."

"The queen really doesn't like insubordination, Em. That you've gotten away with it for so long is a testament to your unique abilities and value to her."

I gripped the paper a little too hard and it crinkled in my fist.

"I'll leave you to sort this out." Paul turned toward the door. "There's a bonfire tonight and I don't plan on missing out."

"Don't you dare." He couldn't possibly mean to leave me alone with this jerk.

My brother paused at the door long enough to wink at me before he walked out.

I stood by my couch, blinking at Ace in complete silence. He made no move to leave or speak, and simply stared back at me with that serious face of his.

"For the record," I said. "I don't like this."

"For the record, neither do I."

I scoffed. "You should be thrilled to work with me. I don't know whose ass you kissed to get this arrangement, but Queen Titania doesn't usually pair newbie hunters with me." She didn't pair anyone with me.

"I'm new to hunting for the queen, not new to hunting. I haven't spent these years twiddling my thumbs and relaxing." He shrugged, and his gaze dropped to where Nala curled up to sleep on the couch. "Besides, how good can you be if you allowed your familiar to get injured?"

Ice flowed over my skin, and I clenched my hands into fists, the letter from the queen scrunched into a ball.

"Get out," I said.

He jerked back, his gaze narrowing. "We have things we need to discuss."

"We can discuss whatever you like tomorrow when I'm less likely to try to stab you," I said.

He clamped his mouth shut and glowered. "Fine."

Without another word, he spun toward the door and walked out of the cabin, pulling the door shut behind him. I would've slammed the door, but he didn't. Instead, Ace closed it gently, and for some reason that made things even worse.

Maybe I was a princess.

Maybe I was spoiled and used to getting my way.

Maybe I was immature and needed to grow up.

Regardless, I'd show this asshole why I got away with it tomorrow.

But first, I had to write a message to the queen and

report the hunters. My hour was up, and it was back to business.

9

The fire in the center of Perga roared, its blazing flames leaping and licking at the night sky while casting dancing shadows on the faces of the gathered crowd. The scent of smoke and spices wafted through the palpable heat. Amidst the crackling of burning logs, a steady hum of chatter filled the air. As the night wore on, the conversations would escalate to shouts as the alcohol flowed and everyone's inhibitions faded.

As soon as I arrived, Sley rushed to me with open arms and gave me a warm hug. "I was worried you'd skip the bonfire again to stay in and read a book," she said.

"Reading is not a bad way to spend an evening," I replied. "In fact, it sounds like a perfect phaaning night."

Sley let go to stand beside me. "Then why are you here?"

It was a valid question. A great one. I had no idea.

Originally, I'd tried to find Blake to give him a

message for the queen, but he wasn't home. When I started to head back, I heard the commotion of the bonfire and hesitated. Suddenly, I couldn't stand the idea of staying cooped up in my cabin tonight...like the meek little mouse Ace always accused me of being. If I stayed in, I'd be confirming everything he already thought of me. Even though I knew I shouldn't care what he thought, it still bothered me. I stayed. He left. This was my town.

I scanned the faces of the group gathered around the bonfire, acknowledging anyone who met my gaze with a nod. I was familiar with everyone in town, and the thought of someone among us stealing made my stomach turn. I might not like a lot of the residents, and more than a few of them disliked me, but a thief? I couldn't wrap my brain around one of our own stealing from the community.

As the flames of the bonfire swayed and crackled, orange and red light played across the faces of the crowd. With a confident stride, Ace moved through the gathering, his fluid grace giving away his training as a fighter. His dark eyes reflected the orange glow of the fire as he scanned the crowd and took in his surroundings.

He wore leather hunting pants and a matching vest. A dark cloak hung over his shoulders and swished behind him as he moved. The metal handles of the daggers strapped to his thigh glinted in the orange light with each step.

He looked dangerous.

And way too alluring considering he was such a jerk.

Next to me, Sley released a low whistle, her gaze fixated on him like a predator stalking its prey. As she relaxed her tense posture, a faint smile crept onto her lips. "Who's that?"

"Actaeon," I said.

"Hunter?"

"Yes."

"Maybe I'll abandon my dreams of a phaanon warrior and settle for a ripped hunter new to town."

I hesitated and tried to shake off the tension in my shoulders. Objectively speaking, he was a good-looking man. But he certainly wasn't the phaanon warrior of Sley's dreams with a nine-inch schlong.

"What?" Sley pressed. "Are you already banging him? Phaan. That's just not fair."

"I am not banging Ace."

Sley studied my face and sighed. "But you want to."

"Absolutely not," I said. "Don't let me hold you back from your dreams."

Sley shook her head. "Besties before bangs, my love. Who is he?"

I sighed. Sley had always been good at reading people. "Remember when I mentioned my old friend from when I was a teenager?"

She straightened and narrowed her eyes. "The guy who vanished after telling you he loved you?"

"Yeah." I gestured toward Ace with a wave of my hand. "That's him."

Sley rocked back on her heels, her mouth dropping

open. "Well, he's officially on my shit list. And also officially off limits."

"That's not necessary."

Sley shrugged, but she'd already made a decision. I could tell. She always made up her mind with a sense of finality. Like when she decided we'd be best friends. She pegged me as the village introvert, adopted me as her best friend and declared that we were friends forever. I'd never been happier to have no say in a matter.

My attention drifted back to Ace in time to watch Maria, the baker, glide over to him and hook her arm around his waist. Her plump lips turned up in a mischievous smile, and a sharp pang of jealousy stabbed my chest.

Sley tensed next to me. "Guess we hate Maria now."

"No, we don't." I sighed and tried to shake the agitation clinging to my spine. "We're not going to hate another woman just because she has her own dreams and desires. She's not intentionally trying to hurt me. Besides, I love her pastries, especially the cinnamon rolls."

"Sure, but...we could despise her." Sley bit her lip. "Maybe even a little."

I shook my head, and Sley let out a frustrated sigh.

"You're always so reasonable," she groaned.

"Wait, are we talking about Emi?" Orion chimed in as he joined us. "The guardian known for causing chaos wherever she goes?"

"I do not cause chaos." I placed my hands on my hips and huffed. I caused death, if we were going to get technical about it.

Orion smirked but didn't bother commenting.

The baker had moved even closer to Ace, her ample breasts pressing against his chest as she whispered in his ear. Ace must've mumbled something incredibly hilarious, because Maria started laughing and smacking his arm.

Ace smirked and looked up. Our gazes locked from across the roaring bonfire, and he stilled, his smile slipping. Before I could make a snide gesture, his attention slid to where Orion stood beside me. He stiffened and his lip curled into a snarl.

At the same time, Graham and Gavin passed where Ace and Maria stood, bumping into Ace's shoulder before making their way toward us.

"Ugh...Looks like Graham's headed this way," Sley announced. "I'm out."

My friend disappeared into the throng of people.

"You seem a little preoccupied tonight." Orion leaned down. "Want me to help you forget your troubles?"

I let a slow smile spread across my face. That was exactly what I needed.

Orion reached out and traced his finger along my arm. "With Blake back already, it won't be long before you receive your next mission. We should enjoy the time we have."

The mention of the messenger's name snapped me to attention. "He's back?"

Normally, he would have stayed overnight in Wast instead of travelling at night. After finding his cabin empty earlier, I'd expected him to arrive tomorrow at the earliest.

Orion groaned and closed his eyes. "I knew that was the wrong thing to say the moment it came out of my mouth."

"Sorry." I flashed him a sheepish smile. "Raincheck?"

"Of course."

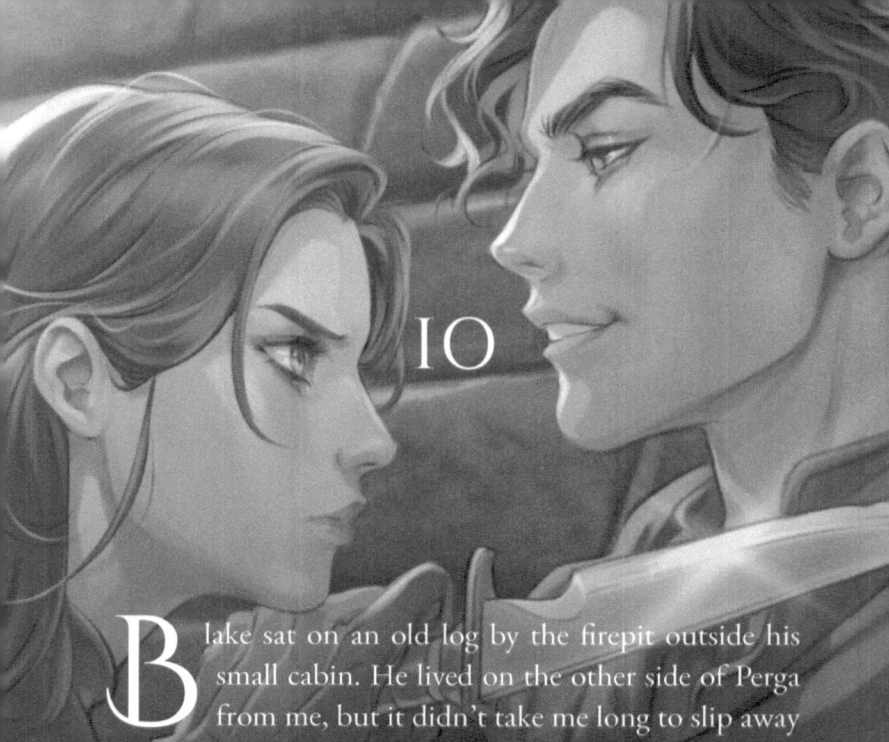

IO

Blake sat on an old log by the firepit outside his small cabin. He lived on the other side of Perga from me, but it didn't take me long to slip away from the bonfire to make my way to his place. Even in the dark. I knew the path well.

Blake looked up at my approach and groaned.

"I just got back," he said.

I understood Blake's weariness all too well. The burden of constantly communicating with the queen's court lay heavily on his shoulders. Normally, I'd wait until morning, but the urgency of the situation outweighed any desire to provide Blake a break.

"Sorry..."

"No, you're not." Blake's tired gaze flashed with a mix of curiosity and resignation as he motioned for me to sit beside him on the log. The fire crackled and danced, casting shadows across his face. "What do you have for me?"

I held out the message, the wax seal proudly presenting my guardian crest. "It can wait until early tomorrow morning."

"But you couldn't?"

I shook my head. "I didn't want to risk missing you before you headed out."

Blake nodded and plucked the letter from my hand. He studied my face in the flickering light, his frown deepening with each blink. "Are you okay?"

My mind immediately went to my wolf familiar's injury, and then to Maria plastering her beautiful body all over Ace. "I will be."

Blake opened his jacket to slide the message into an internal pocket and turned back to me. Normally, I would've already made my way home, but I made the mistake of sitting down.

My feet felt so heavy, my eyelids droopy. Why did I talk myself into going to the bonfire party tonight?

"You need sleep, Emi," he said. "Time for bed, I think."

Before I could explain how my limbs were too heavy to move, Sley crashed through the forest and halted near the edge. The orange glow from the fire cast her in harsh shadows, making it appear as though she was burning up in front of us. "Are you kidding me, Blake?"

His mouth dropped open. "Wha..."

"You avoid me but see no problem propositioning my best friend?" Her gaze twinkled with mischief.

"No, I—" Blake leapt to his feet. "That's not what I—"

Sley held up her hand. "Save it, messenger. You can explain it to me tomorrow. Right now, I need my friend before she falls asleep and lands in your fire pit."

"Me?" I jabbed my chest with my thumb.

"Yes, you." She stepped around the fire to latch onto my arm and haul me to my feet. "There's been another theft."

I blinked away the sleepiness still clinging to my mind as Sley's words registered. Another theft? My gaze slid to Blake.

"Oh, he already knows, remember?" Sley said.

"Not about the new theft."

She shrugged. "Hard to keep a secret in this town. Everyone will find out soon enough."

"How did you find out? We were just at the bonfire together."

"Had a feeling."

I tilted my head and tapped my foot.

Sley sighed and looked away. "I was avoiding Graham and went by the storage house to check on it. Maybe even to hide in it. I found the door open."

Sley had absolutely planned to hide in the storage house. "What did they take this time?"

"Do I look like someone who walks into a dark building at night by myself?" she asked.

"You were literally going to hide in it."

"That was before I found the door open, and it made everything creepy." Sley dragged me toward the path that led to the storage house through the forest. "We need to investigate," she said, her voice laced with determination.

Blake watched us with a mix of concern and confusion. "I'll go with you," he volunteered, his earlier weariness temporarily forgotten.

"No." Sley spun to him and jabbed her finger in his direction. "You stay here. We don't need any distractions."

"We?" I whispered.

"Shh." Sley tightened her grip on my arm, silently urging me to walk away with her. With a final nod to Blake, I stepped into the shadows of the forest and let Sley lead me to the large storage house on the edge of town.

"He wasn't propositioning me, you know," I said.

"Oh, I know."

I raised an eyebrow.

Sley turned to me and winked. "If he had, he'd have a black eye."

I barked out a laugh and nodded. Violence wasn't always the answer, but if Blake had offered me a warm bed while avoiding my best friend—who liked him a lot more than she let on—I wouldn't have been sitting casually beside him on a log, struggling to keep my eyes open. "I'm not sure I would've actually punched him. Not unless he was being a jerk about it."

"Maybe not, but you would've had some things to say." Sley hesitated. "Did he...ask about me at all?"

"We only had time to discuss the queen's business before you showed up. Sorry. Do you want me to—"

"No," she said, her shoulders drooping.

Sley released my arm and motioned for me to stay

quiet as we approached the storage house. Moonlight filtered through the gaps in the trees, casting a silver glow over the weathered exterior of the building. A gust of wind made the old boards creak and groan while sounds of laughter and loud conversation from the nearby bonfire trickled through the forest.

"Did you close the door before you came to get me?" I asked.

"No."

Great. We had a considerate thief.

"Wait here," Sley whispered, disappearing into the shadows.

"Why?" I called out after her.

"Getting some light."

I eyed the ground, soft with thick moss and debated whether I had time to lay down for a bit before Sley returned. But a nap wasn't in my agenda for this evening, at least not right away. Finding the thief was more important. We depended on those supplies for harsh winters and if the chill in the air was any indication, this winter would be particularly nasty.

Minutes turned into an eternity before Sley reappeared with a lit torch in one hand, her expression a mix of triumph and caution. "Let's go see what we can find," she said, beckoning me to follow her inside.

I tiptoed behind Sley, my heart pounding as we entered the dimly lit storage house. Maybe I should've returned to my cabin to grab my bow. I only had a few daggers strapped to me.

The air was thick with the scent of aged wood, grain,

hay and dust, making it difficult to breathe. My throat closed up and my eyes strained to adjust to the darkness as I scanned the shelves and crates lining the walls.

While I searched for possible villains to leap out of the shadows, Sley walked to each shelving unit, stack of crates and cluster of barrels, mentally cataloguing supplies.

"I think I found something," she whispered.

"Another scarf?"

"Come here." Sley led me toward a bunch of barrels stacked in the corner of the room. She crouched down, her nimble fingers moving smaller boxes out of the way before she pointed at the ground. "I thought so."

"You found dirt?" Not exactly a surprise in this place.

She rolled her eyes and jabbed her finger in the air again. "Look harder, guardian."

I squinted, trying to discern what Sley was pointing at. Then, I saw it. A trap door, hidden beneath a crate. The thief must've been in a hurry because the crate hadn't covered one of the edges of the trap door, leaving it partially visible to anyone looking close enough. Unlike everywhere else in this place, no dust had settled over the surface, meaning it had been used recently.

"Did you know this was here?"

"Of course not."

My heart skipped a beat as anticipation coursed through my veins. We'd stumbled upon something significant. I crouched down beside my best friend and together we moved the crate, revealing an iron latch. It took some effort, but we managed to pry it open, revealing a narrow staircase leading into darkness.

"Where does it lead?" I mused.

"How would I know? We just found it."

"The question was rhetorical, Sley."

"Doesn't matter." She shrugged. "Do I look like someone who would descend mysterious stairs into utter darkness?"

I grinned and leaned forward. "But I would."

Sley nodded. "That's really why I'm friends with you. Your complete disregard for danger and the tasty wine you bring home from Wast."

"Come on, *Sleyer.*"

"I told you to stop calling me that," she huffed.

"Never." Taking a deep breath, I unsheathed one of my daggers and descended into the unknown, Sley following close behind me. The air grew colder as we ventured deeper underground, the faint scent of damp earth filling my nose. Our footsteps echoed along the stone walls and Sley's torch flickered and hissed as it provided a small glow of orange light.

We followed the tunnel in near silence, my heart rate speeding up with each step.

"Where do you think it leads?" Sley asked. "I'm already turned around."

"I don't know," I answered. The warm glow of the torch illuminated the uneven surface of the rocky tunnel. "But there are no cobwebs."

"Support beams are old," Sley noted, holding the torch closer to the large slabs of wood that supported the sides and roof of the tunnel. They had grayed and cracked with age. Some had visible signs of rot.

"I practically grew up in this town and I didn't know this tunnel existed," I said.

"So, we're looking for someone older than us?" Sley asked. "I can't see any of the old timers in town doing this."

"Someone older or someone even nosier than us."

"Impossible," Sley said.

"That's what I thought, but evidence suggests otherwise."

Sley pursed her lips. "Looks like we're finally coming to the end."

We'd walked for at least half an hour and Sley's torch burned low. The tunnel had to be at least three to five kilometres long. My skin had long grown cold, and my bed cried for me. It would take just as long to walk back, and we still didn't know what waited for us on the other end.

I climbed the cut-out steps in the dirt and studied the trap door above. Again, no cobwebs. I pushed on the weathered wood, and it moved without complaint. "Ready?"

Sley squeaked in response.

I gently eased the trap to the ground, lowering it gradually to keep quiet. No hinges squeaked. No dust or dirt fell into my eyes. Instead, fresh frigid air whooshed into the tunnel.

As we emerged from its depths, gnarled trees loomed overhead, their branches reaching out like grasping hands. Shadows danced across the forest floor as beams of cool moonlight filtered through the canopy above. Goosebumps prickled my skin as we stepped farther out of the tunnel.

"Where are we?" Sley whispered.

I wish I didn't recognize the bent tree in front of me or the nearby trail that ran under an old oak with a large burnt branch. I wish it had been any other place than this. My heart sunk in my chest. "The forbidden forest."

II

I slung the leather strap of my quiver over my shoulder and stomped to the main area of Perga. Hunters met at the fire pit at dawn before heading out on their regular routes. I hadn't told Ace when or where to meet, but my brother probably did. If Ace didn't show, I'd have to track him down and part of me really hoped for that outcome. I'd give him a wake up call he'd never forget.

My tall leather boots crunched the dirt, rocks, and damp leaves as I took the narrow path through town. My muscles complained—tired and sore from the hunters' attack and my midnight tunnel sleuthing with Sley. We had to find out who was behind these thefts before they cleaned out the town's entire winter stores.

After a long walk back home from the Danu Forest, we decided to lock the trapdoor to the tunnel. The town already knew about the theft, so logically, the thief or thieves had to know we were onto them as well. But I had to push the storage theft to the side for the immediate future. I had other things to deal with.

Like Ace.

Sure enough, he sat on one of the logs by the town's central fire pit, my brother at his side. He'd chosen dark brown hunting leathers today and opted to go without a cloak.

The sight of my brother beside him disappointed me. I wasn't surprised to see Paul, though. These two had been remarkably close growing up. Within weeks of arriving in Perga, Ace and my brother had become besties while I got delegated as the third wheel. That had been a hard transition and part of young-me would've hated Ace for it, but I'd been too obsessed with him to hold anything against him besides my naked body—not that he'd noticed me at the time.

That all changed, of course, when Ace left without so much as a goodbye.

My brother obviously excelled at forgiveness more than I did. I wasn't the only one Ace had hurt.

"Have a good time last night?" I asked, keeping my tone light and definitely not trying to recall how Maria pressed her tits into his body.

Jealousy was such an ugly emotion, but apparently, I wasn't above experiencing it.

I didn't even like the jerk anymore.

Paul grunted and stretched his arms over his head. I hadn't seen him last night at the bonfire at all, but that wasn't out of the ordinary. He usually found a willing bed partner or partners early and spent the rest of the evening in a private celebration.

I gagged a little in my mouth.

"A good time?" Ace mused. "I certainly received a warm welcome."

I narrowed my eyes. I didn't want to ask what he meant, though the suggestion was clear.

And why did I even care? I hated him and needed to focus on more important things.

Since Ace's arrival, I'd had time to cool down and think on the sequence of events over the last few days. Something just wasn't adding up. I'd been attacked twice, sure, but the queen would've only known about one of those attacks before she assigned Ace my partner. Something else was going on.

"What happened?" I asked Paul.

"From what I hear, Maria threw herself at our friend here." Paul jerked his thumb in Ace's direction.

"Not my friend and not what I was asking."

"Took all night to extract myself from her in case that's what you're asking," Ace chimed in.

"Is that what we're calling it now?" I shook my head. I had no desire to discuss Ace's *extractions*. "And again, not what I was asking. Something bad must've happened for Queen Titania to order me to take a partner and then threaten me, her most skilled hunter, if I didn't comply."

Paul and Ace exchanged a look. The latter shrugged and looked away, leaving it to my brother to tell me the truth.

Irritation made my skin itch and heat traveled up my neck and cheeks. My brother should've told me everything already. I shouldn't have had to ask in the first place.

"A body was found in the forest," Paul said.

"So? I am fairly sure I left about six there the other day."

"It was Dita."

I froze. "Dita?"

He nodded.

How was that possible? Dita was a galeon descendent with a bonded familiar. She was as indestructible as me, though she chose a different role in our society.

"How is that possible?" I asked.

"We don't know."

"What happened to her familiar?"

"No sign, but given Dita's death, I would assume the familiar met a similar fate."

"But how is that possible?" Maybe if I asked the same question twice, I'd get a different answer.

"Like I said, we don't know," Paul repeated, a little more sternly. "There were no animal markings or wounds other than a single arrow shot to the chest." Paul nodded at Ace. "Having more hunters around isn't a bad thing. Having someone watch your back isn't a bad thing. I don't think the queen meant for Ace to be punishment. I think she's trying to protect you."

"We'll have to agree to disagree on that." I didn't need Ace's protection. I had Nala.

Ace folded his arms over his chest.

"How did she die?" I asked Paul. Ace didn't deserve any of my attention.

"The arrow in the chest doesn't give it away?" Ace asked.

"An arrow isn't enough to kill someone like Dita." I glared at Ace. "There had to be more to it than just a well-placed arrow."

"And why would you think I'd know the answer to that?" Paul asked.

"You're Queen Titania's golden child. You always know everything that's going on."

"Well, I don't know this."

"Can you get me in to see her?" I asked.

"What?" Paul snapped his head back as if I slapped him, his eyes widening. "You want to see the queen voluntarily?"

"Not the queen. I want to see Dita's body."

"Why the phaan would you want to see a dead body?" Ace asked.

"Don't tell me you're squeamish about bodies? You're here to hunt, not pick flowers."

He scowled at me, his entire expression turning dark and deadly.

"Well?" I turned to Paul. "Do you think you can get me in? Pretty please. I'm your favourite sister, after all."

A single arrow shouldn't have been enough to take down Dita. As far as I knew, nothing existed that could kill a bonded immortal, at least not anymore, but it wasn't like immortals lined up, offering to act as guinea pigs for maiming, beheading, and getting set on fire, so not everything could be discounted.

A memory of the pain spreading through Nala's body flashed through my mind and made my stomach twist in a knot. Was that arrow killing Nala? Would it have eventually killed both of us? But then, why did I survive?

"You took a shot through the heart," Paul said.

"I did." I reached up and rubbed my chest at the memory. Luckily, Paul didn't say when. Ace didn't need to know about any of that. The incident had happened a long time ago. Abandoned at an early age, Paul and I had grown up in an orphanage and later on fled the physical and emotional abuse to live on the streets of Wast. After Paul took what should've been a fatal blow to the head with a bat, the leader of our gang suspected Paul was a galeon. To test that theory, he shot me in the chest and his suspicions were confirmed.

Without familiars, we both should've died anyway, regardless of our immortality–but we didn't.

Queen Titania had been the one to find us. Or rather, the queen had been who the gang leader approached as a prospective buyer for us. Luckily, she hadn't dismissed his claims and paid the low price of fifty gales for our lives. She'd told us never to speak a word about what had happened. People would ask questions we didn't have answers to.

"When did you take an arrow to the heart?" Ace raised his eyebrows. "I think I would've remembered that."

I shrugged, not looking over at my brother. "A lot has happened since you left."

My brother and I kept our promise to the queen and kept the information secret. I didn't like the queen for a lot of reasons, but I trusted her to protect her own interests and I just happened to be one of them.

"Must be nice having a familiar." Ace scratched his jaw.

I exchanged a look with my brother. Not many knew about our lives before we moved to Perga on Queen Titania's orders, and we both preferred it that way. Ace and Paul might've become best friends during those formative years, but nothing and no one would ever get between my brother, me, and our secrets.

"So? You'll get me in?" I squinted at Paul.

"What exactly do you think you'll find that the examiner won't?" Ace asked.

I shrugged, not quite sure of the answer myself. "Maybe I just need to see her for myself."

"Did you know her?" Ace asked.

"Yes." Who didn't? Dita was beautiful and charismatic and always kept the nobles from other cities company when they visited. She made sure they remained allies instead of enemies. And if they had bad intentions, she took care of them with quick efficiency.

Not many people knew Dita was one of King Oberon's many assassins. Where Queen Titania commanded the ragtag group of hunters to monitor and manage both humans and animals alike in the forests surrounding Wast, the king focused his attention on exclusively controlling the people within his city and nearby towns, and he was merciless in his control.

Not only did he have an army at his disposal, he also employed an unspecified number of assassins who he didn't hesitate to utilize.

Paul glanced at the lightening sky. "I'll see what I can do, but I'm not making any promises."

"That's all I ask."

Paul scoffed and turned to walk away, shaking his head.

I didn't need to hear his thoughts to know what he wanted to say–I was asking a lot. Maybe I was a princess. But I gave as equally as I got.

Ace watched me with that eerie stillness of his—as if his rage coiled like a spring and was ready for release, ready to burst into motion.

Now I just needed to figure out his triggers to get him to go away. I smiled sweetly. This man's time with me was limited and finite, and he had no idea just how evil I could be.

Things had changed since he left all those years ago.

He thought I was a princess.

He thought I was a sneaky mouse.

Well, I'd show him just how much I could be both.

Ace narrowed his eyes. "Why are you looking at me like that?"

"Like what?"

"Like you're plotting my gruesome murder and taking great joy in the details."

My smile fell away. "Did it ever occur to you that I was attempting to be nice?"

"And that's your being nice smile?" He cringed. "That smile would scare a phaaning toddler."

I pressed my lips together and glared. "Toddlers are easy to scare so that's not saying a whole lot."

"Go around scaring a lot of toddlers, do you?" He tilted his head.

"Are you done, now?" I asked.

"Done what?"

"Insulting me?"

"Not quite."

I waited.

"I know this must be terribly shocking to the almighty Artemis, the sole guardian of the sacred forest of Danu, but I don't need your help. I stood there and listened to you complain about getting assigned a partner, and you're so stuck up and self-absorbed you never once considered that this wasn't exactly what I wanted either. This isn't the welcome home I'd hoped for, nor the job I wanted."

Ouch. Every word he said stung, and it shouldn't have. I shouldn't care about him or his opinion anymore.

"Well, let's go then. Let's get the truth out in the open. What is it you want? To run off unsupervised in our sacred forest? You might have spent your youth in Perga, but that doesn't mean you're going to get a free pass."

"Are you actually arguing to keep me as your partner?"

"No. I think someone else should be your partner, but I'm surprised you wouldn't want to be with the best."

He snorted. "You're so arrogant."

"It's not arrogance when it's true."

"Is it though?" He cocked his head to the side.

"Is it what?"

"True?" He folded his arms in front of his chest again. "I've heard the stories, but until a few days ago, I'd assumed they were just made up. Everything I heard about you while I was away didn't fit the meek little girl I remember growing up nor the naïve young woman you were when I left. It's hard to know what is true and what is embellished."

Was he questioning my ability? Surely not. "I am one hundred percent real and so is my record."

"Then you wouldn't be opposed to a little demonstration?"

"I have nothing to prove," I said, lifting my chin. Shortly after Ace had left, I'd found Nala, but I'd been a great hunter even before I gained the powers that came with a bonded familiar.

I might've followed Ace and Paul like a lost little mouse, but I'd never been meek a day in my life and he phaaning knew it.

"I disagree," he said. "I am doubting your value as a guide and mentor. Prove me wrong and show me you're capable."

I stuttered, torn between swearing at him, and just stomping off to the forest without him.

His lips quirked up in the corner, almost as if he was waiting for my outburst, almost as if he baited me on purpose. Just as I'd planned to do to him. Was he trying to find my triggers?

Well, I wouldn't fall for it.

I took a deep breath and rolled my shoulders back. This was a perfect opportunity to show him who he'd work with, to remind him how fierce and badass I was. "It seems like we are at an impasse."

"How so?"

"You doubt my worthiness as a guide, and I question your value as a partner. Clearly, there is only one solution."

"Scaring toddlers?" He quirked an eyebrow.

"Of course not. That's only for weekends."

The muscles along his jaw line popped as he clenched his teeth. "What's the solution then?"

"A competition," I said. "Unless you're afraid to lose to a girl?"

He unfolded his arms and leaned closer. "You're on."

"Who died?" Sley's voice fractured the silence. "You look so serious, Em."

I jumped and whirled around to find my friend sauntering into the clearing. I opened my mouth to explain when Sley's gaze slid away from me and snagged on Ace. Her mouth turned down and she looked over at me, worry etched in her brow.

I sighed and shook my head, hoping she'd take the hint and save the questioning for tomorrow. "Sley, meet Actaeon."

"It's Ace," he grumbled.

Sley flashed him a half, closed-lipped smile before pointing at the target laying at my feet. "What's going on here?"

"Friendly competition," Ace said.

"Minus the friend part," I added.

Sley clapped her hands, her gaze sparkling with a conspiratory gleam. "Excellent. You need a witness."

"We don't—" Ace started.

"Absolutely. We're here for your entertainment." I winked at my friend. She had excellent timing.

The sun had crested to its midpoint by the time Ace and I finished setting up the targets in the forest near my cabin. Before Sley showed up, we'd struggled to agree on the test, but we finally settled on three distances for each target. The best shot at each target would win that distance, and the overall winner would have to win at least two of the three targets. I wasn't worried.

I'd win all three.

After we'd settled on the structure of the competition, we hadn't spoken—no friendly banter, or polite conversation. Certainly no catching up after all these years.

Instead, we moved around the clearing with quiet efficiency and cold determination.

I dealt with insufferable men questioning my ability to stand amongst them my whole life. In fact, Ace was probably my first teacher on how to deal with that particular attitude.

I wouldn't step to the side or let some rookie come in and cast doubt on my worthiness ever again.

Was this pride? Yes.

Arrogance? Probably.

Ego? Also, probably yes.

And maybe it wasn't healthy to centre my entire identity and worth on my ability to kill shit with a single arrow, but it was all I had going for me. It was what got me and my brother off the street and what continued to place food on the table.

Ace sat down and pulled his bow from his shoulders to inspect the string, his eyebrows angled down severely, his gaze narrowed.

"Ready?" I asked. I'd already checked my bow and my arrows' fletching before I left home this morning.

Ace stood in one fluid motion and waved at the closest target. "Ladies first."

I scoffed and pointed at him. "Fine, but you could've just said you wanted to lead."

Sley giggled.

He snapped his head back as if I slapped him. "I was trying to be a gentleman."

"Look." I cocked my hip. "We both know I'm not a lady and you're certainly not a gentleman so let's cut the crap and fake cute shit. You're the challenger, so you go first."

He pressed his lips together and stomped over to the line I'd drawn in the dirt with a stick. Without a word, he pulled an arrow from his quiver, notched it, and released. The arrow sunk into the target.

My gaze snagged on the board, and I sucked in a breath. Well, shit.

Bull's-eye.

Sley whistled.

I glanced over at my friend, and she slapped her hand over her mouth and shook her head. She didn't need to apologize or hide her reaction, though. I appreciated her loyalty. Sley always had my back.

It was a fantastic shot, maybe even more impressive by his lack of prep. He hadn't taken any time to sight the target after he notched the arrow.

My skin prickled as all the little hairs on my arms stood up. This wasn't the Ace I remembered. The teen boy had grown up and somehow levelled up while away.

"Looks like I won't need those additional shots," he said, a smug smile spreading across his face.

Of course, he wouldn't. He couldn't beat a bull's-eye.

But I could.

I shoved him out of the way and stepped to the line drawn in the ground. Letting the magic flow around me, I kept my gaze locked on Ace's smug face as I drew and fired a single arrow without looking at the target. My magic hummed in the air. Wood splintered and I smiled at Ace.

Truly smiled.

I didn't need to look at the target to know what had happened. I might not understand my magic, but it had never failed me.

Ace narrowed his eyes and his smile faltered. Slowly, he turned away from me to look at the target. His mouth dropped open. My arrow had split his down the shaft to strike the bull's-eye.

Sley squealed and clapped her hands again.

"Phaan," he muttered and ran a hand through his dishevelled brown hair.

"Looks like I won't need those additional shots, either," I said.

"Let's see if you can repeat that." Ace raised his bow and fired at the target.

Another bull's-eye.

Damn. He was good. And I didn't detect any power humming in the air around him. He didn't have the benefit of magic to help his arrows hit home, yet he was shooting as if he did.

My friend's mouth dropped open in a perfect "o" as if she read my mind. We exchanged a look before I returned my attention to Ace and the targets.

Stepping to the line, I drew a new arrow. Ace leaned in, his body heating my back, his breath fanning the sensitive skin around my ear. "It's okay to admit defeat."

I lifted my foot and slammed my heel down on his boot.

He hissed and stepped back.

"I hope you remember those sage words when it comes time for you to cede." I fired my shot. Wood splintered, the arrowhead piercing the target. My magic hummed around me, happy.

Ace cursed loudly as my arrow split his for a second time.

"What's going on here?" a familiar voice asked.

"A *friendly* competition," Sley called out.

Orion emerged from the path that led to my cabin. He'd bathed recently, his shirt clinging to his skin, and his damp blond hair curling around his ears.

"A competition," I clarified again. Sure, I was being snarky, but Ace's return to my life stirred up a lot of feelings.

Orion raised a brow and shifted his gaze to Ace. The two men considered one another in silence. Ace's lip curled down as if he'd tasted something rotten and Orion squinted at Ace as if trying to figure out if he had symptoms of the plague.

"And this is your friend?" Orion asked.

"This is Actaeon. We grew up together, but he left Perga before you arrived. He's recently returned as a hunter and the queen assigned me as his babysitter. He had the audacity to question my suitability for the role," I explained.

Ace grumbled.

Sley whistled again. "Yeah, I guess there's nothing friendly about this. Not with those fighting words." She cast Ace a wary look.

Orion laughed. "I swear Queen Titania gets more ridiculous each year."

"Are you insulting the Queen of Wast?" Ace asked.

"Me?" Orion placed his hand on his chest. "Never. Nice to meet you Actae—"

"It's Ace," he said. "I go by Ace."

"Of course, you do," Orion said.

"What the phaan does that mean?" Ace asked.

Orion plastered a fake smile on his face and shrugged. "You look like an Ace."

Ace scowled and stepped forward.

"Ace," I interrupted before they both resorted to chest thumping. "This is Orion. Or Rye. He's our local healer, and very good at what he does." Basically, don't piss him off.

Ace clamped his mouth shut, visibly thinking twice about whatever he'd planned to say next. Healers were rare and hard to come by and no one risked angering one.

"I came to check on Nala," Orion said. "How was she this morning?"

"Much better. I left her inside, but feel free to let yourself in."

"I'd rather watch this *friendly* competition, if that's okay." He nodded to where Sley sat.

"Of course," I said, at the same time Ace barked, "No."

I turned to the other man. "Are you afraid of an audience? I can understand not wanting witnesses to your defeat, but it's a little late for that. Sley's already here."

Ace cursed and turned away. "You're the most insufferable person I've ever met."

"You either don't look in the mirror or you don't get out much," I said.

"Who's winning?" Orion asked.

"You have to ask?" Sley scoffed.

"I am," I said, at the same time, Ace said, "We're tied."

Punching the air between us with my pointer finger, I hissed at him through my teeth. "Split arrows place me above you. That's why there's an advantage to going second."

Ace's gaze darkened. He whipped another arrow from his quiver, stalked back to the line for the first target and shot. The wind whistled as the arrow flew through the air. The sharp arrowhead reflected golden sunlight before it sliced through my arrow, splitting it just as mine had split his before. The special feathers of my arrow's fletching fell to the side, the magic fading away with a whimper.

I held my breath and watched him move to the second target and repeat the same thing—another split arrow, punctuated by the crack of wood, and the sound of the arrowheads sinking into the target.

Orion's eyebrows shot up to his blond hairline.

Ace spun around and raised his arms, his bow grasped tightly in one hand. "Guess I used my second shots after all."

He lowered his arms with a wide smile that split his face.

"I didn't know that was possible," Sley whispered, loudly.

"It's not supposed to be," Orion said.

My skin prickled and my body heated as rage swept through me. Normally, I hunted in a relaxed state of being, my feelings locked behind a wall of neutrality so I could emotionally detach from the kill.

But not today.

Not right now.

This was personal.

Ace stepped to the side and headed for the last target. Once he was out of the way, I pulled two arrows, and notched them both. With magic and adrenaline pumping through my veins, I released the two arrows at once. They sped through the air, the fletching whistling a tune that matched the humming of magic in my heart.

When my arrows split Ace's arrows in unison, he froze where he stood a few feet away. He slowly pivoted to look at the targets.

"Are you phaaning kidding me?" he asked. "How is that even possible?"

Magic, but I kept that little tidbit to myself. Magic made a lot of improbable things possible.

Orion howled with laughter, doubling over to brace himself on his knees with his hands. Sley beamed at me and clapped her hands.

I winked at Ace. "Why don't we spare our arrows and your feelings and end the competition here—if we shoot for a third time, the result will be the same."

Orion managed to straighten up and wipe his eyes. "That was priceless."

Ace scowled over his shoulder at the healer. "I really don't need the commentary."

Orion continued to chuckle and shook his head. "What you need to do is admit defeat—though you're clearly a skilled marksman, and probably the closest in skill I've seen to Emi, you won't best her. You may as well accept that now and take pride and comfort from knowing the queen paired you with the best. There is no beating her."

My smile spread across my face. So much for being a humble winner.

No, scratch that. I was never going to be a humble winner.

"And you," Orion turned to face me. "You need to accept that you work for the queen, not the other way around. I might not agree with every order that comes out of the palace, but I can't find any fault with this one. The queen didn't send you some amateur to stumble after you in the forest. She found someone competent, and as close to your skill level as she could possibly find. You should be content and satisfied with her decision."

Lately, Orion had only voiced criticism for the royals, unhappy with their decision not to promote him to a royal healer as well as their blatant favouritism for bonded galeon descendants. For him to agree with the queen...

"Traitor," I said.

Sley shook her head. "You might be immortal, Em, but you're not invincible. Nala's mishap clearly shows that. You shouldn't be alone in those woods and if you won't take Orion with you, then you should take this guy." She jerked her chin in Ace's direction. "If not for your own safety, for Nala's."

Shame spread through my body like a cold wave of ice. My skin pickled, and my stomach churned. I hadn't thought about how this would make Nala safer.

And I should've.

I should always put my familiar first—period—before myself and certainly before my ego.

I swallowed, my mouth suddenly dry, and nodded.

Orion straightened, glared at Ace one last time, and stomped off to the front of my cabin. Hinges creaked as he opened the door and let himself in to check on Nala.

Sley slid off her perch. "I've got to head out too. I'll catch you later?"

I nodded and she waved goodbye. "Nice to meet you, Ace," she called over her shoulder as she left.

"So..." Ace said after Sley was out of earshot. "That's your previous partner? I saw the two of you together at the bonfire last night."

"Sley?"

"No. Onion."

"Orion."

"Whatever."

"Rye and I have hunted together often over the years, but we were never officially assigned as partners by Queen Titania."

"He doesn't seem to like me," Ace noted, his dark gaze flicking to my cabin.

"He literally just convinced me to accept you as my partner."

"He didn't do that alone. Sley provided a pretty convincing argument." Ace gave me a pointed look. "And regardless, he certainly didn't do that to help me out."

"Is that so?" I crossed my arms over my chest. "Please. Tell me what inner motivations drive a man you just met?"

"He wants you to take me as a partner for the same reason your friend does," Ace said. "He wants you and that familiar of yours safe. But that doesn't mean he's a fan of being replaced."

I snapped my mouth shut.

"Is that the partner you slept with? Or was that someone else?" Ace asked.

"That would be none of your business."

He glowered and stomped over to the second target while I retrieved arrows from the first one. While I could reuse some of mine with minimal or no repair, the shafts and fletching of Ace's arrows were rendered useless from my shots. If he was willing to put in some work, he could take his damaged arrows apart to salvage the arrowheads. It was tedious work but worth it to reuse materials.

I tossed him the remains of his arrow. He caught it by the shaft, scowled at the chipped arrowhead, and dropped the whole thing to the ground.

And he called me a princess.

If he left it there, I'd pick it up later and salvage the arrowhead myself.

Waste not, want not.

"What is my business then?" Ace asked after moment of silence. "I should know who I am trusting to guard my back."

I examined the fletching and the arrowheads of my arrows to determine if they needed repairing. "What would you like to know? You practically grew up with us. There can't be too much you still question."

Ace picked up one of the targets to move it back to the storage shed. "You know, now that you mention it, I was always curious about where you and your brother came from. You both showed up out of nowhere, shuffling behind the queen and refused to talk about it. You practically clung to the queen's skirt, and you were one raised voice away from a breakdown."

"I did not cling to her skirts," I lied. I remembered that moment with crystal clarity.

The queen had rescued us from the street gang and brought us to Perga to learn how to hunt and survive. She hadn't left us with an adult to oversee our day-to-day survival. Maybe she sensed the rebellion that would've ensued if she'd tried. Instead, she gifted us with a cabin— the one Paul still lived in—and sent orders and money every week, essentially grooming us to be her perfect soldiers.

Ace was right, though. Not that I'd ever admit it. I had clung to Queen Titania's skirts when we first arrived. I'd also cowered and adopted a meek expression. But I didn't do those things because of fear or intimidation.

I did those things for survival.

I'd held a dagger in my hand and used the queen's ridiculously voluminous skirt to hide the weapon. I was a child of the streets, and learned at an early age how appearances could be deceiving. I used that knowledge to my advantage. The kids our age constantly underestimated me due to their first impressions.

Even Ace underestimated me in those early years because he thought I was a meek little mouse.

He still did.

"Where did you and your brother come from?" Ace pressed. Setting down one target, he moved toward the next one.

I stilled, too busy reminiscing to realize the danger of Ace's words and the direction of his thoughts.

The truth was, I didn't know—not exactly—though the queen had guessed. We were abandoned on the front steps of an orphanage as infants. Maybe we could've learned more about the circumstances of how we were left if we'd stayed, but...

The fresh crack of a whip echoed in my memories, and I flinched. We were starved of affection, sometimes starved of food, and we faced the whip or strap when we messed up, as children often did.

We'd fled to the streets when we were old enough to escape and I tried not to think about our time under Headmaster Marcus' care.

Neither of us remembered anything from before the orphanage, but the one thing Paul and I knew for certain was we were twins and we stuck together.

"After I left Perga, I heard stories about you and Paul," Ace continued. "They were always so odd and never fit with the memories I had of either of you. There's an explosion of information about the work you've done for the queen, but there's never any stories of where you came from. Nothing about you prior to when you arrived in Perga. It's as though you were plucked from a void and placed for the queen to find."

He wasn't far off—except we didn't come from a void. We came from the streets and a painful past neither my brother nor I cared to discuss.

Ace waited expectantly as if I'd suddenly open up

and start spilling my secrets and trauma just because I begrudgingly accepted him as my new partner.

"I'm not going to share intimate details of my past—"

Ace barked. "Intimate? That's not something I want to hear about. I was thinking more about your childhood, your parents, where you're from. That sort of thing."

"What about you?" I waved at him with my hand. "We grew up together, but I don't recall you sharing much about your childhood before we met, either. And after you disappeared, I didn't hear anything about you at all. What have you been up to since you left? You suddenly pop up out of nowhere armed with skills you didn't have before. I mean, you were good with a bow when we were young, but now..." I bit back the compliment. He didn't deserve it. "How did you become such a great shot without me hearing a single phaaning thing about it? If we're going to be partners, the information needs to flow both ways. If you want some secrets from me, you're going to have to spill some of your own."

The wind swept through the trees and Ace paused to consider the forest and the rustling leaves.

"Well?"

"You think I'm a great shot?"

I narrowed my eyes. "What happened to you?"

Ace glanced down at me and shrugged. "My past is my past."

"Yet you expect me to share mine with you?"

"No." He shook his head and considered the forest

again as he set the second target down. "Looks like we both get to keep our secrets a little longer."

"Guess so." I followed his gaze, peering into the forest shadows. I didn't see anything. "Meet me here tonight at sundown."

"Are we going to dual? A fight to the death?" His lips quirked up at the corners. "Do I need to bring Sley as a witness?"

"No." I scoffed. "We're going hunting."

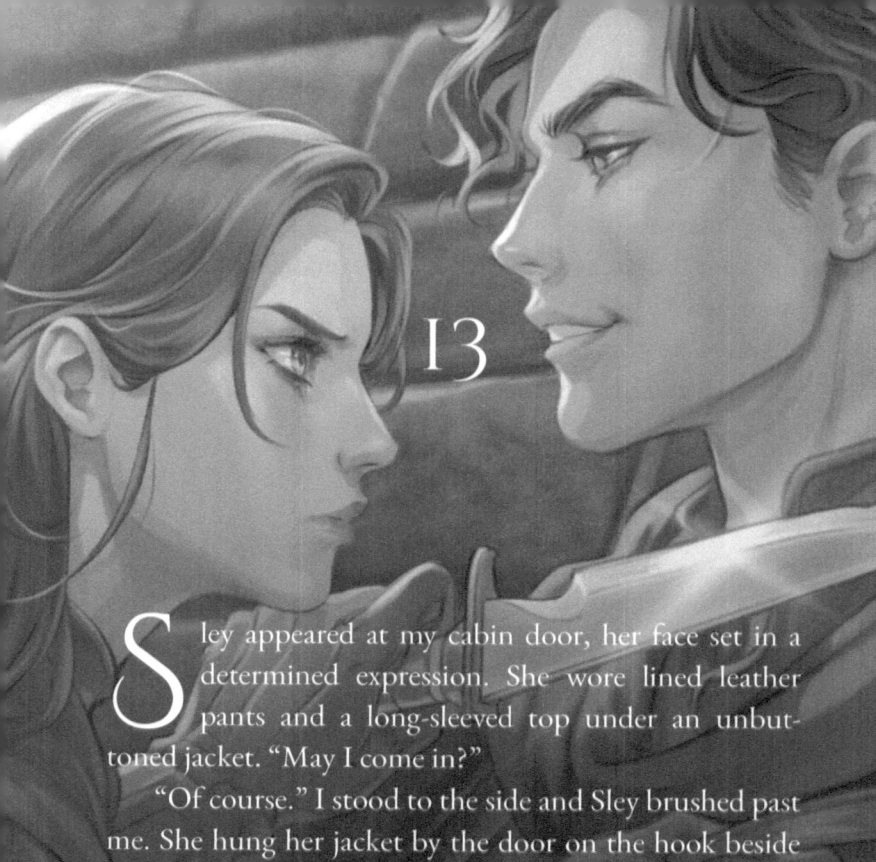

13

Sley appeared at my cabin door, her face set in a determined expression. She wore lined leather pants and a long-sleeved top under an unbuttoned jacket. "May I come in?"

"Of course." I stood to the side and Sley brushed past me. She hung her jacket by the door on the hook beside my bow before gracefully settling onto my couch.

Nala raised her head briefly during the interaction at the entrance, but as soon as Sley sat beside her, my wolf plopped her head in my friend's lap and sighed. Sley absently stroked Nala's soft fur.

The warm glow of candlelight flickered off the wooden walls of my cozy cabin, casting dancing shadows across her face.

Sley studied my leather hunting outfit. "Heading out?"

"Not for a few hours," I answered.

"Are you sure that's a good idea? What about Nala?"

"She'll stay home. Rye said to take it easy, not hole up and starve. I'm going to get some food, not hunt poachers in the forbidden forest." I paused to study my friend. "Are you here to talk about the thefts or Blake?"

"Both?" She dropped her head back on the couch and closed her eyes. "Neither?"

I nodded and headed toward the kitchen. "I'll get the wine."

Sley was still petting my now-snoring familiar with her eyes closed when I returned with two glasses filled with cherry wine. I'd traded a fur pelt for a couple of bottles last summer when the travelling merchants had come to Wast. "So...shall we start with Blake?"

Sley groaned and her eyes popped open. "Phaans, no."

"Okay...thievery it is." I handed one of the glasses to Sley. "We know the thief has been around town long enough to discover the secret tunnel under the storage house and that they may or may not have recently lost a red scarf. Though the scarf seems a little weird...why would anyone rob a storage facility wearing something flashy?"

Sley took the glass and raised it in the air in a silent salute before taking a sip. "I guess we don't have very much to go on."

"Not yet. Our amateur detective days aren't numbered yet, though. Don't give up on your dreams."

"That's not even close to my dream and you know it." Sley sighed dramatically.

"Ah, yes. Your phaanon obsession."

Taking a sip of my wine, I settled into the armchair across from her. "Well, if Blake is off limits, and we're done summarizing our investigation. I guess we'll have to focus on finding more clues," I said. "No distractions."

Sley gave me a mischievous grin. "There's only one place I know of that's perfect for gathering information."

I groaned and downed my wine. "Gossip, you mean."

"It's the same thing." She leaned forward, her eyes gleaming with amusement. "That's what keeps this town interesting. Grab your shit. We're going to the pub."

THE AIR IN THE PUB WAS THICK WITH AN ACRID mix of sweat, ale, and burning wood. The flickering flames from torches lined the uneven stone walls, casting dancing shadows. As Perga's only pub, everyone walked through these doors with the same purpose—to unwind. Well, except me and Sley. We came to gather information.

I sat on a worn-out stool at the bar, nursing a glass of something amber that tasted like liquid fire. Sley leaned on the rough-hewn counter, her eyes scanning the dimly lit room.

"Maybe we're going about this the wrong way," I said. "Instead of thinking about who could possibly steal from us, maybe we should start listing who wasn't at the bonfire." I traced my fingers idly along the rim of my glass.

Sley's gaze lingered on the corner table where Gavin, Graham and Maria loudly discussed something requiring a lot of hand gestures and laughter. "Is it just me, or do they seem chummier with each other?"

I peered over at the rowdy group, currently bashing their glasses together in a sloppy cheer, splashing beer over the tabletop.

"Graham and Gavin have always been close, ever since Graham moved to town to live with old man O'Reilly. I'm surprised Maria joined them. I thought she had better taste than that."

Sley cleared her throat. "Did you forget I had Graham in my bed just last week?"

I took another sip of my drink. "I thought you had better taste, too."

Sley sighed and tipped her glass in my direction. "No wonder Maria was throwing herself at Ace. There are limited options in this town."

"The town is eighty percent male, and we get new hunters coming through each season. There are other options." Not really. The new hunters rarely stayed.

"Is that so?" Sley raised her eyebrows. "Then why..."

"Let's stick to the case. No distractions, remember?"

Sley giggled and nodded. "I don't remember much about the bonfire, to be honest. I wasn't exactly taking notes. I didn't see Blake there, and I know because I was looking. We both found him after we left."

"Wait..." My heart started to race as my mind snagged on a memory. "Doesn't he have a thing for flashy scarves."

"Who has a thing for flashy scarfs?" Maria fell into the bar with a giggle, her wild curls cascading down her shoulders.

"Blake," Sley bit out.

"Oh yeah, he used to wear that red one, all the time." Maria's emerald eyes glittered with mischief as she continued, "But he hasn't worn it recently. Got rid of it weeks ago."

Sley's eyes widened with realization. "That's why it looked familiar! Damn, I knew I'd seen it before."

Before we could ask Maria more questions, the door swung open, and Ace sauntered in. His dark brown hair caught the light as he approached, and his piercing gaze scanned the room, landing on me with a disapproving frown.

"Drinking before our hunt, little Mouse?" he asked, his tone a mix of annoyance and anger.

I shot him a defiant look, swirling the contents of my glass. "We're working, Actaeon. A little liquid courage never hurt anyone."

He leaned against the bar, arms folded. "You can't afford to be sloppy."

"Who said anything about getting sloppy? I can handle myself," I said. "Besides, if drinking before a hunt was such a big deal, why are you here?"

Before he could reply, Maria squealed from behind me. "You came?"

She ran past and threw her arms around Ace's neck. His narrowed gaze met mine over her shoulder.

"You know...I think I have had enough," I said to Sley. "Time to go hunting."

"I'll stay here," she said. "Maybe I'll discover more information."

I nodded and pushed away from the bar, leaving my drink behind for Sley to finish. Ace's gaze lingered on me for a moment before he sighed and followed, slipping out of Maria's arms.

Maria whined somewhere behind us. "You promised."

"Not tonight," Ace said over his shoulder. "I have a hunt to go on."

As Ace and I stepped into the dimly lit streets, the sun had dipped below the treeline, casting the town in shadows.

"You don't have to come," I said. "I would hate for you to miss out on the festivities."

"Jealous, Mouse?"

"Not at all." But I was and I hated my traitorous heart for feeling anything other than hatred for this man. "Let's go."

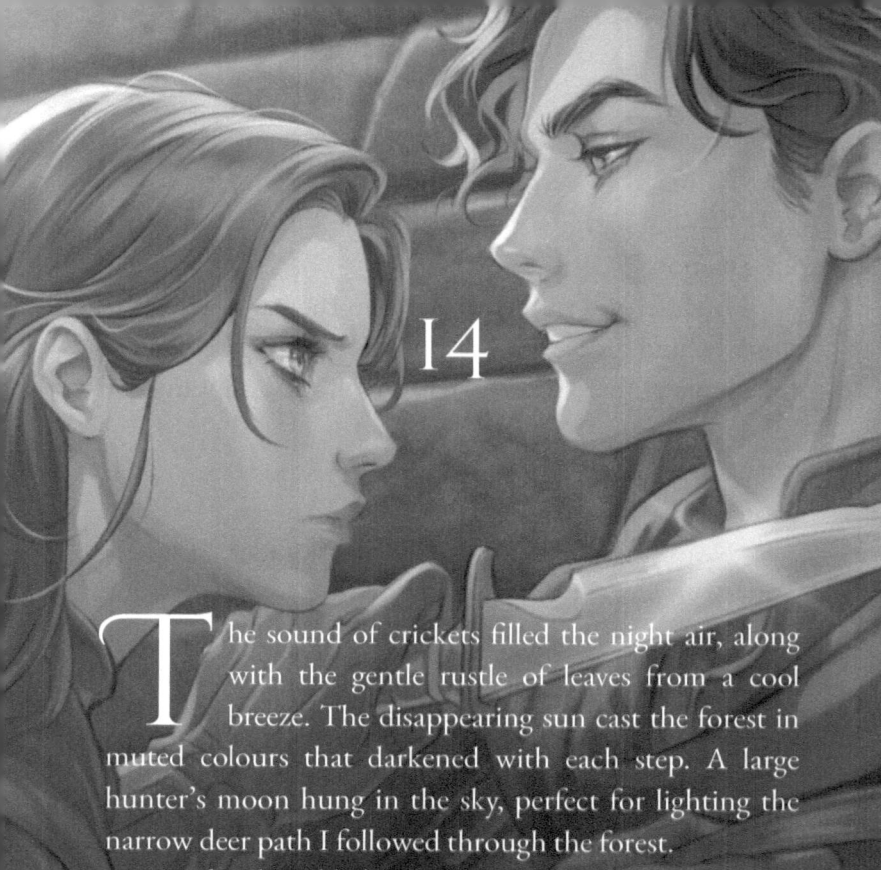

14

The sound of crickets filled the night air, along with the gentle rustle of leaves from a cool breeze. The disappearing sun cast the forest in muted colours that darkened with each step. A large hunter's moon hung in the sky, perfect for lighting the narrow deer path I followed through the forest.

Ace lumbered behind me, occasionally cursing when his boot caught a rock or upturned root.

"You're about as quiet as a stampeding herd of horses," I muttered. He might be great at hitting targets, but he needed to work on stealth. "Are you trying to hit everything on the path?"

"Why are we hunting at night?" he asked. "This is stupid. We should be using daylight."

I pushed a branch to the side of a narrow section on the already narrow path and walked past. With a smile, I released the branch in time for it to snap back and slap Ace across the face.

He grunted and grabbed the branch in his large hand. The snap of wood echoed through the forest. "Cute."

I thought so.

In our youth, we'd stuck to hunting during the day and this little jaunt through the woods confirmed my theory that Ace hadn't worked on any night hunting skills since he left.

Had all his training focused on hitting targets?

He moved with the fluid grace of a fighter and if I had to bet my last gale, I'd guess he'd spent time training as a warrior.

So far, though, I had only suspicions, no facts. But Ace was hiding something.

"Hunting requires stealth," I said. "I'm relying on senses other than sight. This is the perfect opportunity for me to see what I'm working with."

"And you didn't see that during our *friendly* competition?"

"Sometimes shooting an arrow is the easiest part," I said. "There's more to hunting than that."

"I'd like to point out that I'm perfectly capable of stealth in a familiar area or a city, day or night," he said.

"Of course. There's no need to get your ego in a bunch."

He cursed but walked along the path for another few steps before speaking again. "Now that you find me lacking, are you going to go back to your brother and argue some more about not wanting me as your partner?"

I cringed, my step faltering. With a shake of my head,

I continued forward, hoping Ace remained too focused on not tripping to notice.

The more I thought about it, the more I realized how his first impression of me when he returned to Perga really was one of an entitled brat. I could've handled the situation better. With maturity. Instead, one look at his stupidly handsome face and I was ricocheted all the way back to an angsty teenager.

I'd insulted him and tried to get out of the partnership, but it wasn't like we didn't know each other, and it wasn't like he didn't have some answering to do. So almost immediately after feeling bad for my knee-jerk reaction, rage consumed me. I kept waffling between regret for my behaviour and justifying my anger.

And I did not waffle.

I was stronger than that.

I usually just killed shit.

"Look," I said. "I'm sorry about how I greeted you. My reaction to your return had little to do with you as a hunter or partner so much as the heavy-handedness of it all. I should've pulled Paul aside to have a private conversation, and I should've considered your feelings. I'm sorry."

Silence answered me and I resisted the urge to spin around to see his expression.

Ace cleared his throat. "Thank you, but you didn't answer the question."

What question? I ran through the last bit of our conversation in my head. "No, I'm not going to demand more changes. You might move loudly through the forest at night, but that's something I can work with."

"Is that so?"

"I am assuming you can take direction," I shrugged. "Or maybe I'm wrong and all that shooting skill will go to waste. Time will tell."

Ace snorted. "I can take direction, Mouse. Just tell me what you want."

My cheeks warmed. He didn't mean that to sound like an innuendo. Why would he? But it placed my mind in the gutter anyway because, apparently, I wasn't done acting like an angsty teenager.

"I want you to forget your sight right now," I said.

"With this view?"

I stopped in my tracks, and Ace ran into me. He bounced back before I spun around.

"What are you doing?" I asked.

"What?"

"Are you...flirting with me?"

He scoffed, his lip curling up. "How much did you drink tonight?"

I narrowed my eyes.

"No, Mouse. I wouldn't dream of trying to *flirt* with you."

"Good," I said over my shoulder. "Now focus on the path. The key to moving through the Danu Forest is to embrace your senses. Get a feel of the wind and the crunch of your boots on the dirt. Smell the pine and the decaying berries. They all paint a picture of the area and then you let the moonlight fill in the details, the cracks.

We rely too much on our sight and not enough on our other senses. Hunting at night places us on a more level playing field with the animals we hunt. It also allows us to become more like them, to move like them. This in turn helps us connect with the very things we hunt."

"Which is? Only the big predators are out at night."

I scoffed. "And why is that? They're hunting too." I glanced over my shoulder to see Ace snap his head back, gaze calculating. "This forest in particular is rife with night bunnies."

"Night bunnies?" His mouth twitched. "Is that their official name?"

"Of course not. But who cares? They're bunnies that come out at night." I started walking again.

"I gathered as much from the name. Most rabbits are diurnal, not nocturnal. I'm just surprised. I don't remember night bunnies on the menu when I was a teenager."

He could be surprised as much as he wanted, it didn't change that these bunnies had evolved to become more active at night—probably to avoid humans, which were the biggest source of predation during the day next to hawks.

"We're coming up to the field where they usually roam," I whispered. "So, ask your questions now. Once we get to the treeline, that pretty mouth of yours needs to stay shut."

"You think my mouth is pretty?"

He knew it was. "Focus, *Ace*."

Ace moved to stand beside me, his hulking frame

blocking the moonlight and casting me in shadow. He jerked his head at the tree line and the field bathed in a silver glow. "What's the plan?"

"We take only what we need. I am hunting tonight for myself and a few families." I didn't bother revealing my plan to trade the meat for new supplies to replace the stolen goods from the storage house. "I plan to take five, maybe six max. We're downwind, so they won't detect us unless you start stomping around again. Barring that, once the first bunny falls, they'll scatter. We'll shoot in unison. This guarantees us two kills if we shoot fast. More if we're lucky. I like to keep this field nicely stocked and won't be back for at least a month."

"Are there other fields?"

I pulled my bow from my shoulders and smiled. "Of course."

He mirrored my actions and followed me to the tree line. I pressed my finger to my lips. His gaze tracked the movement and he nodded.

Moonlight cascaded down on the open field and illuminated several bunnies in the tall grass. They blended in well, but not well enough when I knew where to look.

I pulled an arrow from my quiver and slowly stepped to the side to make room for Ace. He needed a clear view of the targets as well.

I notched the arrow, and under my breath, whispered, "Three, two, one."

On cue, Ace released an arrow at the same time I did. The arrows flew, whistling through the air with the sharpened points catching the light. They both struck their targets, with sickening thuds.

The night bunnies scattered.

Having already pulled and notched another arrow, I released the string and reached for a third. I fired that one, too, and then drew another and another. With my heart rate elevated, I forced the arm holding my bow to lower to my side even though the magic wailed in my blood to keep shooting.

More.

The power flowed through my veins, demanding I continue, demanding I shoot them all until none remained.

I took a deep breath and released the magic. My body shook, my limbs trembled. Letting the power go seemed harder and harder each time, but then again, I always managed. Maybe this quiet battle was all in my head.

Ace studied me, expression unreadable.

"What?"

"You took out five in the time it took for me to shoot two."

"Did you forget your earlier defeat in our little competition so quickly?"

He shook his head. "Those were fixed targets. These weren't." He swallowed, the moonlight catching the bob of his throat. "Could you have cleared this whole field?"

I opened my mouth to lie and promptly shut it. I didn't like Ace much, but something inside me didn't want to lie to him. He might've been gone all these years, but some things didn't change. Not only did he value brutal honesty, but he could always tell when I lied.

"Yes," I admitted.

He pressed lips together and nodded. "All right, Mouse. Let's get our dinner."

I shook my head. "You get them."

"Why me?"

"You're the new guy."

He took a deep breath and rolled his shoulders back as if physically preparing to fight me. Instead, he held out his bow. "Hold this."

With a wave of my hand, I directed him toward the clearing while I stood back, trying not to appear too smug.

The moon's silver glow bathed the clearing, casting graceful shadows among the trees and forest floor. The night air hung heavy with the fragrance of damp earth and pine needles, still moist from recent rainfall. I leaned on a nearby tree, my arms crossed over my chest, Ace's bow resting on the bark beside me.

Ace grumbled as he stomped over the dense moss toward the night bunnies we'd shot. He managed to glare at me over his shoulder each time he had to bend to pick one up.

Movement at the edge of the clearing caught my attention. A massive mountain lion emerged from the shadows like a phantom from a nightmare. Magic whispered along the moss with each step it took toward us. My breath caught in my throat. Before I could warn Ace, the mountain lion lunged.

It happened so fast.

The predator smacked into Ace with an audible thump, sending them both crashing to the ground. Ace swore and they rolled on the forest floor.

With my heart racing, I dropped Ace's bow and drew my own weapon. I needed to get a clear shot and they were moving around too much.

Why did the feline attack Ace? They didn't normally hunt humans and there was a forest full of easier prey all around us.

I tracked their movement, but I couldn't get a clean sightline on the mountain lion. Maybe I should grab my dagger and jump into the clearing? I had a better chance of helping Ace from here, though. I just needed a clear shot.

My breathing scraped my lungs and my hand itched to grab the hilt of my dagger as I watched Ace fend off the attack down the straight line of my arrow.

With a growl, Ace pushed the feline away from him. In mid-air, she twisted her body, landing between me and Ace. She hissed and moved to the side, her ears pinned back, her sharp teeth barred, as if protecting the northern section of the field.

Realization hit me and my stomach sunk.

"A little help here!" Ace shouted. Drawing his dagger, he crouched low.

I had a clear shot now, but I didn't take it. Instead, I threw down my bow and ran toward them.

"Stop," I yelled as I unleashed my magic.

Ace stumbled sideways and the mountain lion tensed. Her piercing gaze flicking between us.

"I apologize," I said, allowing my magic to flow over her. "We haven't been in this area for over a month and didn't know you had made a den here."

The cougar stopped hissing and perked up her ears. In the shadows behind her, two little fuzzy heads popped up—her kits.

I held my breath.

My heart still hammered away in my chest. One day, it might just give up.

I'd left my bow at the edge of the clearing and if I reached for my dagger now, she'd probably attack us both.

I'd gambled our lives on my intuition.

Slowly, the mountain lion turned away and retreated into her den. Magic shimmered along her fur and sprung up from the moss with each step. Her kits followed, leaving me and Ace alone in the clearing with a pile of dead night bunnies.

I let out a deep breath.

"Thanks for having my back," Ace grumbled behind me.

"I had your back," I said. "I would've shot her if there was no other option." I turned to face him. He stood a few feet away, panting, clutching his dagger. His leather top had rips, showing the claw marks of the cougar but no blood. "Are you okay?"

"Fine," he said.

He looked physically unharmed, but I continued to study him under the moonlight because something else was off. Would he have preferred I kill a mother and leave two kits to die of starvation over winter? My main role in this forest was to protect these creatures, not harm them. After all, her kits could end up as someone else's familiars one day.

Did I need to explain that to him? Make him understand?

"Okay, fine," he said, breaking the silence. "My ego is a little bruised."

I frowned. "From what? You fought off a mountain lion with your bare hands." He'd even managed to push the beast off him. Though I'd heard of adrenaline fueling super-human feats, Ace's strength was still shocking.

"That's one way to look at it," Ace said.

"What's the other way?" I asked.

"I just had my ass handed to me by an overgrown housecat."

I shook my head and gathered the spoils of our hunt. "Let's go."

Before we stepped away from the clearing, Ace grabbed one of the bunnies in my arms and left it near the entrance of the den.

15

The fire crackled and popped, sending floating embers up into the night sky, along with billowing plumes of smoke. Cooking meat sizzled and spat on a spit over the flames and added a mouthwatering scent to join the pine and smoke in the air.

"That smells delicious," I admitted.

Ace grumbled. The light from the fire cast him in shadows and accentuated the hard lines and chiselled features of his face.

"Careful, Mouse." He pulled the meat from the spit and handed me the skewer. "That almost sounded like a compliment. I know how you loathe to give me any."

I accepted the food and held the stick up in my hand, waiting for it to cool down.

"It was a compliment," I said. "Paul's hopeless at cooking for himself."

"Still?"

"Mmhmm. Despite my best efforts to help him. Where did you learn?" He used to be at the same skill level as Paul.

Ace pulled the second skewer from the fire and stared down at the meat for a moment. "Five years is plenty of time to learn a lot of things, Mouse."

I narrowed my eyes. That was vague.

He took a bite from his skewer and sucked in a deep breath. He most likely burnt his tongue, and the thought made me smile.

"You spent five years training to cook, fight, and hunt?" I asked.

"Who said anything about fighting?"

"I did." Would he try to deny it?

Ace shrugged. "Cooking is a key element of survival, and I figured out quickly that I wanted to live. Why wouldn't I work on this survival skill along with everything else?"

He had a good point. Yet, I knew that would never change Paul's view on cooking.

Waving the skewer in the air, I leaned in and bit into the tender meat. Flavour exploded on my tongue.

"Danu, that's good." I closed my eyes and moaned. I took another bite and enjoyed the flavours, letting the taste flow over my other senses.

Dirt crunched as Ace shifted in his seat on the log opposite of me. I popped open my eyes to find him staring at me strangely.

"What?" I asked.

He looked away, clenching his teeth together. His

hair had a slight wave to it and a lock had fallen across his face. "Nothing."

I took another bite, and it was just as good as the last. After skinning and prepping the meat, Ace had used some sort of rub with herbs. He said he always travelled with it.

My new life lesson was discovering the recipe.

I sank my teeth into the meat, the grease spreading over my lips and coating my tongue.

Ace cursed. "Do you need a room?"

I lowered the skewer and licked my lips. "Are you upset I'm enjoying the food?"

"Do you always make those sounds?" he asked, his gaze darkening.

"I always make these sounds when I'm satisfied, yes." I took another bite and moaned again, maybe a little louder than before. Maybe a little exaggerated. If it bothered Ace, then I planned to keep doing it.

"Phaan." He sprung from his seat and stomped into the inky darkness, taking his dinner with him.

I laughed and took another bite. The food really was delicious. Irritating Ace was just a bonus.

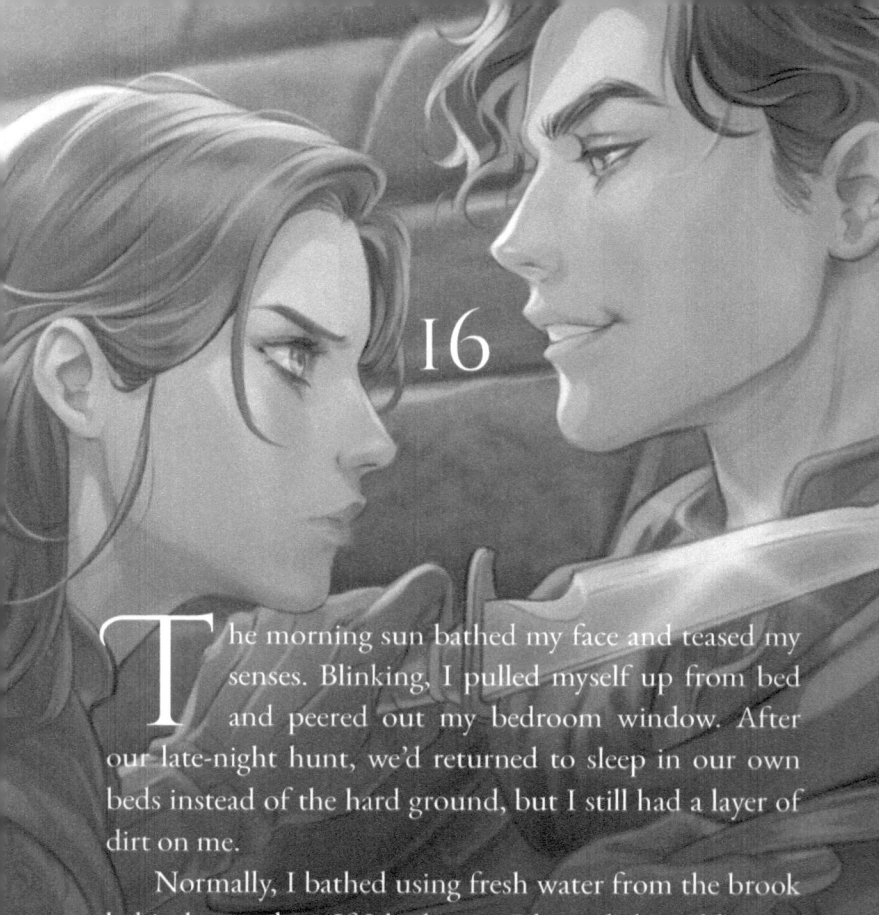

16

The morning sun bathed my face and teased my senses. Blinking, I pulled myself up from bed and peered out my bedroom window. After our late-night hunt, we'd returned to sleep in our own beds instead of the hard ground, but I still had a layer of dirt on me.

Normally, I bathed using fresh water from the brook behind my cabin. If I had time, I heated the cold water over the fireplace first. In the summer, I'd jump into the river and cool down at the same time. Now that the air held more of a chill, however, and I awaited new orders, I planned for a more luxurious bathing experience.

Throwing on loose fitting clothes, I grabbed my soap, bow and quiver and headed toward my favourite bathing place located far from our little community. I preferred this place to the closer lake because I knew the others never ventured here.

Nala perked up when I padded into the main room.

"Are you coming girl?" I reached out and ruffled her fur.

She yipped and jumped off the couch. Though she moved slower and with a slight limp, her health had already improved since the attack. She would be back to her old self in no time and then I could track down the rogue hunters. Sure, I might've killed them all, but I wanted to know where they'd come from and if there were more. My fingers itched to pull my bow, my legs begged to run to the scene of the attack, but I'd learned long ago to listen to a healer's advice. Orion had said our bond had weakened and I didn't want to leave on a long hunting mission until Nala was stronger.

With my familiar at my side, I set off into the forbidden forest of Danu.

The birds sang merrily overhead and flittered from branch to branch among the sun-dappled leaves as they followed my path through the forest. A couple of large ravens also trailed after me, occasionally adding their eerie croak to the noise overhead. The morning air still held a slight chill, but I welcomed the bite, knowing full well things would heat up soon, anyway.

After a short jaunt through the forest, I arrived at my destination. A secret hot spring existing near the major river and the edge of the forest. Paul and I had found this place when we were fourteen. Ace had dared us to jump in.

A two-tiered pool system had a large, heated upper pool that cascaded down to a lower pool in a spectacular waterfall before it drained into the river where the naiads sometimes lurked, including the one I'd questioned the other day.

I had no interest in running across that unfriendly creature again.

I set my supplies down near the edge of the lower pool and started pulling off my dirt-encrusted clothes. The morning bite in the air made my skin pebble, but the promise of the warm water propelled me forward. The lower pool wasn't as hot as the upper one, but I wasn't looking to scald my skin or plummet to my death, so the lower pool would meet my needs.

Dipping my toes into the water gently lapping at the bank, I tested the temperature of the hot springs before walking in the rest of the way.

The water flowed over my naked skin and soothed my nerves. I missed this. I missed the calm that came from bathing every inch of my body with heat.

Nala huffed and flopped down beside my stuff on the banks of the lower pool.

"I won't be long," I assured her.

She grumbled and cushioned her head on her front paws.

My wolf preferred that I smelled like dirt, cooked meat and wolf. She hated when I came to the pools.

I turned away from Nala and dove into the water. The feel of the current through my hair and the warm water along my skin felt better than any massage session.

After I resurfaced, I dove again.

I could do this all day, but that wouldn't be fair to

Nala, and my brother probably expected us back by lunch.

I grabbed my soap and headed for the waterfall.

It wasn't a powerful stream of water. I could stand under the cascading water without getting crushed. Using the soap, I lathered my body, running my hands over my breasts, arms, and the flat of my stomach. The heated water washed away any of the dirt too stubborn to come off earlier. I bent to scrub my legs and groin next when Nala barked.

I straightened immediately and turned toward my familiar. A chill ran up my spine despite the temperature of the water.

Nala wasn't looking at me. Instead, she stood and faced the opposite bank of the lower pool.

I turned slowly to follow her gaze and froze. There, standing at the edge of the water, Ace watched me, his expression unreadable from this distance. He held his bow in one hand but had lowered it to his side. His mouth was partly open. Instead of attempting to cover myself where I stood, I dove into the pool and let the water shield me from his gaze.

What was he doing here?

When I resurfaced, I found Ace standing in the same spot. Why hadn't he left? Why hadn't he looked away? I let my feet touch the pebbled bottom of the pool and stood. The water came up to my neck, the steam lifting from the heated surface to caress my face.

"Did you get a good enough look?" I asked. What

would he do if I walked out of the water and draped myself over his body like Maria had at the pub?

Ace snapped his mouth shut and a dusty rose colour spread over his cheeks. "I asked your brother if anyone still risked coming to the hot springs in the forbidden forest and he said no. I wouldn't have come if I knew you'd be here."

"Yet, you definitely stayed." I cocked my head. "I've killed men for less."

He straightened, his gaze finally meeting mine. "Have you?"

I ignored his question. Of course, I hadn't. I killed men for hunting in the forest. "If Nala hadn't alerted me, how long would you have kept watching?"

Ace held his hands up. "As lovely as I'm sure the view is, I wouldn't get your panties in a bunch. You were too far away for me to see anything. I was trying to figure out if it was you, or some sort of hallucination when your familiar barked."

That was the lamest excuse I'd heard in a long time and said as much. "Why don't you go bathe in the river? There's a naiad visiting. I'm sure she'd love the company." Maybe if I was lucky, she'd drown him.

Ace jerked back as if burned, his face turning white. "A naiad? Here?"

I nodded. "Super unfriendly, too, so you'll probably hit it off."

Ace cursed and turned around. He bent to retrieve the bag he'd dropped. "I'll see you back in Perga."

"That better be all you see of me," I shouted after him.

He shook his head and stormed off into the forest.

The audacity of that man.

I scrambled out of the warm water and started to dry myself. Had Paul sent him here intentionally, knowing I preferred to bathe in the mornings or had this been an innocent mistake with Ace caught in the middle?

Scowling, I threw my towel down. Nothing my brother did was a coincidence. This had his meddling signature all over it.

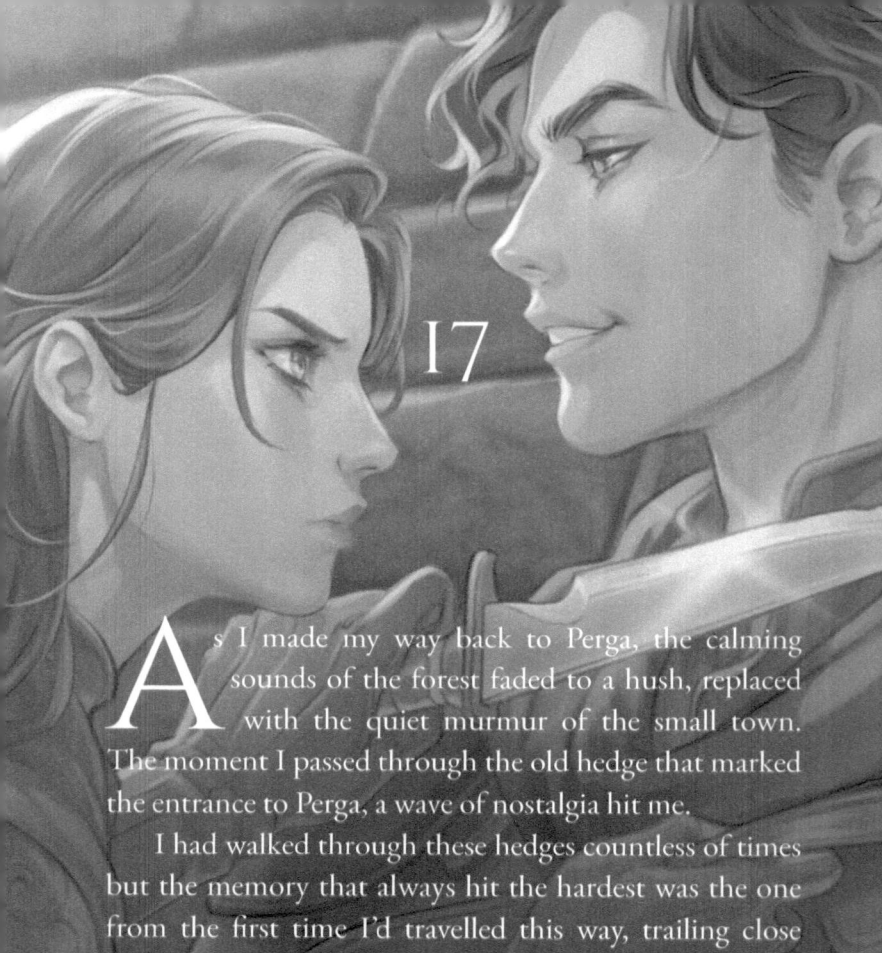

17

As I made my way back to Perga, the calming sounds of the forest faded to a hush, replaced with the quiet murmur of the small town. The moment I passed through the old hedge that marked the entrance to Perga, a wave of nostalgia hit me.

I had walked through these hedges countless of times but the memory that always hit the hardest was the one from the first time I'd travelled this way, trailing close behind the queen and her guard. Fear had filled me, but another emotion had clung to my heart—an emotion I hadn't dared feel before. As I clutched my brother's hand and stepped into this town all those years ago, I'd been filled with hope.

The trees stood tall, and the leaves whispered in the wind. With Nala trotting beside me, I walked down the main street through town. Old cabins with thatched roofs lined the old road. Chimneys puffed out smoke into the crisp air and the overgrown grass along the side of the street swayed in the breeze.

Home.

Growing up in an orphanage, and later on the streets, I'd never considered anywhere home before Perga.

Some of the locals milled around outside and greeted me with nods as I made my way to my cabin on the opposite side of town. I was good enough to defend their forests and stock their storage house, good enough to acknowledge if they accidentally made eye contact with me, but not good enough for most of the town to befriend.

I was too different.

Too scary.

They didn't understand my power, so most of them avoided it.

Maria stepped from the entrance of her bakery, her curls bouncing around her face. Despite her habit of throwing herself on Ace, Maria had always been kind to me. She didn't know I had a past with the new hunter in town and even if she did, my history with Ace didn't give me any claim over him.

Not that I wanted one.

"Back already?" Maria called out. "Didn't you just leave?"

"And stay away from this charming place? Never," I said. The charm being my bed, books, Sley, and my familiar. "Besides, I just left to bathe."

Maria leaned forward. "Speaking of charming, is it

true you're involved with Ace? I couldn't help but notice something between the two of you last night."

"Me and Ace?" I shook my head and ignored the knot twisting in my stomach. "Absolutely not."

Maria bit her lip as she visibly considered her next words. "That's not what it looked like."

"What did it look like?"

"Like you have history," she said.

"I have no claim on him," I said. Nor did I want any.

My chest tightened and I cursed my body for betraying what my mind already knew—Ace and I would be a disaster together. Another heartbreak and heartache and Ace didn't deserve the opportunity to do that to me again.

"But you guys used to be friends, right?" Maria asked. "I heard Ace lived here before and you all grew up together with Graham and Gavin."

I nodded, not liking where this conversation was going. Graham and Gavin had obviously shared a lot more than beer with Maria last night. "Did Graham and Gavin also share that they used to call me, Paul and Ace the orphans? Or that they tormented me relentlessly?"

"Um..." Maria looked away.

"I thought not."

"Those two are harmless," she assured me.

"Sure," I lied. "I've moved on from that and I'd like to think we've all changed. If I'd known I'd count on Graham's arrowheads or Gavin's woodworking, maybe I would've been a little nicer back then, too."

Maybe they could've been a lot nicer.

"I would argue old man O'Reilly hasn't changed at all," Maria quipped.

I felt a chill run down my spine and checked over my shoulder instinctively in case he stood behind me. He wasn't. "That's the most truthful thing I've heard all morning."

"You know he's been asking about you lately."

"Who has?"

"O'Reilly."

A shiver ran through me again, and I scoffed, trying to hide my unease. Nothing good could come from that cantankerous old man asking about me. "I don't want to know, but at the same time, I need to ask. What did he want?"

Maria sighed and looked around as if she too worried the old man would leap out from the shadows. "He thinks you're hiding something about the forest and says it's unnatural for someone so young to bond with a familiar."

"Well, some things really don't change. He's been saying that for years. I'm well aware of O'Reilly's opinions of me." The old man had always been a little too nosy about the forbidden forest and overly suspicious of my reluctance to respond to his questions about it. Most of the time, I remained silent because I simply didn't know the answer. And other times, he sought information that wasn't mine to share. He'd accused me of lying, of spying, and of casting Perga under a spell at town council meetings. Multiple times. Though I'd grown used to O'Reilly's constant antagonism, I hadn't grown out of my unease around that man.

"Well, just be careful," she cautioned, her tone serious. "There have been whispers about strange things going on in the forest lately. Unsettling things."

My heart quickened at her words. "What kind of unsettling things?"

She hesitated and reached down to give Nala a pat instead of responding right away. "People have reported hearing strange voices in the forest, of whispers in the dark."

That could be the thieves. "Anything else?"

"There have been sightings of shadowy figures darting between the trees near the forbidden forest, disappearing before anyone can get a clear look."

A sense of foreboding settled over me like a heavy fog. The forest had always held its secrets close, but the unsettling things Maria mentioned could be descriptions of more rogue hunters and thieves. If others had started to notice them, though, that meant their numbers had to be growing.

"And O'Reilly thinks it's connected to me?" I asked, my voice barely above a whisper. My mind had already connected the dots. Why else would Maria bring up the old man and tell me to be careful?

She pressed her lips together and nodded.

"Do you?"

Maria's gaze softened with concern. "I don't know, Emi. Maybe you're not responsible for any of it, but something tells me you're involved somehow. You've always had a connection to the forest—a connection none of the rest of us fully understand."

The weight of her words hung heavily in the air. Gossip spread easily in a town this size, so did misinformation. If the citizens of Perga thought I was responsible for all the shenanigans going on, they could end up on my doorstep demanding my head. "Thanks for the heads up, Maria."

She nodded and ducked back into her bakery while I continued onward through town, lost in thought. Nala walked beside me, occasionally bumping her body into my legs.

"Emi!" Sley called out, running around the central fire pit to reach me. She wore leather pants and a loose cotton shirt, and her breath condensed with each breath.

"Hey."

Sley slowed to a stop in front of me and held up her finger. She bent over and braced her hands on her knees, breathing hard.

"Are you okay?"

She nodded and continued to wheeze. Nala leaned forward and sniffed at her head as if to make sure she was alright.

"That was a pretty impressive run, there, *Sleyer*."

"Phaan...you." She reached out to scratch behind Nala's ear.

"I'm not your type," I said.

She chuckled and shook her head before finally straightening. Her gaze sparkled with mischief.

"Did you just want to run dramatically across town, or..."

She leaned in. "Or I found another clue."

My eyebrows rose.

"And maybe I've always wanted to dramatically run through town."

"In your head was I a seven-foot phaanon warrior?"

She waggled her eyebrows at me.

I snorted, shaking off my unease from my conversation with Maria. I didn't want to tell Sley about it, because she'd rampage through town and chew everyone out for doubting me, which may or may not help my case as far as my reputation in this town went. "What did you find?"

"It wasn't just dry storage," she said. "They also took wool and leather."

I froze, my mind instantly travelling to thoughts of the men from the forest attack. "What colour wool and leather?"

Sley grimaced. "Undyed."

I scrunched my nose. It wasn't definitive proof linking the two events, but it definitely made me pause. The wool could've been dyed green. Someone in town could've supplied the rogue hunters with Perga's supplies.

Sley waited patiently in front of me while my brain worked.

"The hunters that attacked me wore wool and leathers," I explained.

"Everyone wears wool and leathers. It's winter."

I nodded. "But there might be a connection."

"It would be a phaan of a coincidence if they're unrelated." She paused and bit her lip. "You killed them all, right?"

"All the ones that attacked me, yes."

"I guess if the thefts stop, we'll know why." Sley tapped her chin.

"Agreed," I said. "Assuming the thefts you discovered all occurred before the attack. But..." My mind went over the chain of events.

"But?"

"But you found the door open to the storage house after I killed those hunters."

"So there's at least one person involved who survived?" She huffed and crossed her arms over her chest. "What now?"

Warmth spread across my chest as my plan formed in my mind. "I'm going home to eat and then I might go see what I can find out about the rogue hunters. Maybe I'll find your thieves along the way."

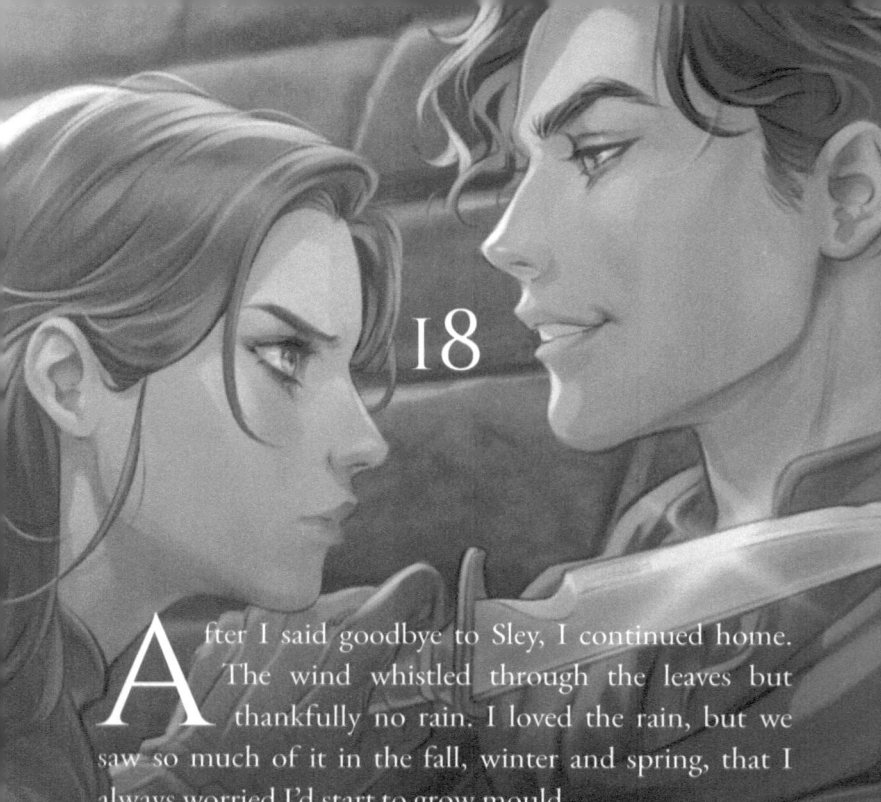

18

After I said goodbye to Sley, I continued home. The wind whistled through the leaves but thankfully no rain. I loved the rain, but we saw so much of it in the fall, winter and spring, that I always worried I'd start to grow mould.

I exited the woods to find Ace and Paul sitting on my front step. Biting back a groan I stopped short. What did they want now?

When the men saw me, they both stood.

Nala whined and broke off into a gentle lope to enter the tree cover. She often did that to take care of business or to stretch her legs. She'd be back.

I turned to Ace. "Didn't you see enough of me earlier?"

Ace had the decency to look away, his jaw clenching.

My brother looked back and forth at us, his brow furrowing more and more with each snap side to side.

"I don't even want to know what that's about," Paul

said, finally breaking the silence. He held out a scroll bearing Queen Titania's seal. "Here."

Snatching it from his hand, I tore through the seal. As I quickly scanned the contents, my stomach dropped. The queen commanded me to investigate the hunters and track down their origins. Queen Titania's orders were not unreasonable, and I already planned to do exactly that. But I still wanted to toss the parchment into the nearest fire. Why did she feel the need to put the orders in writing? Did she think I'd let this go? The only reason I hadn't marched right back into the forest was because Orion told me to wait for Nala to heal.

I shook away the annoyance and focused on my rage. Though Nala wasn't a hundred percent, she had recovered quickly since her healing session with Orion.

I needed to look at this a different way. It was finally time to seek out those responsible for hurting my familiar. Shaking away the annoyance from the letter, fiery determination ignited in my chest. The hunters might've died in their futile attack, but there could be others like them lurking in the shadows, stealing our food and supplies. And if they existed, I'd find them.

The lack of rain worked in my favor—the tracks would be easier to find and follow.

"Do I have to take him with me?" I jerked my chin in Ace's direction. The orders hadn't technically specified the inclusion of a partner.

"Of course," Paul said. "Think of it as a great bonding opportunity."

"Bonding?" Phaaning unlikely. The pervert watched me bathe.

And I'd liked it.

Paul shrugged. "Training opportunity, then."

I glared at Paul, debating whether or not I could convince him to change his mind. But it wasn't really up to him. The queen might've left out the mention of Ace in this order, but her previous letter had been clear. I couldn't disobey her command.

"Fine," I reluctantly agreed. "But he stays out of my way. This is my investigation, and I won't have him slowing me down."

"I'm not incompetent," Ace growled. "I won't get in your way."

"We'll see," I said.

Paul smirked and left without a goodbye. He was entirely too amused with the turn of events, and I didn't appreciate any of it.

"Come on," I said.

Ace trailed behind me as I stepped into my cozy cabin. The lingering smell of last night's fire mingled in the air with glue and leather. As I rummaged through my belongings to gather gear for our hunt, Ace wandered around the living room, his keen gaze scanning the titles on my bookshelf.

Nala scratched at the door and Ace took a break from studying my collection to let her in. She sauntered past to make her way to me. After a few aggressive bag sniffs, she flopped down at my feet.

Ace waved at my bookshelf. "You read a lot of romance."

"Why wouldn't I?"

"It's a little unrealistic."

I shrugged and shoved bandages in my carry bag. "That's how I like my men."

"Fictional?"

"Exactly," I said. "Much more enjoyable than reality."

He held the door open for me. "There's something wrong with you."

"Is there?" I slipped past him and let the fresh air wash over me. How dare he critique my choice of reading? "Come on, girl."

Nala yipped and followed me out the door.

As we left town, I spotted Blake walking past Maria's place. A sweet aroma wafted from the bakery and my stomach rumbled with thoughts of Maria's cinnamon buns. But other thoughts quickly spoiled the temptation of pastries. Was Blake involved with the thefts or was finding his scarf near the looted barrel an unfortunate coincidence? My heart skipped a beat as I watched the queen's messenger disappear around the corner.

"Wait here," I quickly instructed Ace before spinning around to catch up with the messenger. Nala trotted alongside me, her face turned up, her brown gaze watching me intently for a command. I had none.

"Blake!" I called out, my voice cutting through the quiet of the street. He stopped and turned to face me, a smile fading from his lips as his gaze slid to my right.

I groaned inwardly, knowing that Ace must be close behind me, obviously ignoring my order. Now wasn't the time to scold him, though, I needed to talk to Blake.

"Hey," I said breathlessly, only now realizing I hadn't planned what to say once I reached him. I wanted to ask about his red scarf, but now that I was in front of him, I wasn't sure how to bring it up without the conversation sounding like an interrogation. "I just wanted to check if there were any messages for me?"

Blake's eyes flickered with surprise as he looked at me, his expression guarded. "Not today, sorry," he replied. His gaze kept shifting over my shoulder, and I knew Ace had caught up to us.

I sighed inwardly, realizing my attempt at privacy and subtlety had failed miserably. "Right," I muttered, feeling a flush creep up my cheeks. Nala leaned into my legs, and I reached down and ruffled her fur. "Any gossip from town?"

He peered at me as if I were a puzzle he was trying to solve only to realize I was missing a few pieces.

"Not much," he said. "The queen is spending more time out of the castle while the king is rarely seen in public. People are speculating there's trouble in paradise."

"Is there?"

"I'm just a messenger, Emi. They look as equally unimpressed with each other as they usually do," Blake said.

Huh. That sounded about right. The king and queen weren't known for showing affection toward each other.

"Anything else?" I asked. He hadn't mentioned news of Dita, which was odd.

He paused, tapping his chin. "The vendors of Wast are excited about the upcoming visit from Vitor, but that's nothing new."

The monarchs from the two major cities on the mainland were meeting to amicably discuss trade. I'd only been to Vitor a few times and disliked it almost as much as I did Wast. It didn't help that my only knowledge of the city beforehand was that Old Man O'Reilly and his asshole nephew both came from Vitor. That was enough to taint my first impression and to this day, whenever I thought of Vitor, I imagined a whole city of O'Reillys—male, female, young, old, small, and big— grumbling and sneering as they milled around town.

I shuddered at the involuntary image. "Okay. Well, thanks."

He nodded and made a move to leave, but before he could make his escape, I reached out to stop him. My grip on his arm was gentle yet firm. "Wait," I said. "I need to ask you something else."

His expression turned serious as he looked down at my hand gripping his arm. "Okay."

I let go of his arm. "I remember you used to always wear a red scarf."

A faint smile tugged at the corners of his lips as he shifted his weight back. "You wanted to ask me about a scarf?"

I nodded, my cheeks now burning with embarrassment with what I planned to say next. This was going to get awkward, but I was willing to let my ego take a hit to get more information for the investigation. "Yeah, I really liked it and wanted...I wanted to get one for someone else."

Ugh, I was terrible at this.

Thankfully, Nala didn't whine to give away my discomfort.

Blake's eyes flicked to Ace standing behind me and his lips curved up. "Is that so?"

I cleared my throat and pulled at the neckline of my shirt. "Yeah, where did you buy it?"

"Sley is your best friend and a skilled seamstress," Blake replied smoothly. "I'm sure she could make you one."

"And if I didn't want her to know?" I bit my lip and hoped the messenger fell for my poor acting skills. I didn't risk glancing at Ace.

He raised both eyebrows in amusement. "Then there's a merchant who comes to Wast for the Sunday markets with a booth of them. But buying a scarf seems like a silly thing to keep secret."

I winced and nodded, trying to seem sheepish. "Maybe I'll grab one when we get back." I paused and pretended to inspect his neck. "Should I get another for you? I noticed you've stopped wearing yours."

This time, Blake grimaced and looked away. "Maria took it."

"Maria?" Now that was unexpected.

"Please don't tell Sley," he pleaded.

"It looks like we both have our secrets," I said, keeping my tone light and teasing. I was definitely telling Sley.

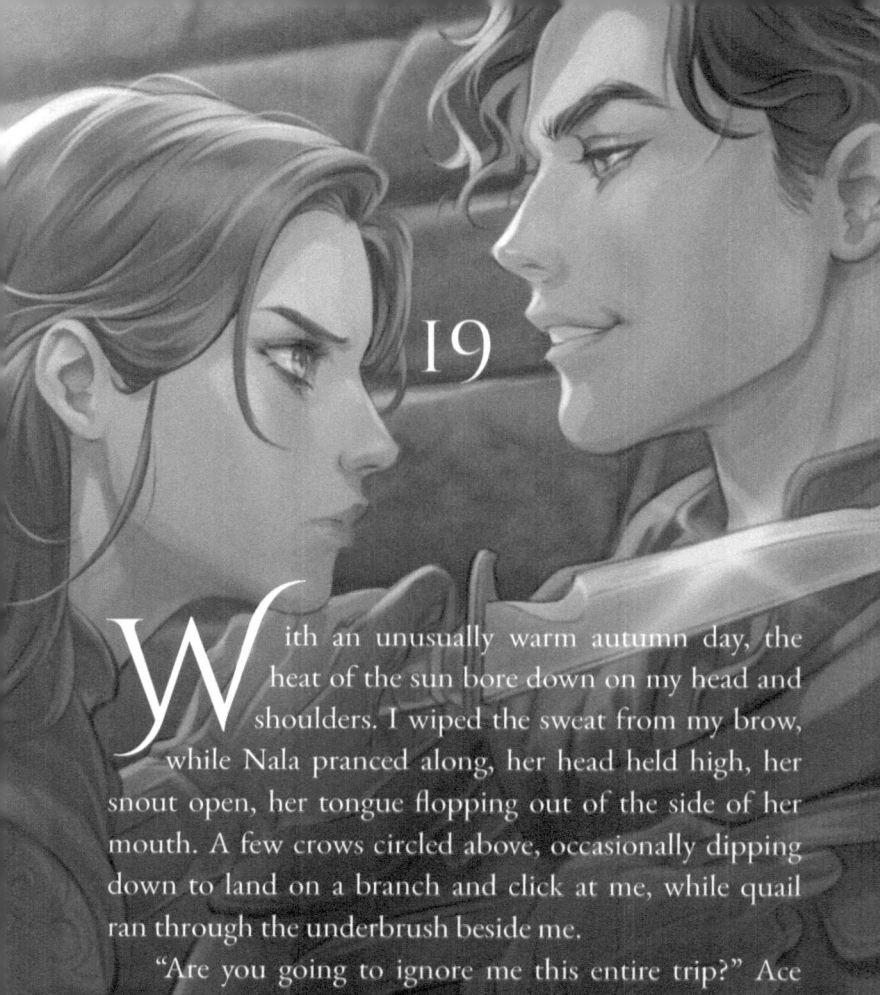

19

With an unusually warm autumn day, the heat of the sun bore down on my head and shoulders. I wiped the sweat from my brow, while Nala pranced along, her head held high, her snout open, her tongue flopping out of the side of her mouth. A few crows circled above, occasionally dipping down to land on a branch and click at me, while quail ran through the underbrush beside me.

"Are you going to ignore me this entire trip?" Ace asked. As if to show his displeasure, the oversized brute stomped through the forest beside me, snapping every branch and crushing every pinecone under his giant feet.

I didn't reply, content to let him sweat a bit.

"I take that as a yes," Ace muttered under his breath.

As much as the idea of ignoring him the entire trip tempted me, even I, with all my childish behaviours and stubbornness, knew communication was key to a good partnership.

"I'm still waking up, and I'm still angry at you," I said.

"It's midday, you bathed and ate. You even interrogated the queen's messenger about his fashion choices. How long, exactly, does it take you to wake up?"

I ground my teeth together and balled my hands into fists. "Oh, don't you worry, buttercup. You'll hear lots from me soon enough and you'll then be wishing for silence."

"I thought you were over this whole partner thing. Why are you still angry?"

I took a deep breath and counted to three. "I am angry because you saw me naked."

"From what I hear, that's a requirement to being your partner."

I spun, my hand drawn back, and struck. My fist connected with his jaw and pain shot down my arm. Ace's head snapped back, but before he could react, I stepped in and drove my other fist up in a vicious uppercut.

But this time, I wasn't so lucky. My blow never landed.

Ace moved.

He blocked my strike, stepped in, and caught my arm under his.

My heart hammered uncontrollably, and I tried to reverse my strike to hit him one more time.

He caught that arm, too. I stood so close to him, my chest pressed to his, my ragged breath hitting his neck.

Nala growled behind me. She'd attack if I gave her the command. Tempted, I opened my mouth.

Ace clicked his tongue and peered down at me. "Violence is never the answer."

"Neither is being a dick."

He smirked. "Seems like you have a few things to learn from me."

"Being a dick?" I raised my eyebrows. "I think I'll skip those lessons, thank you."

He shook his head. "Your bow work is phenomenal, but without it, you're not as dangerous as you need to be to match that mouth of yours."

"My mouth?"

His gaze drifted down to my lips, and I instinctively licked them.

"Your attitude," he clarified, his gaze still fixated on my mouth. "It keeps getting you in trouble. Some things never change."

"You might be good at hand-to-hand combat, I'll give you that." Begrudgingly. "But your manners suck."

Something flashed in his gaze, but he quickly blanked the emotion away. Releasing my arms as if they'd suddenly caught on fire, he stepped back and created space between us. He ran his hand through his hair. "I shouldn't have said that."

"And?"

He frowned.

"Are you sorry?"

His frown deepened. "I said as much, didn't I?"

I shook my head. His apologies were as good as my

brother's, which meant they were terrible. "Like I said, you could learn a few manners."

"Why?" He started to walk along the trail again, and I turned to join him. "Would grovelling on my knees before you change the value of what I said or the intention?" he asked.

"I would like to see you on your knees." I bit my lip. Maybe I'd like that a little too much.

He raised his eyebrows, his gaze cut to the side to watch me as we walked. "Is that so?"

"Not like that." I added.

He scoffed and his knowing gaze told me he didn't believe me. That made two of us.

"Crawl your mind out of the gutter, Mouse," he said. "And explain why you were interrogating the queen's messenger about a red scarf and then you can explain what we are looking for."

"A red scarf was found in the storage house. It may or may not be connected to the thief or thieves who are stealing our town's supplies."

Ace pressed his lips together and nodded. "And you think Blake is involved?"

"Just following the evidence."

"It's pretty weak," Ace said.

I blew out a long breath. "I'm aware of that, but aside from suspicions, it's all we have right now."

Ace shrugged as if my struggle to solve the storage thefts were of no consequence. He studied the forest around us. "And now? What are we looking for?"

"The rogue hunters."

"Obviously," he replied, tone dry and not conveying any appreciation for my forthcoming nature. "I knew that part."

"Did you? That's lovely," I said. "I feel it's safer not to assume a level of comprehension when it comes to conversing with you."

"Allow me to clarify my question." He scowled, his lips pulling back to expose his white teeth. "How are we going to find the rogue hunters?"

"We're going to reverse track the hunters who attacked me and Nala."

"I'm surprised you haven't gone after the hunters sooner."

I waved at the path behind us where Nala followed in her gentle loping pace. Her tongue lolled out the side of her mouth. "I try to avoid venturing into the sacred forest without my familiar, and she needed to heal. I was also busy vetting you, if you don't recall."

Ace scrunched his face as though he smelled something foul. "You're not the only hunter in camp. Why didn't your brother go? Or your boyfriend?"

"My boyfriend?"

"Onion."

"Rye isn't my boyfriend," I said.

"Well, he's a terrible partner or whatever the phaan he is."

"And why do you say that?"

"Because he hasn't gone to check out the hunters. He hasn't tried to track them down. If you were mine, I'd destroy the whole phaaning forest and slaughter anyone involved."

"If I was yours?" That thought both horrified and excited me. I squeezed my eyes shut briefly. How dare I like the sound of that. How dare my heart forget so easily the hurt this man had caused.

He mocked my romance books, for phaaning sake.

Ace took a long-suffering breath as if his comment was somehow my fault. "Don't flatter yourself or start getting ideas, Mouse. It's a figure of speech. I meant if my significant other was attacked like you were, I'd do everything in my power to ensure it never happened again."

"Trust me, I don't find any of that flattering."

He glared at me for another full inhale and exhale before turning away. "You're an infuriating woman and intentionally missing the point. Where is the sense of immediacy? Of retaliation?" He waved his hand at the path in front of us.

"Right here," I growled and thumped my chest with the flat of my palm. "The anger and rage are right here. I don't need my brother or some fling rampaging into the forbidden forest for me when I'm more than capable of doing it myself. I don't know where you've been all these years, but I've been here, working hard earning my place. I'm not helpless. I am not a simpering maiden in need of rescuing or a mouse that cowers from danger, and the sooner you realize that and manage your expectations accordingly, the better."

Ace's eyebrows rose with each word, but he remained blissfully quiet.

"Besides, only guardians can enter the sacred forest. None of the non-galeons are allowed to enter and galeon descendants are forbidden from hunting in these woods as well. They're only supposed to enter it if they're pulled by the call of a familiar or they have a familiar that wants to play in the fields."

"Play?"

I shrugged. I had no intention of explaining the inner mechanisms of familiars when I sometimes questioned my own understanding.

We walked in silence after that while I fumed, and Ace quietly contemplated whatever thoughts ran through that smooth brain of his.

"A fling, huh?" He finally broke the silence.

"Out of everything I said, that was what you decided to fixate on?" I readjusted the strap for my quiver. "You're an ass."

He smiled then, his face almost splitting in two. "The sooner you realize that and manage your expectations accordingly, the better."

20

We crested the bank of the river that led to the field where the hunters had attacked. Nala must've sensed how my nerves frayed with each step because she walked beside me, pressing her furry body into my legs. Whether she did this to reassure herself or me, I'd never know, and it didn't matter, because at the end of the day, we both needed the connection.

When we arrived at the field, I froze on the spot while my mind tried to process the scene in front of me. It didn't make sense. The area was empty. No bodies.

I spun around and scanned the forest.

Nothing.

I searched and found location markers around the area—the tall pine with the snapped branch, the fallen log with moss, the alignment of the mountain range through the twin cedars.

They were exactly where I expected. I hadn't

mistaken the area or somehow lost my way. This was the field. This was the place I killed a bunch of men and one of them shot Nala.

My skin prickled, and I slowly approached where Nala had fallen.

Squatting down, I ran my hands along the pine laden ground. It was damp, and the saturated dirt hinted that a pool of fluid had formed here recently, a pool of blood.

Nala's blood.

My familiar whined.

I reached out and scratched her behind the ears.

"This is where Nala was shot," I explained to Ace over my shoulder. It was about as much as I could say, given the absence of visible evidence.

"There's a notable lack of dead bodies," he said.

I straightened and pointed to my left. "They were over there." I pointed at another spot. "And there."

"I'm assuming from their absence someone must've moved them?"

I nodded. "Or more than one person. Those archers weren't small. It would've taken time and effort to move them."

"It has been days," Ace said, scratching the stubble on his chin. "You shouldn't be so surprised."

"Right." I frowned and looked around again, hoping some sort of secret message with all the answers would fly out of nowhere and smack me in the face. "They had time to move the bodies, but they had to know where to look. So either they travelled this route often, or they did have a spotter." And the worst part—the part I didn't speak out loud because it was now phaaning obvious—there were more of these rogue hunters. We had confirmation I hadn't killed them all.

"Why go to all that trouble?" Ace asked. "Unless their identities gave something else away. Did you recognize them?"

I shook my head and wiped my hands on my pants before straightening. "Not a single one. Their clothes looked different than ours, too."

"How so?"

"Different cuts and materials. Even the colour was different." Perga and Wast hunters tended to wear black or mahogany brown leathers. "They wore green wool and light tan leather."

Ace walked over to one of the spots I had indicated and knelt. "They went to a lot of trouble to get rid of the evidence. They didn't want us to identify them."

"Or they belonged to a group who cared enough to bury them." I pursed my lips. How could a group this large go undetected in the forbidden forest for so long?

He shifted and his gaze swept the ground in front of him, searching. "Do you have enough to track them?"

Instead of answering right away, I walked over to the edge of the forest and considered the directions the hunters must've come from to attack me. The cleanup crew did a fantastic job, hiding the bodies and their own tracks, but they hadn't thought to cover the tracks for the hunters' arrival to the area.

Nala trotted over and sniffed at the ground and pawed the dirt aggressively. I leaned over and considered the thick brush. Small, broken twigs and shrubs caught the light.

Perfect.

Did I have enough to track them? A smile spread across my face. "Absolutely."

Turning toward the shrubs, I leaned down and checked the footprints. "This way."

Nearing winter, the forest sounds were more solemn than the constant buzz and drone of insects in the summer. The crickets had grown silent over the last few days, now too cold, and the migratory birds had long left the woods. Instead, eerie stillness settled over the forest, punctuated by the croak of a raven, a flitter of wings or the sharp snap of twigs and branches under Ace's feet.

We walked in silence through the bushes until we came upon a small trail cutting southwest to northeast through the forest. No more than a deer path, trampled grass, squished moss, and upturned dirt marked the passageway.

I knelt to examine the tracks made by heavy boots. They were multiple sizes, which indicated more than one hunter. These had to be from the same men who'd attacked me and hurt Nala.

Based on the shape of the prints, the tracks came from the northeast and headed southwest toward the field. I was on the right track—pun intended. Straightening, I brushed my hands on my dark leather pants.

"Tell me something, Mouse," Ace's deep and gravelly voice made me jump in surprise. "I get that you were angry the queen ordered you to have a partner, but you're also angry it's me. This is personal, and don't bother trying to tell me otherwise. Years ago, you would've stumbled over your own feet for the opportunity to be my partner."

"Because I had a little girl crush on you?" I scoffed.

"We may have been young when we met, but you were twenty when I left. Hardly a little girl, and hardly a simple crush."

Why did he have to keep pushing? This was the last thing I wanted to talk about. "You need to get over yourself. I certainly got over you."

"Then why are you so angry I've returned?" he asked. "If you're so over me, why all this rage?"

"You're right, I am angry, but it's not because of some crush. I am angry because you left *him*."

"Him?"

"My brother," I hissed. "You were his best friend. His only friend. And you left without telling him, and without sending a word after you disappeared. We didn't know if you simply left on your own or if you were lying dead in a gully somewhere. You hurt my brother. I could handle your return better if it was just me you hurt, if it was just my rejection. But you destroyed my brother, and I will forever hate you for that."

Ace turned to me and opened his mouth, but whatever he planned to say caught in his throat.

A branch snapped in the direction we'd come from, stopping both of us from speaking.

We turned in unison toward the sound and drew arrows from our quivers, our conversation forgotten.

Taking a step away from Ace to create space, I took cover behind a tree just as a large man with blond hair stumbled onto the path.

I cursed and lowered my bow. "Rye!"

He held up both his hands, a sheepish grin on his face.

"What are you doing here?" I stepped away from the tree and glanced at Ace. He was frowning. Again. So that told me nothing.

Nala yawned and appeared completely unbothered by it all.

"I almost shot you," I said.

Orion dropped his hands and rolled his shoulders back. "Well, that would be one way to ruin the evening."

"What are you doing here?" I repeated.

"It's getting dark," he said as if that somehow answered the question.

I looked up. Sure enough, the sky had darkened. My focus on tracking the rogues narrowed so much, I hadn't noticed. "I'm not scared of the monsters lurking in the dark."

I was one.

I was the nightmare parents warned their children about—a cautionary tale of what would come after them if they dared to stumble into the forbidden forest. It was a bit unfair—I'd never harm a child. But the stories were told regardless as a deterrent for hunting where they shouldn't when they grew up.

"We expected you back in Perga," Orion continued. "I was worried."

"I can handle myself." I strung my bow over my shoulders and placed my hands on my hips. "And it's not like I'm alone. I'm with the partner *you* talked me into keeping."

Orion's gaze flicked to Ace briefly before he stepped closer to me. He lowered his voice. "About that. Can we talk?"

"We are talking."

"In private."

Ace rolled his eyes and spun on his heels. Without a word, he walked down the path about forty feet before turning to face us. He crossed his arms over his chest and called out, "Will this suffice?"

That was exactly what I would have done. A flashback from our youth smacked my mind—one of Ace smiling and laughing as we joked around. That was before he crushed my heart and that of my brother's, of course.

Orion scowled at Ace, but when he refocused on me, he hesitated.

"Just spit it out," I said. If he took any longer, it would be impossible to set up camp. We needed the light, and the sun was setting fast. At least one good thing had come from Orion's interruption.

"It's Ace," Orion said.

"Yeah, I get that, but you're going to have to be a little more specific. I already know his name and that he's an asshole. I'm one, too, if you hadn't noticed and my patience is non-existent."

"I don't trust him."

"Again, you have to be a little more specific." I narrowed my eyes. "And why couldn't this wait until we returned to Perga? You could've easily pulled me aside, then, without drawing any attention to us, or this conversation."

His expression closed off, his emotionless healer mask sliding into place. "I did a little digging after you left and it's not safe for you to hunt with him."

Did my brother put him up to this? Those two rarely interacted, so probably not. And Orion didn't usually sensationalize information. He was acting out of character, but why? Why was it so important for me to return home tonight?

"Again, you're going to have to elaborate," I said. "Especially when you were so determined for me to accept him as a partner in the first place."

"I'm worried about you, okay?" His voice rose. "I thought he might use this outing as an opportunity to hurt you and I wanted to warn you."

"So, you decided to follow us in case I needed help defending myself?"

Nala growled.

I nodded at her. Though I didn't speak wolf, I fully agreed with her.

It wasn't that I didn't appreciate the sentiment of him worrying or caring—I did. It was nice that someone other than my brother gave a shit. But I was fully capable of taking care of myself and Orion's actions undermined my capabilities. Actions always spoke louder than words and his said he didn't think I could take care of myself. He didn't think I was smart enough to understand danger. Maybe he was right, maybe he was wrong. But I never appreciated being treated like an ignorant incapable girl. Like a weak mouse that needed protection.

I'd been helpless as a child and made a promise to myself never to be weak again.

Orion glanced at the darkening sky, as if it would somehow provide him with the answers to all his problems. "I know you can handle yourself, Emi. This is not some veiled insult to your skills. You might be immortal, but you're not invincible."

"I literally cannot be killed. That's pretty phaaning close to invincible if you ask me."

"You can't be killed in any way that we *know of*, but galeons and phaanons used to kill each other all the time. There is a way, we just don't possess that information anymore," Orion said. "Besides, there are worse fates than death. You should head back to town instead of making camp."

Well, that took a dark turn.

I glanced over at Ace who continued to glower. "And that's what you think Ace has planned for me? Biological testing or the dreaded but vague fate worse than death? Do you think he's going to start a fire and hope for success? Hope I'll just stand there while he tries to shove me in or cut off my head?" Though, I guess he could wait until I fell asleep.

Orion pressed his lips together, his gaze flicking side to side to study my face. "Two days ago, you were furious to get a partner and now you're defending him. What happened?"

"Nothing happened. I'm still pissed at the queen's meddling and I'm not Ace's biggest fan. Look, I appreciate that you care and are concerned about my safety. I really am. But I just don't understand why you've stomped through the woods to deliver a useless, vague warning. You know I don't trust easily, and I'm already very aware of how vulnerable I am when there are only two of us out here." I dropped my hands from my hips. "I get that you are worried about me, but you seem to have forgotten I am one of the most cynical people in Perga and certainly one of the most dangerous. I might've known Ace years ago, but I don't trust him. We have no idea where he's been or what he's been doing since he left, and he doesn't seem intent on sharing that information. He hasn't earned my trust. It takes more than an archery contest and cooking a meal for that."

Orion frowned. "He cooked for you?"

"Are you two just about done?" Ace called out. "We're losing daylight."

Frankly, I appreciated the interruption. This conversation was going nowhere, and I'd already reached my tolerance for bullshit today.

Orion scowled over his shoulder before leaning in to hold my arm. "He's dangerous, Emi. There's a reason why he's so good at shooting and why he disappeared from Perga five years ago. He's been working for the royals this whole time, just not as a hunter."

"As what then?" My heartbeat picked up as my mind

raced through the possibilities. I kept coming to the only answer that made sense and I didn't like it at all.

"As an assassin," Orion said, confirming my fear. It somehow sounded even worse out loud.

Ice flowed over my skin as the missing piece to the enigma of Ace slid into place. That would explain why he had average skills at tracking and hunting animals through a forest at night yet hit a target just as well as I could. If he was an assassin, he probably stuck to urban areas. He could hunt, just in a different setting. It also explained why he moved like a fighter.

When I lived on the streets, I'd run into a few assassins before, and they always scared the crap out of me. In the back of my mind, I knew it was only a matter of time before one of them got sent after me.

"An assassin?" I mumbled.

"That's what my source said," Orion whispered. "What if...what if he's still an assassin?"

I swallowed and glanced over to Ace. "That doesn't mean he's here for me or anyone else in Perga." He might've decided on a career change.

"Em..."

"I hunt and kill men in the woods for Queen Titania. He hunts and kills them in a city. If you think about it, there's not a huge difference in our roles."

"Just the motives," Orion muttered.

Ace's gaze met mine and without a word, he started walking back toward us. His whole body radiated menace and irritation. His gaze flashed as it snagged on Orion, and he curled his hands into fists.

"Just promise me you'll be careful," Orion said.

"Yes. Fine. I promise," I said.

Ace moved with that centred, fluid gait of his, the movement that screamed danger. Maybe I should be more concerned or scared at learning Ace's history—but if he was here to try to kill me, why the charade of becoming my partner? There was no need.

No need unless he was here for information instead of murder.

Orion pressed his lips together, his gaze bouncing between us.

"I hope you two are done," Ace said. "We're going to have to set up camp and find dinner in the dark at this rate."

"And I need to get back to Perga." Orion nodded before looking at me one last time. "Just...remember what I said."

It took every ounce of self-control I had left not to groan or glance at Ace. "Of course."

We said our goodbyes and Orion left the same way he'd arrived, stomping, and cursing through the bushes.

21

The last rays of the day filtered through the canopy overhead, dancing along the moisture on the leaves and casting long shadows. During dawn and dusk, the few non-migratory birds in the area broke their silence and filled the forest with sounds of their sweet songs. They'd disappear into the shadows soon.

The setting sun took with it the little heat it offered, leaving the chill in the air to grow stronger. Though I wore leather pants and a leather shirt, the cold here soaked through to the bone. We'd need to make a fire soon before my chattering teeth lured large predators out of hiding.

"Do you want to tell me what that was all about?" Ace asked.

"Not particularly."

"Looked like a lover's spat to me."

I snorted and shook my head. "You must be incredibly inexperienced as a lover if you think a quiet conversation like that was a lover's spat."

A sly grin spread across Ace's face. "Nothing could be farther from the truth."

"Is that so?"

Ace leaned down, his dark gaze scanning my face. Before he could say anything, though, Nala growled.

I grabbed Ace's arm and pulled down as I dropped to the ground. Nala only growled like that for one reason, and that was to alert me to danger.

My wolf stared at the forest at the north end of the path.

"Nala," I whispered.

She stiffened but didn't take her attention off the path. She didn't need to for me to know she heard me.

"Go," I ordered.

Without hesitation, she took off, her paws silently pressing into the trampled moss. Nala had been and always would be my number one hunting partner.

My heart thudded heavily, threatening to punch free of my chest, as I waited. Nothing flushed hunters out of the forest faster than an angry wolf.

A man yelled out in the distance, followed by a low snarl. I stood to face the direction of the sound when something whizzed through the air.

Pain ripped through my arm and an arrow sunk into the bark of a nearby tree. An arrow had sliced through my skin, grazing my arm just below my shoulder.

As the pain exploded in my arm, numbness spready

over my body. I was already spinning toward the source of the shot. The archer had to be behind me. In one fluid motion, I drew my bow, and let the arrow fly.

A garbled sound responded, an echo through the night, followed by the heavy thud of a body hitting the ground. Before I could calm my racing heart or slow my breathing, branches snapped and cracked. Large shapes emerged from the woods all around us.

The darkening skies above made it difficult to catch certain details, but the men were large, and they ran toward us with weapons in their hands.

I notched my arrows, one after the other, and let them fly.

The men stumbled and fell to the ground, but more ran out from the bushes. I was almost out of arrows.

Ace pulled his dagger and leaned to the side, narrowly missing a vicious attack. He countered and ran his blade over the man's throat. Without pausing, he met the attack of the next assailant, dancing out of the way before following up with a flurry of strikes that left his opponent staring down at the gaping wounds in his own chest before he toppled over.

I lowered my bow. My heartbeat still raced, and my breath was stuck in my throat.

Ace was mesmerizing to watch.

He became a whirlwind—slashing and stabbing and slipping past defensive maneuvers. When he cut down our remaining attackers, he stood still, breathing, heavy, his hand with the dagger lowered to his side.

"Ace..."

He turned slowly, his face cast in shadows. Suddenly, he jerked upright. Holding his hand out, he yelled, "Em."

An arrow flew by my face and struck something behind me. I spun in time to watch another attacker fall to the ground with a loud thump. His arm had been raised to strike me down from behind with a knife.

And I would've fallen.

I'd been so distracted by Ace's fighting I had dropped my guard.

Stupid. Stupid. Stupid.

I wasn't one of those damsels in distress. I wasn't one of those people who made too stupid to live decisions. I was better than this. I was smarter than this. And I somehow had lost sight of my own bad-assery in the presence of a pretty smile and fancy fighting moves.

Thankfully, Ace wasn't looking at me to witness what must've been a comical transition of emotions across my expression. Instead, he had positioned himself toward the section of the forest where the arrow had come from.

And the person stumbled into the clearing.

"Onion," Ace muttered.

Orion's hand holding the bow shook and his face was paler than usual. "I can't leave the two of you alone for five minutes."

I scoffed. "You were gone for at least ten."

"How did you know to come back?" Ace asked.

Orion frowned at him. "I heard the shouting and came right away."

"Geez, Ace. What does it matter?" I asked before I stepped forward to close the distance between us. My head swam. I stumbled and careened to the side.

22

The world tilted as I stumbled. My feet sluggishly moved underneath me, not quite getting the message. With a few jilted steps, I staggered into a tree, catching myself before I toppled over. My head spun, my stomach turned, and my arm ached.

It hurt so much.

I pressed my face into the rough bark of the tree trunk and breathed in its earthy scent.

"Mouse?" Ace asked.

I waved him off. I was probably just processing a major adrenaline surge. I stepped away from the tree and a sharp pain stabbed my body. I cried out and clutched my arm.

Orion and Ace rushed to my side. Ace gripped my uninjured arm, holding me upright, while Orion leaned forward to examine the area radiating pain. I had instinctively covered my wound from the arrow.

Orion smacked my hand. "Let go."

When I dropped my hand, more pain slammed through my body. Nausea twisted my stomach in a knot and my vision wavered.

Orion pulled the split material of my top to the side to examine the wound. His brow furrowed. "What happened?"

"Nothing," I snapped, my mouth shut on the pain.

"The bleeding wound on your arm suggests otherwise," Orion said.

"An arrow grazed her earlier," Ace said.

Traitor.

Orion stilled. His breathing shallowed as his gaze flicked between my wound and my face. "No..."

"I've been grazed before. It's no big deal," I said, my words slurring together.

Well, that can't be good.

Orion frowned harder and pressed the skin around the wound. "This isn't like your previous wounds. You're in a lot of pain and it's not healing quickly." Orion straightened and shared a look with Ace.

"I'm sure it will be fine," I said.

"Okay. Why don't you try to take another step on your own?" Orion suggested.

Ace let go of my arm.

I staggered forward. Blinding pain shot through my body, my vision swam, and I careened to the side.

Ace grabbed me again before I crashed to the ground and lifted me onto my feet. "I've heard of falling for someone, but this is a little much."

"I wasn't going to fall...jackass...," I muttered, my head still spinning. "Just fail...at standing."

"You're Artemis," he growled. "Guardian of the forest. You may fall down, but you'll never fail." His words sent warmth rushing through my body and gave me the strength to get my feet under my body to straighten.

My gaze snagged on his. Fury flashed across his expression. He looked torn between wanting to drop me or kiss me.

"Something's wrong," I whispered. "I feel so...weak."

"You're the strongest person I know, Mouse. You'll be okay."

I shook my head and wavered on my feet, the world turning sideways. I tried to step away from Ace and fight through the fog consuming my mind.

He pulled me into the heat of his body before I had the chance to topple over again. "You're strong enough to let me help."

I sagged into his chest.

"She can't walk home like this," he said over my head. When he spoke his whole chest rumbled, and vibrated my body while his breath ruffled my hair.

"We could carry her," Orion suggested. "If we cut through the forest and head straight to Perga instead of backtracking your trail, we're maybe an hour or two away."

"It won't be comfortable for her, and we won't travel fast," Ace said. "It will take double that time."

"What are you suggesting?"

"I don't know. You're the healer. Do you have anything that might make her feel better or counteract whatever poison was on the arrow?"

Poison?

Of course. That made sense. The arrow had to be tipped with something to make me feel this way.

Why were my thoughts so scrambled?

"I do," Orion said. The ground crunched somewhere behind me.

"Can poison even harm her?" Ace asked.

"She's a bonded galeon. Usually, I would say no and suggest we wait this out. But it depends on the poison. If it's made with the same magic that courses through her veins..."

"Galeon magic?"

Orion nodded. "That's right. If it's the same, her body will acclimatize and absorb it."

"And if not?"

"It's most likely her system will burn it off, and she'll bounce back."

"But?"

"But someone managed to kill Dita, and Emi has never taken this long to stabilize. She's getting progressively worse. I don't want to assume this is harmless. I don't want to risk it."

I sagged more in Ace's hold, my limbs growing heavier by the second. He tightened his arms around me.

"I'll stay with her," Ace said.

Orion grunted, the ground crunched some more. "I'll be back as soon as possible."

"I'll keep her safe," Ace said. "I'm going to carry her to the clearing by the forest's edge. I don't like the idea of waiting by all these dead bodies."

"I'll look for you there," Orion said.

Ace nodded, his chin brushing the top of my head.

A breeze flowed over my skin and branches snapped in the distance as Orion made his way home. I'd look, but I was now the equivalent of a puddle of mud and couldn't feel my legs.

"Hang in there, Mouse." Ace's voice rumbled. "I'm going to take care of you."

With movement too fast for my addled brain to track, Ace bent and hoisted me over his shoulder. I flopped against his back helplessly, my world spinning.

Ace bent again to pick up something else before he marched through the forest toward the field.

My whole body spasmed in pain and I whimpered. Gray fur flashed in the periphery of my vision. Nala had returned to trot beside us.

"We're almost there," Ace said.

He sat me down a few minutes later, propping me up in a sitting position against a large fallen tree. Nala instantly darted in and sniffed me aggressively. She punted my upper body with her snout until she reached my injured arm. A low growl vibrated her body and her hackles stood up. She sniffed harder and faster while her gaze moved from side to side.

"I'll be okay," I told her.

Her hackles lowered and she stopped growling. With a few more snuffles and glares at my wound, she moved to my side and curled up beside me, her warm body heating my legs. I rested my uninjured arm over her and played with her fur.

While this was going on, Ace had moved around the small clearing near the forest line that faced the field and started a fire. The night held a chill, and the cold had already started to seep into my bones despite having a wolf heater by my side.

"Let me see that wound." Ace crouched beside me and pulled back the leather near my sliced skin. The blood had stuck to the fabric and the leather made a sickening ripping sound as Ace peeled it free.

Blinding pain gripped my body, and I squeezed my eyes shut.

"I should've called you a mule," he said. "You're certainly stubborn like one."

"But...I'm...mouse." My teeth chattered.

"Definitely. And a princess. You'll probably want my head cut off after this."

"After what?"

Ace leaned in, scooped me up and splayed me out on the ground. I've never been tossed around like some sort of ragdoll, and Ace had done exactly that twice in one night.

Numbness with sharp jabs of pain spread over my body.

Fabric ripped.

I didn't have the energy to raise my head off the ground, but if I had to make a guess, Ace tore my shirt off to examine the wound.

My body might be shutting down, but my mind still worked. Sort of. "Pretty lame excuse to get my shirt off," I muttered. "Going to go for the pants, too?"

Ace snorted. "If I wanted in your pants, you would've already stripped for me."

"I should consider myself fortunate to be spared such a disastrous fate, then. Thank you."

More pain shot through my body.

Ace placed his hand over the flat of my stomach and pushed down. A warm sensation trickled over my skin, whispers of a touch that called to my restless magic inside. "Shush. I'm almost done."

"Almost done what?" I tried to focus on the sensation rolling over me in waves, but numbness spread over my body, followed by a chill. I shuddered and tried to sit.

Ace pushed me down again.

He was the most irritating man.

"Okay, Mouse." He leaned over my body and blocked my view of the night sky overhead. "All done."

"Thank you," I said, though I wasn't particularly sure what I was thanking him for. "Did you salvage any of the shirt, or did you just rip it off as another souvenir for your trophy case?"

"Your shirt is fine." He reached under me and lifted me enough to place me back against the log. My shirt sleeve hung open, but the rest of the garment covered me as before.

Nala got up to move closer, flopping down in the dirt beside me, her head over my lap and her legs sprawled out. She hadn't voiced a single protest while Ace manhandled me.

Ace sat beside me and pulled some seasoned jerky from his pocket. "Want some?"

I nodded and instantly regretted it as pain washed through my entire body.

When I didn't reach up to take the meat, Ace shrugged, ripped off an end and held it to my lips. I opened my mouth, and he plopped the meat onto my tongue.

"I thought I would enjoy seeing you speechless," Ace said. "I find myself mistaken."

I gently chewed the meat. My body still screamed in agony, but the pointed sharpness began to ebb with the fading pain, and the cold chill in the night air beginning to seep in.

Hopefully, that meant my immortality super healing was kicking in. Normally, it didn't take so long to act, but I'd also never been poisoned before.

Nala curled up beside me in a tight ball, tucking her snout into her body and hind legs. An owl hooted nearby, concealed by the inky darkness of the forest.

The salt from the cured meat hit my tongue and made my mouth water. "This is good," I said, chewing more.

"She speaks." Ace's gaze swept my body. "What do you need?"

"I'm cold." My teeth had begun to chatter, and ice prickled my skin.

"Not much I can do to help you with that. I don't

want to risk a larger fire." He swung his arm over my shoulders and pulled me into his body. Heat flowed around me where I nestled into his side.

"This helps."

"Are you feeling better?" he asked, his voice unusually light.

"I think so. It was worse before, but I think I'll bounce back. At this rate, I might be able to walk on my own in a few days."

He squeezed my shoulders. "I'm not sure how much you caught of our conversation earlier, but your lover boy went to grab some healer shit. He shouldn't be too much longer now."

"He's not my lover boy."

Ace chuckled and shifted a little where he sat. "If you say so."

But I did already say so. Repeatedly.

"What's your problem with him?" I asked.

He glanced down at me, his expression tightening. "I don't trust him."

Well, I guess the feeling was mutual. Orion said the same thing about Ace.

"You don't trust him because he's being so suspicious?" I frowned. "What exactly has he done to not earn your trust?"

"He's not acting suspicious. He's letting his feelings cloud his judgment. Emotional hunters are unpredictable and dangerous and that's why I don't trust him."

"Am I to believe that in addition to being an expert in hand-to-hand combat you also excel in therapy?"

"Psychology is probably more accurate."

I rolled my eyes, and a wave of nausea instantly made me regret it. I took a deep breath and waited for the wave to pass.

"Can you elaborate?" I asked.

"He obviously cares about you very much."

"You're right, totally suspicious."

"You know what I mean," he said.

"Caring for me is hardly a crime."

"Too much. He cares for you *too much*."

Seriously? "You really know how to give a girl a complex. Am I not worth adoration? Am I not worthy of someone's affection or of being cared for?"

He jerked his head back and blinked. "Of course, you are. That's not the issue. The issue is that he stomped loudly through a forest with possible killers in it because he was worried about you and let his own fears outweigh logical thought and reasoning— you were and are perfectly capable of protecting yourself. You're not some rookie in need of protection or coddling. He probably led the hunters straight to us."

I shut my mouth.

"He didn't pause to think about the consequences of his actions."

"He doesn't trust you," I whispered. "That's why he came to see me. He wanted to warn me."

Ace's smile somehow morphed into something cruel and sad at the same time. "Have you figured out why yet?"

"Because you're new to him and a stranger. And most likely gained your experience from killing people."

"You kill people too," he pointed out. "That hardly makes either of us untrustworthy."

"Did you kill Dita?"

He jerked to the side, taking away some of his warmth. "Of course not. I don't know of any way to kill a bonded galeon descendant."

"You just kill regular people."

Ace scoffed. "That's not why Orion doesn't trust me."

"Do tell then."

"It's because he views me as competition. Men who are jealous are dangerous."

"He's harmless."

"I disagree and the hunter he killed probably would as well," Ace said. "It's clear he doesn't trust me because he's worried you're going to fall for my considerable charms, and he's trying desperately to interfere and distract you."

I peered up at him. "Considerable?"

Heat flashed in his gaze, and he leaned down close enough to kiss, bringing back his warmth. Our breath mingled. The ebb of pain in my body faded away.

"You have no idea," he whispered.

I tore my gaze away. "I remember you and Paul having pissing contests on O'Reilly's back fence. I wouldn't go making baseless claims." My cheeks heated at the words because I remembered everything, and Ace's claims weren't baseless at all.

"We were ten," he said.

"Thirteen and fifteen, actually."

Ace rubbed at the stubble along his jaw. "Whatever happened to O'Reilly?"

"Nothing. He's still there, being a miserable old bastard. Haven't you seen him around?"

"Fortunately, no, I haven't. Is he still running the smithy? It might be difficult to avoid him."

I shook my head. "He gave the smithy to his nephew a few years back."

"Graham?"

"Yeah."

"He's still a dick," Ace said.

"We agree on something it seems." Silence descended over us, and I let the sounds of the night forest flow over me as I thought on Ace's comments. "Maybe I should tell Rye the good news so he can relax a little."

"Good news?"

"Haven't you figured it out yet?" I lifted my chin and glanced at him. "I haven't fallen for your *considerable charms* at all."

"Yet."

The one word set my skin on fire. I sucked in a breath and made the mistake of looking up at him again. Our gazes locked. Tension danced between us, and his gaze slipped to settle on my lips. My heart raced.

A memory of us standing together on the grassy hill by the bridge to Wast blazed in my mind. He'd held me in his arms under the moonlight not so different than this one, the scent of spring flowers danced around us in an uncommonly warm wind. He'd told me he loved me. He'd told me I was everything to him. He'd leaned down to kiss me and—

"You two look awfully cozy." Orion's unexpected voice dumped ice over my senses.

I jerked back and whipped my head to the side to find Orion standing a few feet away.

My vision swam, and I had to take a deep breath and blink a few times until the details of my surroundings crystallized once again.

A sheen of sweat covered Orion's face and it glowed in the fire's light.

Had he run the entire way from town?

"Seems you can be quiet when you need to be," Ace drawled, and stood up, his arm slipping from my shoulders. His departure left my side cold, and I shivered.

"We were just counting all the ways I despise him," I said, dropping my head against the log behind me.

Orion had blanked his expression, slipping on his healer's mask. He stepped closer and crouched in front of me. "If your sass is back, you must be feeling better."

I stretched my neck, tilting my head from shoulder to shoulder. I didn't throw up, so that was a win. "A little. Whatever was on that arrow did a number on me, though. At this rate, it will likely take a few days for me to fully recover."

Orion frowned. "You normally only take a few hours..." He glanced over his shoulder at Ace. "Did you find the arrow and save it?"

Ace smirked. "Of course."

Orion shook his head and reached into the satchel hung over his shoulders. "You really are lucky, Em. If that arrowhead hit you centre mass, you might have ended up like Dita."

"Did you see her?" I asked, watching Orion pull a leather pouch from the bag. "Did you view her body?"

"Of course not," he said. "They've made it clear they don't need my services in Wast."

Orion knelt beside me and untied the leather pouch. It opened like a flower to reveal white paste with an acidic floral scent.

"What's that?" I asked.

"Smells awful." Ace wrinkled his nose and took a step back.

Orion ignored us and dipped two fingers into the smooth, creamy paste. With careful precision, he reached forward and gently peeled back the bandage that Ace had tightly wound around my injury.

As soon as the paste touched my skin, a rush of coolness spread through my body like a gentle wave, refreshing and invigorating. I took a deep breath and the pain slowly dissipated, replaced with a tingling sensation that left me feeling light and rejuvenated. I tested my range of motion, stretching my neck from side to side. There was no dizziness, discomfort or nausea, just a comforting sense of healing seeping into my skin.

Orion watched me expectantly.

Ace glowered where he stood off to the side, but he watched me just as intently, tracking every move with his dark gaze.

I straightened my back and shifted to get my legs under me. Without help, I stood and waited for light-headedness to make me waver and topple over. But the dizziness never hit. No fainting, no stabbing pain.

Ace whistled. "That's some magic stuff you got there, Onion."

"It's Orion." The healer stood and wrapped the balm in the leather pouch. "Thank you."

"Is this the special potion you've been working on?" I asked. "You've been holed up in the cabin like a mad scientist for weeks."

Orion stashed the pouch in his satchel. "I'm surprised you noticed."

I looked away. Of course, I noticed. The key to successfully avoiding someone was to always know where they were.

Ace smirked.

Awkward silence fell over the small clearing.

"Guess we head back now?" I spoke when the silence threatened to kill me.

"Guess so," Orion said.

23

We stood around my small dining table and stared down at the arrow. Orion and Ace notably kept as far away from each other as possible and had only exchanged the briefest of words on the trip home.

Ace ran his hand down the arrow and magic stirred in the air. I jumped and spun to face him, my mouth falling open. My power came in the form of connecting with my weapons and focusing on a target, but I could usually tell when others accessed magic because it made the hair on my arms stand up.

What the phaan was going on? Ace had magic? When the phaan did he get magic?

I shut my mouth and narrowed my eyes.

People were either born with magic or not. It wasn't something gained by a ritual or eating some magical fruit, but sometimes the magic took a while to manifest, or required a bonded familiar to be released. Ace had never let on he had magic when we were younger. Did his not manifest until later? Or had he always known he had magic and kept it hidden? Whatever the case, he definitely had it now.

My mind spiraled back to the clearing where he'd dumped me on the ground. He'd done something to help me heal before Orion arrived. I'd been too out of it to question him at the time, but it didn't take away the memory of his magic whispering along my skin and sweeping into my body. What was his power? And what else did he hide? And what was he doing right now?

I wouldn't ask him about his magic in front of Orion. Not because Orion wouldn't have noticed the magic, but because there was no way Ace would open up in front of a stranger. Ace had always been a private person.

When we were alone and I was feeling better, though, I planned to get the truth out of him—or at least some of it.

"It's laced with something," Ace announced. "The poison has a magical element to it, but I am not sure what it is." His brows angled down in a deep frown, and he pressed his lips together. He didn't need to voice his thoughts for me to understand he hated not knowing something. It was written all over his face. "Can you tell what it is?"

We both looked over at Orion expectantly.

The healer stepped toward the arrow and repeated the same action as Ace. His magic filled the room with its calming effect that reminded me of the hot springs and lavender. His magic felt familiar, and comforting. He'd accessed his power around me often, and he'd used his magic on me to heal...and do other things.

My cheeks heated and I shifted my weight on my feet.

Nala huffed and flung her paw over her snout where she'd sprawled near the fire.

Orion had the ability to heal and examine magical auras. He could also use it to caress someone else's power. It was hard to explain it, but it felt amazing in bed.

"It's immortal magic," Orion announced, apparently, unaware I was reliving our passionate night together.

How would Ace's magic feel if he used his power on me like Orion had?

Orion stepped back and when his gaze landed on my face, he frowned. "What's wrong with you?"

"Nothing."

"You're flushed." Ace narrowed his eyes.

"I feel a little warm," I admitted. "Must be a side effect of healing." I looked down at the arrow to avoid looking at either of them.

Ace snorted. He might've been gone for five years, but he'd known me from the ages of twelve to twenty during my angsty youth. He knew my tells. Lying to him was pointless.

But I hadn't lied for him. Not technically.

"Interesting," Orion said. "I'll make a note of that."

"Can you tell anything else about the immortal magic?" I asked.

"It's very...raw," Orion said.

"Raw?" I asked.

"When someone uses their power, it feels smooth and focused. This doesn't have that same feel."

"What does that mean?" I asked.

Orion studied my face for a second before answering. "I don't know."

Well, crap. We had a little more information but none of the pieces to the puzzle were fitting together.

"If you'll allow it," Orion spoke again. "I'd like to take the arrow to my shop and study it some more. Maybe there's a way for me to trace it."

I waved at the arrow, and he reached forward to pluck it off the table, careful not to touch the arrowhead. With a curt nod, Orion walked out of my cabin.

I waited until the door to the cabin clicked shut before I turned to Ace.

"You have magic," I blurted out. "You helped me back there in the forest and I want to know what you did."

"I cleaned and bandaged your wound, nothing more. Sometimes flushing out the poison can buy you more time or help speed up recovery. Obviously, that helped."

Bullshit, but from the hard set of his jaw, he wasn't sharing any more information. At least not tonight. I'd find another way to discover the truth. "What about just now? You accessed power to study the arrow."

He shrugged. "I have the ability to detect magic. I can't label it or track it, but I can recognize energy signatures that I've come into contact with before."

"And did this one feel familiar?"

"In a way," Ace said. "There was something familiar

about the magic, but if it was like seeing someone's face, the image was blurry. I couldn't focus on enough of it to identify who it belonged to."

"Has this happened before?"

Ace shrugged.

"You're not going to tell me?"

"Are you going to tell me why you were really blushing a few minutes ago? I thought there wasn't anything between you two."

"There's not." Not anymore. Not now that my mind couldn't stop thinking about how the press of Ace's power would feel along my skin.

Phaan.

He raised eyebrows. "Poor guy."

I growled and spun around to walk away. "You've been away for awhile. Things have changed. If you want to make any friends here, I recommend you stop antagonizing everyone you come across."

"That's rich coming from you," he said.

"What's that supposed to mean?"

"You have two, maybe three friends, and one's your brother and another just wants to sleep with you."

I opened and then shut my mouth. I knew I wasn't the friendliest person in town, but I was trying. Trust didn't come easily to me, not with my history, and I always had to hold a little of myself back to keep my secrets safe.

"I don't have to dish all my secrets to be liked, Mouse," Ace continued. "Nor do I need a heart to heart to get laid."

I snapped my mouth shut to take a deep breath in and out. "No. But you don't have to be a dick about everything, either."

"You seem awfully fixated on dicks." Ace followed me into the other room. "And anyway, what gave you the impression I was trying to make friends?"

"You'd prefer to be miserable and alone?" I spun to face him. "That's quite fitting, actually. Sad. But fitting."

He leaned toward me, somehow dangerously close without any effort. "I prefer not to get distracted."

"Then we have something in common."

He rocked back on his heels. "How so?"

"I also don't want to get distracted, and that's what a relationship with Rye would become. I don't feel the same way he does about me and that would also be unfair. So now you know the whole sordid truth about me and him. Probably not what you were expecting but that's all there is to it."

"Harsh." Ace nodded. "I like it."

"I don't really care what you do and do not like as long as you keep your opinion to yourself and stop asking me personal questions."

Ace smirked and crossed his arms over his chest. It made his biceps bulge and strain against his shirt sleeves.

I absolutely shouldn't be noticing details like that and the fact I did annoyed the phaan out of me.

I looked away. Orion might be worried about me for my own safety or because he was jealous, but he raised a good point earlier. I didn't know Ace very well, and I couldn't trust him.

When I thought about it, I didn't know a lot about Ace back in our youth, either. At least not about his past. I knew he liked honesty and despised going to the city. He had a dry sense of humour and preferred evenings to mornings and coffee to tea. I knew those sorts of things. But not wanting to share about my own sordid history meant I'd never questioned Ace about his. Nor his need for the same level of secrecy. And as far as I knew, Paul hadn't pried either. We'd formed a trio with me as the awkward third wheel and we all knew so much, yet so little about each other.

But now I had more pressing things to learn about my not-friend Ace. Did he still work as an assassin? Was he here for more nefarious purposes and that was why he didn't want to make friends or get distracted? Was all this just a part of a longer game or hunt? Who was his target?

"I still don't trust him," Ace said.

What? Had Ace been reading my mind?

No. Wait.

He was referring to Orion.

"I trust him," I said. "With my life. He's saved it enough times."

Ace sneered. "How can he save the life of someone who can't die?"

"He just saved my life. Twice. Just now with the poisoned arrow and before with saving my familiar. Seems like I can conclusively say he's not out to get me."

Ace smirked.

I flashed my teeth. If I were a wolf, I'd bite him. "You know what I mean."

Ace looked me up and down. "That was cute, I half expected you to stomp your foot."

I hated him. I truly hated this man.

"Besides, I would argue lifesaving and trust do not necessarily go together. At least not for you."

"What are you talking about?"

"I saved you, and yet you don't trust me at all."

I paused. Dammit. He wasn't wrong. "Point taken."

Something in Ace's expression softened. "I'm going to head out. Are you going to be okay on your own?"

"Why wouldn't I be?" I snapped back and immediately regretted it. Maybe Ace wasn't the only one who needed to work on his people skills.

Ace shook his head. "You really are a stubborn goat. Maybe I should've called you that instead of mouse."

Mouse, princess, mule and now goat. Had he ever used my actual name?

"Emi... I've loved you since you called me a phaaning ass and kicked me in the shin."

"So you continued to be an ass, because...?"

"Your anger was glorious. I wanted to see the fire in your gaze." He ran his finger along my jaw before tilting my chin up. *"The same fire I see now."*

I squeezed my eyes closed on Ace's words from the past.

Lies.

That was what they were. Lies.

Why else would he have run away the next day?

Ace headed toward the door oblivious to my flashback. "Just don't be so stubborn that you die all alone in this cabin. Nala might be forced to eat you."

Nala and I exchanged a look and my familiar whined.

Sometimes, I swore that wolf understood more of what we said than she let on. I would make a terrible meal—too bitter.

Ace left and shut the door to any protests I might've made. Pretty hard to argue against the truth, but something about that man made me want to argue out of spite anyway.

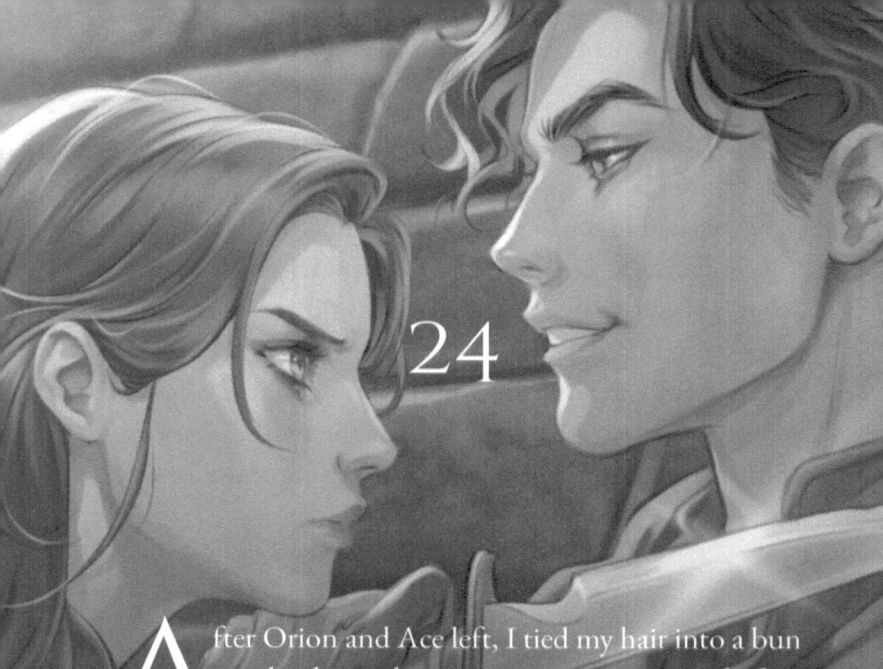

24

After Orion and Ace left, I tied my hair into a bun and changed into cotton pajamas before deciding to cook. Whenever things became chaotic in life, I found calmness in completing the most mundane tasks—bathing, cleaning, cooking. I moved around the kitchen and hummed the tune Sley had sung in my shop, though I didn't know the words.

The peace didn't last long.

Paul crashed through my front door without knocking and skidded to a stop in my cabin. Ace followed him through the entranceway and closed the door with an amused smirk. Hadn't he just left? Didn't he have something better to do with his time than saunter around my place and judge me?

"This feels eerily reminiscent of your last visit." I set the plate of cooked meat down and straightened to cross my arms over my chest. "Have you tried knocking?"

My relaxing evening plans consisted of snuggling with Nala on the couch and reading a book. And once again, as if he anticipated my plans and sought to ruin them, my twin was in my face, leading trouble through my door.

Paul wore his regular, short-sleeved navy shirt and dark pants combo, whereas Ace had changed into dark leather hunting gear with a cloak to stave off the cold. Instead of wearing a back quiver over his cloak, Ace had opted for wearing one around his hip. Tall, leather boots rose to his knees, the leather pants clung to his thighs, and the shirt looked a little too snug on his shoulders and arms.

Why did he have to look so good?

I waved at his outfit. "Shopping at the bargain stalls at the market again? You need to go a size up."

Ace flashed his teeth at me—either an attempt at smiling, or an attempt to hide his trademark sneer. Either way, he wasn't fooling me.

"Play nice, Em." Paul waggled his finger in my face. "I have urgent news, and I thought it prudent to grab Ace along the way and bring him with me so we can plan together. Also, I hate repeating myself, so this was just easier for me."

"A plan?" I raised an eyebrow.

"Yes, but first I want to hear what happened to you." He glanced at Ace. "Your *partner* indicated that the tracking mission didn't go well but didn't have a chance to elaborate before I hauled him to your cabin."

I glanced at my food, still hot and smelling delicious. My stomach growled.

Paul followed my gaze and licked his lips. "Any chance you have more?"

Of course, I had more, and he knew it. Paul breezed in and out of my life and my cabin. I always made extra food just in case.

With a quick pivot, I plucked my plates off the table, and headed back into the kitchen. "Do you want a plate too?" I asked Ace over my shoulder.

"If you have enough," he answered.

"She does," my brother added as he rubbed his hands together.

I plated two more dishes and set them on the small dining table as Ace and Paul joined me. I spent the next twenty minutes recounting the events in the Danu Forest with Ace occasionally interjecting to add details.

Paul forgot he had a plate of meat in front of him and just stared at me, and then Ace, and then me again, his mouth progressively dropping more open with each movement.

"Holy shit," Paul said after I finished the story. He didn't look shocked anymore, just angry. His gaze flashed with barely contained rage and his magic simmered below his skin, calling to mine.

Paul didn't have a familiar, but he had magic like me. The power raced in his veins, but he'd never found an outlet for it like I had with shooting. One day, though, when he found his familiar and his purpose, he would be spectacular.

"You must have a horseshoe up your butt, Em," my brother said.

"I thought you always said it was a broomstick?" I stabbed my meat with a fork and cut off a piece.

Paul waved my comment away as if his past insults should be forgotten.

Never.

Ace had busied himself with finishing the meal. He ate quickly, practically shovelling the food in his mouth. He paused and lifted his head, his gaze met mine. "What?"

"You should try breathing in between mouthfuls. I don't feel like saving your life tonight."

"Ah...so you don't reciprocate." He pointed his fork at me. "You're all take, no give."

I leaned back in my chair and moved some of the food around on my plate with my fork. "I never said I wouldn't save you. This isn't about reciprocation. It's about needlessly placing yourself in danger."

He scoffed and took another bite. After he chewed and swallowed, he pointed at the empty plate with his fork. "This was good. Thank you."

"You're welcome. Though I can't help but be a little annoyed at your surprise."

He placed his fork on the plate and straightened in his seat. "You just seemed so appreciative of my cooking, I assumed it was because you had nothing else of quality to compare it to."

I blinked at him for a few seconds, unsure of how to respond. The truth was, I had been an average cook at best before Ace left. It was only after Sley came to town and shared her cooking tips that I had developed any skill.

Deciding on not responding to Ace at all, I turned to my brother. "You said you had news and needed to plan. Time to talk, brother."

Paul nodded and dabbed his mouth clean with a napkin. It was silly really, he'd hardly eaten any of his meal. "Another body has been found."

I pushed away from the table and bolted to my feet. "What the phaan, Paul? Why didn't you lead with that?"

He had the audacity to shrug.

"You let us blather on about our story, but that could've waited," I said.

He pushed back from the table to stand as well.

Ace stayed sitting and eyed the leftovers on the kitchen counter.

I rolled my eyes and waved my hand in the direction of the food.

Ace jumped up from his seat with his dish in his hands to get another helping and a stupid, small part of me delighted in knowing he enjoyed the meal.

Ugh.

I would die before I shared that thought.

Paul watched the scene with a grin spreading across his face. "Your story could've waited, true," Paul said. "But so could mine. Shona won't be any less dead from waiting the twenty minutes."

He had a point.

"I don't know much about Shona," I said.

Paul nodded. "Shona was a galeon descendent as well. Also bonded. Her familiar was found a few feet away with no signs to indicate the cause of death."

"Did they ever find Dita's familiar?"

"Yes. Back at her house. She must've left her familiar behind, but it didn't save the animal. It was also dead. There were also no signs of trauma on Dita's familiar. So, we have to assume they died because their bonded galeon died."

There hadn't been a galeon death since the war with the phaanons, and the history books were vague on how they occurred. What wasn't vague was the connection between a familiar's life and that of their galeon. If one died, so did the other. There would be no visible wounds for the second death, because it was the death of the soul.

"And Shona? Were they killed with a single arrow shot to the chest as well?"

Paul nodded. "Yes. I think you and Ace are right to suspect a link between your attackers and those deaths." He paused, his body tensing.

"What?"

"I think it's also safe to say that attack on you in the woods a few days ago was a botched attempt. Not the one where you and Nala were ambushed by a bunch of men, but the one before that." He curled his hands into fists. "Maybe you were meant to be the first victim."

A shiver raced up my spine and I shook the unease away. Paul wasn't saying anything that hadn't already crossed my mind.

Ace, on the other hand, had stopped chewing and now glared at Paul. "Other attack?"

Right. While I hadn't told my brother about the attack directly, he would've heard about it from either the town's gossip or the queen herself—I submitted a report after all—but Ace didn't have the same connections.

"I was attacked coming back from Wast. I wasn't harmed." What I didn't mention was that I had help from a mysterious wolf. I didn't want to dwell on how close I'd come to death.

Ace grunted and pushed away from the table. He picked up his empty plate along with mine and carried them over to the kitchen sink.

"We really need to see the bodies," I said. "If we can detect the same magic on the bodies as the magic on the arrow that struck me, then we can confirm the connection. It will give us at least a direction to go in, and we'll be a step closer to figuring everything out."

Paul glanced at Ace. "You told her about your magical senses?"

Okay...where mild irritation had percolated before from Paul's drawn-out theatrics, I was now fully annoyed.

What else did Paul know about Ace that I didn't? What other secrets had these two kept from me. And more importantly, what secrets had Paul shared? Some of his weren't his alone.

Ace grunted in response before turning on the tap to wash the dishes.

"You've been dealing in secrets, brother," I hissed under my breath.

"Never yours," Paul said, his gaze softening. He jerked his chin in the direction of the couch, and I followed him into the living room with irritation still prickling my skin.

We settled on the couch, leaving Ace in the kitchen. Nala hopped onto the cushions between us and curled up. My brother reached out and ran his hands along her fur. Sadness briefly pinched his expression.

I didn't need to read his mind to know his thoughts had travelled to his own familiar—or rather the lack of its existence.

"There's another reason I am here." Paul raised his voice from a whisper. If Ace could hear over the sound of washing dishes, he could probably listen from the other room.

"I won't help you get into Sley's pants. You've tried so many times to seduce her it's just getting embarrassing now."

Ace's chuckle travelled from the kitchen.

Paul smacked my arm lightly. "No, but now I'm rethinking my gift."

"Oh?" I raised my eyebrows. "What gift?"

"I've arranged to get the two of you into the Death House to view the bodies, but it must be tonight, and I only managed to get you an hour."

A dish clattered in the kitchen and Ace stomped over to join us. He had a mouth full of food, so he had to angry chomp and swallow before he could talk. Had he used dishwashing as a cover to shovel even more food into his face?

"Phaan, Paul," Ace said. "That gives us no time to prepare."

"Why didn't you lead with that?" I flung my arms up for what felt like the millionth time today. Pain streaked down my body, and I grimaced, quickly lowering my arms. I might've recovered from the wound, but sudden movement still caused twinges of pain. Hopefully, this side effect would go away soon now that my accelerated healing had kicked it.

"Calm down." Paul moved his arms up and down as if trying to soothe wild animals. "We have some time, and the plan isn't super elaborate—we go in, you sniff around, we get out."

I glared at him.

"On a scale of one to ten, how much do you want to smack me right now?" Paul flashed his cheeky grin—the same grin that got him out of as much trouble as it got him into.

"I'd say I am at a pretty solid eleven," I said.

Paul waggled his finger in my face and tsked. "Family first, sister dearest. No murdering me today. Besides..." He paused to brush his shirt. "It's the best I could do."

I sighed and looked up to find Ace watching me.

"What do you want to do?" he asked.

"What I want to do is go to bed and sleep for the next week." I frowned and considered our options. It didn't take long because we didn't have many. "What we need to do is take advantage of this opportunity and go see those bodies."

Ace nodded. "How long do you need to get ready?"

"Fifteen minutes. You?"

"I was born ready."

I rolled my eyes. If this mission didn't kill me, Ace's overuse of clichés might do the job.

I stomped off to my bedroom. "See you in fifteen."

25

A gentle breeze swept through the chilly air, bringing with it magic and a silent warning. I halted in my tracks as the wind tousled my hair and flicked up the hem of my cloak. Nala bumped into my legs. Gripping my bow firmly and plucking an arrow from my quiver, I turned toward the Danu Forest and stepped off the well-worn path.

My familiar whined.

"Emi?" Paul grumbled. "We don't have time for this."

"Then go on without me," I replied.

"What's happening?" Ace growled somewhere behind me.

"The forest is calling me," I answered, though it was more than that. Danger lurked nearby and though the wind carried no words, the feel of power lingering on my skin told me a familiar was in trouble.

The wind drifted to a section of the forest where several people had stepped off the path.

Hunters.

The message from the forbidden forest's magic was clear. There were poachers in the Danu Forest.

Leaving Paul and Ace behind, I followed their trail through the dense foliage, picking up speed as the magic tugged at me to move faster. Nala quietly moved behind me as I used broken twigs and tangled threads of wool to guide me.

It didn't take long to catch up with the hunters. There were three of them. Three too many.

They leaned over a moving net, the trapped creature struggling beneath the tightly woven fabric. The hunters all wore light tan leather pants and green wool sweaters—a now familiar outfit I was sick of seeing.

Rogue hunters. Poachers.

I couldn't tell what they'd caught, but it was large and angry. The identity of the animal didn't matter, though. These men were trespassing in the forbidden forest and the penalty for their crime was death.

With Nala by my side, I moved silently around the edge of the clearing, staying hidden amongst the trees and carefully avoiding any stray branches or dry leaves that could betray my presence. Even the birds kept their distance as if they, too, wanted to help keep me hidden.

My leather gloves creaked as I tightened my grip on my bow, poised to strike once I found a better position.

Every fiber of my being thrummed with anticipation. My magic danced within me, mingling with the forest's call.

I was the guardian of the forest.

I would protect what was rightfully ours.

The hunters were too preoccupied with their prey to hear my silent approach. Taking cover behind a thick oak tree, I drew back the bowstring, the familiar tension bringing me a sense of calm. With a steady exhale, I let go of the arrow. It soared through the air and struck the first hunter with deadly accuracy.

Panic erupted as the man fell to the ground beside the thrashing net. Without hesitation, I emerged from my cover. I didn't give them a warning. They didn't deserve a chance to surrender. Instead, I swiftly took out the two remaining hunters with well-aimed shots.

Stepping into the clearing, I scanned for more hunters. Seeing none, I approached the creature trapped under the weighted net. It had stopped struggling and lay still as if waiting for me.

Nala followed, a quiet presence behind me.

I grabbed a corner of the net and pulled it off.

The creature sprung to its feet, a flurry of white fur and feathers, and I stumbled backward.

She was breathtaking.

Shaking off the rest of the netting from her shimmering fur, a unicorn stood before me. The moonlight danced along her sleek body and the magic in the air whirled around us. I had never seen a unicorn before. I hadn't known they existed. Weren't they just mythical creatures from storybooks?

The unicorn's power curled around me. Both familiar and foreign, it tugged at my heart and called the magic pulsing in my veins. I stared in awe as the unicorn rose onto her hind legs and pawed at the air, a piercing whinny fracturing the silence while her mane flowed down her back.

Her mane...

Instead of horsehair, her mane and tail were made of long white feathers that glowed under the moonlight. With movement, they shimmered with the metallic colors of the rainbow. The same feathers I used in my arrows' fletching.

"It's you," I whispered. A unicorn had left its feathers for me to find and use.

She landed gracefully on all fours, basking under the moonlight. She looked at me with her large black eyes over her shoulder before sprinting into the forest in the opposite direction of the trail, kicking up dirt and patches of moss in her wake.

I let out a long breath while my heart still tried to punch through my breastbone. I looked down at my familiar.

Nala sat by my feet, her tail thumping on the thick moss beneath her.

"Did you know?" I asked.

She panted, her long tongue lolling out.

Someone whistled behind me.

I spun around to find Ace standing at the edge of the clearing, his eyes wide. "I don't know what's more terrifying, seeing a unicorn with fangs or watching you tracking and taking down three hunters without making a sound."

Fangs? I hadn't noticed. I'd been too mesmerized by

the feathers.

"Now I know why you're the monster they warn everyone about."

26

Moonlight bathed my skin as I walked through the forest behind Ace. He'd pulled his cloak up to pluck spurs from the hem and I tried not to appreciate the unobstructed view of his leather-clad ass. I needed something else to fixate on to distract my mind from seeing a unicorn and unfortunately for me, that meant checking out Ace's objectively nice physique.

After retrieving my arrows, we left the hunters where they'd fallen and returned to the path. We didn't speak about the unicorn or the rogue hunters, nor did we discuss any possible theories as to what they were up to.

Maybe because neither of us had a clue what was going on.

Neither of us mentioned the unicorn to my brother when we met up with him, silently agreeing to keep that information to ourselves. Paul's only response to seeing us emerge from the forest was to ask if we were done playing around. I'd managed a nod.

Paul had chosen not to follow me or Ace into the forbidden forest. Maybe he trusted me to protect myself, or maybe he wanted to conserve his energy, but a part of me wished he'd followed to see me in my glory, to witness how badass I was, and to be there if I needed him. There was a time we always had each other's backs, a time when we had no secrets.

"Exactly how did you arrange for us to see the bodies?" I asked Paul who still walked ahead. "And why does it involve us sneaking into the city?"

Paul grunted and crouched behind a dense patch of salal bushes. He waved for us to join him.

I knelt down, the moisture of the moss soaking into my black pants. I should've opted for leather like Ace.

I'd never admit that though.

"I made a few deals with the city guards. We must sneak in because galeon descendants walking through the streets tends to gather more attention than we want or need. Especially if one of us is the famous guardian."

"No scaring toddlers for you tonight." Ace wagged his finger in my face.

I frowned, my brow furrowing and my lips pressing together, and I clutched my bow. Not a lot of hunters were female and my bow and quiver full of arrows with rainbow fletching made me rather easy to identify. "I'm going to have to leave this behind, aren't I?"

Paul nodded.

"Why didn't you say something earlier?" I peered

over the bushes at the top of a gentle hill that led to a small pedestrian bridge. The city of Wast glowed under soft lamp lights beyond. The moon above illuminated the stark buildings that rose around the streets and the quiet din of chatter hinted at people still up at this un-danu-ly hour.

I pulled free my quiver of arrows and stashed it alongside my bow under the bushes. Ace followed suit, and if his scrunched expression was any indication, he was just as pained to leave his weapons behind as I was. Though he wouldn't be easily identified, a bow would still set him apart in the city. We needed to leave the bows to have a better chance at blending in.

Ace turned to me. "Do you have a knife?"

I smiled wide and let my teeth speak for me.

He grunted and peered over the bushes. "You could've just said yes."

"How would I maintain my air of mystery?" I asked.

"I don't really like my partner to be a mystery. I want to know what to expect, what you're thinking and how you'll react when things don't go well. None of those things should be a mystery."

He had a point and I hated him a little more because of it. "Can you tell what I'm thinking right now?"

"No," he replied. "But knowing your predisposition for fixating on dicks, I'm pretty sure it's phallic in nature."

I took a deep breath and counted down from five. "I have two boot daggers, a long dagger strapped to my thigh and a shorter dagger on my hip. The last two you could've seen for yourself if you took a moment to look."

He nodded. "Good."

"And..." I prompted.

Ace turned to me and raised an eyebrow.

"What about you?" I asked.

"Don't worry about me." He smirked and looked away.

A low growl erupted from my lips.

Ace laughed.

He actually phaaning laughed.

I turned to my brother, scowled and jerked my thumb in Ace's direction. "Why'd we have to bring him?"

"Better option than Onion," Ace said. "You need someone to assess the weapon and injury."

Paul glanced at the sky and groaned. "Will you two please attempt to keep your petty squabbles to a minimum once we're in the city? We need to be a united team."

Without waiting for either of us to respond, Paul stood and stepped around the bushes, giving us the option to either follow or get left behind.

"Nala, stay here."

My familiar huffed and flopped down beside my weapons. At least I knew they'd be well-guarded. As I walked past Ace, I flipped up my middle finger.

"Very mature," he said with a flat voice.

I moved forward, my footsteps muffled by the soft grass beneath me. The knoll sloped gently downward, leading us toward a narrow bridge that spanned over a rushing river. As we crossed the bridge, it swayed under our weight, the wood creaking and groaning.

The towering outer wall of Wast cast a cold shadow that seemed to stretch forever and offered no warmth. As we approached the stone wall, the guard perched high above the small entrance to the city turned away, his sharp gaze scanning the horizon instead of inspecting us. Armor clanked as other guards stationed along the wall moved away from the entry point.

My brother winked.

We passed through the small gate where another guard was supposed to be stationed, but wasn't, and headed down a quiet side street.

"We have an hour," Paul said.

I still didn't get why we had to sneak through the city like thieves. I understood why announcing our presence at the city gates would be ill-advised, but why couldn't we come during the day when the gates were open and not controlled?

I swallowed my questions and followed my brother into the city and onto the bustling street.

The noise and closeness of other people made my skin crawl. I might've lived on these streets when I was younger. I might've arguably thrived in the setting at one time, but now, all I felt was a stifling discomfort, and the need to run away to my forest.

The smell of cooked meat, hot stones, campfires, and body odour flowed over me, and I shut a mental door on the memories trying to resurface.

"We are almost there," Paul said over his shoulder, as if I didn't know where the Death House was myself. When we fled the orphanage, we'd ended up running with a gang of young misfits. We took shifts and specific areas, and mine was often to stake out the Death House. No one guarded a dead body, and if street rats like myself hadn't ripped off all the valuables at the time of death, it meant a treasure trove of possible stolen goods awaited my attention at the back entrance while the Death House workers unlocked the gates.

I shook off the memory and focused on the here and now.

Paul turned back to the road but halted and threw up his hand. I stopped at the same time as Ace, and we exchanged a look. Ace shrugged.

He had no idea why we were stopped either.

"Move." Paul quickly jogged to an alley and pressed his entire body to the stone wall to shield himself from view.

We followed.

The stones were cool on my face. My heart raced, the beat of it consumed my hearing.

What were we hiding from? Galeons weren't outlaws. People with magic were welcome in the cities. We worked for the queen.

I was from the city, for phaan's sake.

A group of guards walked into the courtyard. In the center, a woman with long silver hair moved with fluid grace, her head held high, her chin tilted up. She wore a scandalous dress. The neckline dipped down to the belt line, exposing a generous portion of her full breasts and double leg slits lead all the way up to the underside of the belt line so she flashed the entire length of her well toned legs with each step. A raven with shiny black feathers perched on her shoulders.

Queen Titania.

"Phaan," I whispered.

Standing behind me, Ace leaned over my shoulder and whispered in my ear, "Is that the queen?"

"Don't you recognize her?" Paul asked.

"I was fourteen when she came to Perga. I remember how Mouse cowered behind her skirt, but I don't remember much about her face," he said.

The queen often used her magic to distract people from noticing her and she'd taken us to Perga with only one guard. Though I still didn't understand the queen's motives, it was clear looking back she wanted the trip to remain a secret. She wanted us to remain secret.

"Didn't you meet her again when she assigned you as Emi's partner?" Paul asked, his eyebrows furrowed.

"Can't say I had the pleasure," Ace replied.

I rolled my eyes, but my mind reeled. How did Ace get assigned as my partner without meeting the queen?

How did he work as her assassin if...

"She was away for some meeting when I arrived," Ace continued. "Sent her regrets along with my orders which included tracking down your ugly ass so I could give you her letter for Emi and also so you could help me break the news to your sister."

"I'd assumed you met," Paul said.

Of course he had, I assumed the same. Queen Titania had a borderline obsession with the hunters and oversaw everything. Why would she avoid Ace?

Unless...

Unless they'd already met and Ace lied, or he didn't work for her at all.

"You worked for the king," I said.

He glanced down at me and grunted.

"And he transferred you to work for his wife. Are you still..."

"I asked for the transfer, Mouse. I no longer work for the king. He wasn't pleased. And now I wish I'd stayed in town and waited to meet her." Ace continued to speak right into my ear, his breath ruffling my hair and tickling the sensitive of skin of my neck. "I probably would've received a warmer welcome."

I jerked my elbow back hard and caught him in the gut.

He grunted and staggered backward.

"If you think you'd get warmth from that woman..." Paul jerked his chin in the direction of the queen and her guards, now heading out of the courtyard in the opposite direction. "Then you really haven't been paying attention to any of the rumors."

"Why bother?" Ace asked. "Those same rumours said all sorts of things about you and your sister and so far, the only thing that appears true is the aiming stuff."

"Are you trying to get me to kill you?" I asked.

He winked. "Is it working?"

"You're an asshole."

"And you're a stubborn hermit. So what? We're here to do a job."

Annoyance bubbled up inside me, and I clenched my hands into tight fists, itching to strike. I debated the satisfaction of punching him squarely in the throat when a sudden blur caught my attention from behind. My reflexes took over and with a swift sidestep past Ace, I grabbed hold of the thief's shirt. Thread-bare fabric tore beneath my grasp. With a forceful thrust, I slammed the thief against the cold stone wall. I closed the distance between us, pressing the edge of my dagger to their exposed neck. The tension in the air became palpable. My hearing buzzed with adrenaline.

No taller than five feet, thin as a reed, the youth's eyes widened. They had an androgenous look—a mixture of both feminine and masculine features. How old were they? Ten? Twelve?

"You should know better than to target three armed people cloaked in black hiding in an alley," I said.

"Phaan you," the pickpocket spat.

I shook them, careful to not puncture their neck with the sharp edge of my blade. "What did you take?"

"Nothing."

I pressed the dagger into their skin.

"Front pocket," they yelped.

Keeping my dagger at their neck, I used my free hand to pull a billfold from the youth's front pocket—all black leather. I held it up to Ace's face. "This yours?"

He snatched it from my hand.

"Did you take anything else?" I asked the thief.

"Not from you, you crazy bitch."

I glanced at Ace, who just finished patting himself down. He nodded. The youth told the truth.

I didn't need to ask Paul. He'd never let a pickpocket sneak up on him. Instead, I turned my attention back to the pickpocket. "Is Allen still running the streets?"

The youth blinked at me. "That old guy? Phaan no."

Allen couldn't be more than thirty-five. I was insulted on Allen's behalf and my own.

"Gabe's running things?" I guessed. Gabe was a few years older than me and Paul, and always aspired to take over one day. It was all he ever talked about, and he was not only ambitious, but sneaky enough to accomplish anything he put his clever mind to.

The youth's gaze widened. "He was stabbed last month. Olly's running things now."

Huh. I always liked Olly. I never pegged him for taking over a ragtag group of thieves and misfits though. Then again, life had a way of veering off-course.

"Em..." Paul warned.

Right. This wasn't what we were here for, and we were running out of time.

"You need to stay away from us, okay?" I warned the youth. "I'm going to let you go, and you better run away. Fast. As fast as your little legs can go, okay? If you don't, you won't get a second chance. Do you understand?"

The youth swallowed before nodding.

I stepped back and let go at the same time. I didn't lower my dagger so much as moved it out of the way. I might've scared the thief into compliance, might've even impressed them, but I wasn't naive enough to trust they'd listen to me.

The youth caught their balance quickly. With one last look over at our group, they ran into the shadows, blasting past us, just as I had asked.

"That was unnecessary," Ace said.

"Because you don't need me to protect your honour or wallet? I'll tell you what wasn't necessary—getting robbed by a phaaning five-year-old while we're on a job."

Ace pressed his lips together. "They needed the money more than I did."

I snapped my head up and peered at Ace. The shadows played with the hard angles of his face. "What?"

"I knew I was getting robbed, and I let them do it, okay? If they were going for a weapon, I would've done something because I need those, and my weapons are hard to replace. But I don't need the money as much as they do."

I blinked at him for a couple of seconds, while my brain scrambled to process his words. "You're an idiot."

"I mean, I think it was more empathetic, generous, honorable..." He shrugged.

"No, it was idiotic. You let that poor kid think they got away with robbing you. Now, the next time they see a dangerous warrior in an alleyway, they'll be more tempted to try their luck again."

"Aww. You think I'm dangerous," Ace said, leaning forward and flashing his teeth. "You're positively gushing about me. Please, continue."

"You're giving them a false sense of success along

with your gales," I hissed, ignoring his comment altogether.

"Gales can be replaced." Ace narrowed his eyes and leaned in. "You're really fired up about this."

Crap. I was giving away too much. More than I wanted. "I'm not. I just think there are better ways for you to be empathetic while also teaching the kid a lesson."

"So, telling you to calm down right now wouldn't be appropriate?" Ace asked.

"When has it ever been appropriate to tell a woman to calm down?" I snapped back, placing my hands on my hips. "And when has it ever worked?"

Paul grunted an agreement. "She's got you there."

"You know, when you and your brother arrived in Perga, there were rumours you came off the streets and you certainly acted that way." Ace tapped his chin, putting the pieces together. In truth, he probably already had, but instead of coming right out and asking about it, he left his comment to hang in the air as an opportunity to share some personal information.

If a comment was a physical thing, I would've smacked it away. I had no interest in offloading childhood trauma.

"Are you two about done?" Paul interjected. "We're running out of time."

"Yes," I said at the same time Ace growled, "No."

I shook my head and waved at the courtyard ahead of us. "Paul's right. This can wait. Let's go."

With a grunt, my brother spun on his heel and walked out of the alley. I quickened my pace to catch up.

"Are we going to talk about why we're avoiding you know who?" I asked Paul.

"Nope," he said.

"Does it have anything to do with why we're slinking around town like common criminals in the dead of night or is your avoidance for personal reasons?" I'd always wondered about the closeness between the queen and my charming brother over these last few years. He always denied there was anything more than what there was supposed to be.

The problem was, as much as I loved my brother, as much as it was us against the world growing up, I didn't believe him. He'd always have my back, but everything else was shrouded in shadows.

"We're not slinking," Paul snapped over his shoulder.

"Speak for yourself. I'm definitely slinking," Ace chipped in.

We rounded the corner. The Death House sat in a halo of streetlamps at the end of the road.

27

Under the moonlight and the unnatural magical glow of streetlights, the Death House waited for us. Three stories high, the rectangular building took up half the block. We approached from the shadows of the alley, letting the darkness shroud our presence.

"This way." Paul led us around the side of the large rectangular building. He pointed at the decrepit fire escape ladder someone had left down.

"Are we breaking into the city's death house?" I blinked at Paul.

"More like visiting without permission," my brother said. "Besides, it's not breaking and entering if we don't break anything." He jerked his chin at the ladder. "Start climbing."

Guess that explained the need to move through the city without being noticed.

Ace shrugged. He did that a lot. He just went with

things. He must be confident in his ability to get out of trouble.

I grabbed the metal railing and pulled myself up. Step by step, I made my way to the second floor with the other two behind me. After I reached the small landing, I peered down at my brother. "What now?"

"Usually people open the door." His tone was dry and full of unappreciated sarcasm.

"Ass," I muttered. I half-expected him to make me use a secret knocking code, but when I turned the knob, the door clicked open. He must've paid, bribed, or asked a guard to leave the escape down and the door unlocked.

As far as I knew, the Death House wasn't usually subject to break-ins, but the highly unusual deaths should've drawn some attention, should've piqued some interest. But there was none.

No one knew.

Someway, somehow, the royals had kept the deaths a secret. There was no other explanation. If the residents of Wast had learned of Dita and Shona's deaths, they wouldn't be unaffected or disinterested. Something like this usually made it into the gossip flyers that flittered around town, but I hadn't heard a peep about it. Blake certainly would've said something. He was such a gossip.

I pulled the door open and stepped inside. The air was cool and clean, with a hint of chemical cleaner.

"Did you know they used to call Death Houses morgues?" Ace spoke behind me.

I jumped a little. "What?"

"Before the great war when electricity ran the world instead of magic. They called these places morgues."

"You're a historian, too?" I fluttered my eyelashes. "Such a complete package."

"Oh, I have a complete package—"

"Can you guys shut the phaan up?" my brother said.

I held the door open for the men and stepped to the side. Once they both made it into the hallway, I released the door. After it snicked shut, darkness encased us. The soft glow from farther down the corridor provided enough light to highlight the edges of the hallway, but Ace's and Paul's faces were shrouded in shadows.

"This way." Paul led us down the hall, around the corner and into a large clinical room with surgical steel everywhere.

Well. Almost everywhere.

Two corpses lay on separate slabs in the centre of the room with sheets covering the entire length of their bodies—presumably Dita and Shona.

"I need to take care of a few things. You have about half an hour before we leave." Paul slipped out the door and left me alone with two dead bodies and Ace.

"Shouldn't they be stored on ice or in one of those magic freezing rooms?" Ace waved at the wall of cadaver storage.

"Maybe? I'm not a coroner. Maybe they only get stored there after the autopsy is concluded. But it's more likely Paul arranged to have them left out for us."

"Then let's get to work." Ace approached the first body and pulled down the sheet to expose her face.

I sucked in a breath. Dita.

Ace's gaze slid to study my face. "Did you know her?"

"Not well." I lifted my chin in the direction of Dita's body. "Just hard to see someone I knew like this, you know? It's the colouring and stiffness that makes it not seem quite real."

Ace nodded and pulled the blanket down farther to expose Dita's chest. Right between her ample breasts, a gaping wound stared back at us. Arrows usually made clean cuts going in, but someone must've ripped out the weapon roughly because the edges of Dita's wound were jagged and hideous.

"The arrow went straight through the breastbone." Ace studied the injury. "Phaan of a shot."

"Phaan of an arrow." The breastbone was strong. The archer had to have used quality arrowheads and must've drawn a bow large enough to exert that much force.

Ace grunted and pulled off one of his gloves, tucking it under his arm. Without a word, he laid the flat of his palm over the wound. He closed his eyes and magic stirred in the air.

"What are you doing?" I jerked forward to stop him. By the time I took the three steps to reach him, he'd already removed his hand and stepped back to pull his glove back on.

I shoved his shoulder. "What the phaan?"

He scowled over his shoulder. "I took a sample of the magic. That's why we're here isn't it?"

"I thought you were going to do the same hover thing you did with the arrow. I didn't think you'd touch her. You can't disturb the evidence." I waved my hand at the dead body. "What if you left magical residue?"

Ace lifted both eyebrows. "Last time I checked, I'm not some sort of serial killer leaving the city guards my calling card. Even if they pick up my magical signature—which I very much doubt—they won't have anything to compare it to."

"Yet." I folded my arms over my chest, and mentally formulated a lecture about why tampering with the evidence could be disastrous for an investigation.

"The magic could be important, and I can only do my *hover thing* over inanimate objects, not people," he said. "It can't be coincidental that bonded immortals are dying, and you were struck by an arrow that managed to incapacitate you so drastically."

"Did you get anything?"

He smirked.

"Oh, come on. The damage is already done, and you made a compelling argument. Can you tell if it's the same magic that was on the arrow that struck me?"

"Yes, I can tell."

I wanted to throttle him. "You know, if you have a strangling kink, you could've just said so. I'd be happy to oblige. No need to be coy."

He chuckled and shook his head. "Yes, I can tell, and yes, it's the same."

My vision wavered, and an icy chill spread over my skin, prickling my scalp. Though I'd expected as much, though all the evidence—as minimal as it was—pointed to a connection, it was jarring to hear. Suspecting and confirming someone tried to murder me and would've succeeded if they'd aimed better packed two different punches. I'd never faced mortality before.

I didn't like it.

Squeezing my eyes shut, I took a deep breath to try to banish the shivers running along my spine. I hadn't just recuperated from a poisoned arrow shot. I'd avoided death. I had come remarkably close to being a third body on a slab in this room.

"You were lucky," Ace said. Apparently, he not only followed the same line of thinking as I did, but he also liked to state the obvious.

Or maybe my silence disturbed him, and he was trying to fill the void.

I nodded and swallowed down the fear. Now wasn't the time to let my emotions rule my thinking or actions. "But why? I've been attacked twice now. Why me? Why these galeons?"

Ace turned to me, his brow furrowed, and opened his mouth.

My gaze snagged on an arrow laying on the slab beside Dita's body. The fletching unmistakenly familiar, the arrowhead splintered and ruined. It might've pierced through the breastbone, but a large fragment had broken off.

"Is that..." I swallowed, unable to voice what was so obviously right in front of me.

"The arrow that killed her, yes," Ace said. He reached forward and hovered his hand over the weapon.

My weapon.

I'd know that fletching in the dark.

Cold washed over my skin as I replayed the few facts about these killings—immortal magic, perfect shots, my arrows...

They hadn't tried to shoot me with my own arrows. I would've noticed that.

I was being framed.

But why would someone or a group of someones go to the effort of framing me to then try to kill me? Or had they tried to kill me first and then when that failed, moved to set me up to take the fall? The sequence of events didn't quite make sense or fit either scenario.

Before Ace could say anything more, the slap of shoes on hard tile echoed down the hallway outside the room. I held up my hand and listened.

Ace snapped his mouth shut, but I knew the moment he heard the footsteps as well, his whole body stiffened, and his gaze scanned the room. The footsteps grew louder, the person was heading toward us.

It might be Paul.

Or it might be someone else.

We couldn't risk getting caught with the dead bodies of a murder investigation, especially when my arrow was the murder weapon. I flung the sheet over the body and frantically looked around the room. No windows. No other exits. And I'd rather get caught then slide into a cadaver freezer.

Ace reached forward and grabbed my wrist. He pulled me toward a tall metal cabinet, the kind that was the size of a large wardrobe. He flung the door open to reveal several lab coats on hangers, and work boots lined up underneath.

I didn't need any further direction. I pushed the lab coats to the side and hopped in. Ace followed, somehow squeezing into the remaining space before shutting the door behind him.

No sooner than the cabinet door closed, the mystery person swung open the door to the room.

"My lovelies." A woman's voice crooned.

28

The coroner spoke to herself as she moved around the room to set up for the autopsy. Meanwhile, we remained stuffed in a metal cabinet, pressed into the man I despised.

He smelled like pine and campfires, and he had no business feeling so nice beside me.

Maybe I needed to get out more. Start dating. Phaan, maybe take Orion up on his offer.

"Single arrow shot to the chest. Poor thing. Why didn't you heal? You're a bonded galeon and supposedly immortal and indestructible." The corner kept talking as she studied one of the bodies. Metal clanked and her shoes scuffed the floor as she moved around.

"The arrow struck the breastbone, shattering it. The arrowhead fractured on impact." Metal clanked in a bowl, and I envisioned the coroner pulling out a fragment of the arrowhead to drop it into the collection dish.

"Only a very skilled archer could make this shot.

234

Immortal magic of some kind is coating the arrow. This may have acted as an inhibitor to healing, or maybe it was the true death blow. Small slivers of bone, wood and metal travelled through the chest cavity and sliced the superior vena cava. Death was quick for you, assuming your immortality didn't prolong your suffering. The lungs are also filled with blood, so a fragment must've punctured that, too. You would've collapsed quickly, if not immediately—hard to tell with galeons—but you suffocated. There is no evidence of healing. I'm so sorry, Dita. That's not the way anyone should have to go."

The coroner changed utensils again. "But just between you and me, we both know there were a number of people who wished you dead."

I perked up and leaned forward. So, Dita had enemies. Were they behind this? Did they also dislike me and Shona enough to wish us dead, too? What linked the three of us together aside from being bonded immortals?

I frowned, my mind racing to connect the dots.

The door to the room slammed open, and I jumped back, smacking into Ace. Another set of footsteps announced someone walking into the room.

I tensed. Did the doctor have a lab partner? And would they head straight to the cabinet to get their gear?

I held my breath and waited.

The coroner set a utensil down on the metal surface and let out a long, dramatic sigh.

"What are you doing here?" she asked.

"Carla, I'm shocked," my brother said. "Do I need an excuse to see you?"

"Yes."

"That's not what you said the other week."

Seriously? My brother could charm the pants off anyone.

"A moment of weakness," Carla said, but her voice held a smile.

Paul scoffed and sauntered farther into the room—at least I assumed he did. He rarely entered a room any other way. "Come on, Carla. I haven't seen you in a week and you promised we'd go out for drinks if I did that thing with my tongue."

Gross.

"It's the middle of the night," Carla said.

"Yet you're here."

"I like working late at night. Less people." She paused and another item hit the collection dish. "Less people who breathe."

Silence fell over the room. Normally, Paul would take the hint and leave, but he wasn't here to get laid, he'd come to extract us so we could escape. He was buying us time.

"If it's not too late for work, it's not too late for a drink."

More fragments hit the collection tray. "You're very persistent."

"You're very enchanting," he countered. "One drink."

"Coffee."

"One coffee. Which is a drink, by the way."

Carla sighed again and she must've pulled off her

gloves because something snapped and hit the collection dish.

"Let's go," Paul said.

I held my breath, the entire time, waiting for the sounds of their footsteps to fade away completely.

Ace threw open the cabinet doors. "Let's go, before that woman comes to her senses."

"Or I have to hear more about what my brother does with his tongue." I shuddered as I hopped out. I carefully pulled the lab coats back to where they'd hung. Or close enough before bending to organize the work boots. We had moved them around a little in our attempt to fit into the cabinet.

"Good enough." Ace grabbed my wrist and pulled.

"Should we examine the other body?" I peered over at the other prone shape under a sheet.

Ace shook his head. "We've seen enough. I think it's safe to assume Shona died the same way. Let's get out of here before the coroner comes to her senses and turns your brother down."

"Good point."

Our boots slapped the hard tile floor, echoing our escape as we walked through the empty hallways. My heart raced in my chest, caught between exhilaration and fear. Someone yelled behind us. With a jump, I started to run, and Ace kept pace beside me. The man drew closer, letting out a string of curses as he gave chase. I pumped my arms and dropped my chin. Each step was driven by a desperate need to go faster, to go farther. I refused to get caught in the Death House, especially when I was the only hunter known for carrying a quiver full of magic arrows. The same arrows that would match the murder weapons used on two bonded galeons.

The man behind us yelled again, calling for us to stop, but it didn't matter. It was too late for him to catch us now.

With Ace close behind me, I burst through the doors and into the cool night air, barely slowing as I half slid, half jumped down the fire exit. With another rush of adrenaline, I rounded the corner and entered the shadows of the city.

Only when we were a few blocks away did we finally stop running. Hidden in a dark alley, I bent over and gasped for air as I tried to slow down my hammering heart.

Ace leaned against the rough brick wall of a nearby building, his eyes closed, and his head dropped back in exhaustion.

"Well, not the smoothest exit," I said. Did we have to run? Maybe. Maybe not. It wasn't worth the risk of getting caught and I didn't care to discover what happened if we overstayed our welcome in the Death House.

"Let's get a drink," Ace said.

"What?"

He pushed off the wall and studied me, his lips teasing up at the corner. "We made it out, but probably drew a lot of attention. They're likely to watch the city gates. It's what I would do." He nodded in the direction of the one entrance to the city that remained open at night. "It's not against any rules for us to be here. We should go for a drink, discuss what the phaan is going on and let the heat from our hasty exit cool down. We can leave in a few hours or even wait until the morning."

I glanced up at the night sky. "Morning isn't that far off anyway."

Nothing he said was incorrect. But while his idea made the most sense for evading capture, it still felt dangerous. And I was sick of being in danger.

No, that wasn't quite right.

I lived a life of danger and was used to constantly feeling on edge, on guard. But lately things had become chaotic. When I hunted poachers in the Danu, I had control, knowledge, and skill on my side. Now, I felt uneasy because I was in the dark about so much, too much. I had been attacked, ambushed, and now apparently, set up as a murderer.

And it all started when Ace arrived.

"Well?" Ace asked. "Shall we grab a drink?"

Before he could react, I grabbed the leather strap across his chest and pushed him against the cold wall, my dagger pressed to his throat.

"A no would've sufficed," he said. His dark gaze sparkled with amusement, and he reached up to prick the tip of the dagger with his gloved finger. "Oooo. Sharp."

I glared at him, trying to find a way to voice the turmoil in my mind. Taking in a deep breath, I focused on why I was so angry.

"Maybe try using your words?" Ace suggested.

"All this shit started after you arrived," I finally said. "It's one phaan of a coincidence."

Ace swallowed, his Adam's apple scraping along the cold edge of the blade, but he continued to smirk as if I couldn't end his life with a flick of my wrist.

"Not a coincidence at all," he said. "I think the queen knew something was going on and wanted you protected."

I pressed the edge into his skin, and blood pebbled around the blade. My leather gloves creaked as I clutched the handle tightly.

"Maybe," I said. "Or maybe you're the reason I'm in danger in the first place. That was my arrow beside Dita's body. You've had access to my weapons the entire time."

"Only split ones," he said, his gaze blazing. "Besides, everyone in town has access to your arrows. You have a large trap door big enough to allow Nala and pretty much anyone else into your workshop. Perga isn't exactly a secure location, either. It's mostly just an incestuous free-for-all."

My mouth twisted down. "Gross."

"Yet accurate." He leaned forward, pressing his throat into the blade without any apparent concern for his life. "I'd also like to point out you were attacked once before I arrived."

Phaan.

He was right.

And I was...wrong.

I pushed off the wall, removing my blade from his neck. An angry red line decorated the delicate skin.

He gingerly touched the wound on his neck and examined his gloved fingers. The bleeding had already stopped. The wound was a scratch, but a pang of regret stabbed my stomach.

"I was wrong," I said, the words turning sour on my tongue. "I shouldn't have done that."

"And?" Ace's lips twitched. "Are you sorry?"

I shook my head, realizing he was throwing my own words back at me. Apparently, my apologies were as terrible as my brother's, too. "Would grovelling on my knees make it better?"

A wide grin split Ace's face. "I'd definitely like to see you on your knees."

"Pervert."

"Are we going to go for that drink now or what?" Ace asked.

"Fine, but you're buying," I said.

Ace turned toward the alley's exit. "Phaan that. This isn't a date. You can pay for yourself. After that stunt you just pulled, you should be buying me drinks."

"Phaan that. I didn't bring any money, and this was your idea," I snapped back as I followed him, sheathing my dagger. "Besides, if you were more upfront and honest with me, instead of continuing to hide information, I wouldn't distrust you so much."

He hesitated and glanced over his shoulder. "Fine. I'll buy the drinks but don't get any ideas."

Like I'd ever.

29

I stood outside the rundown two-story bar with wood siding, half expecting it to topple over and crush me where I stood. "This is your bar of choice?"

Ace leaned in. "I come for the booze and to be left alone. This place is perfect."

"I'm surprised you know of any places in the city. You never used to venture here, and you've been away for a long time."

"Yes, but that doesn't mean I haven't been here." He left me to gape at him and pulled open the door. The hinges creaked loudly. "I used to live in the city, too, you know."

Ace held onto his secrets when we were growing up, but he held more now. I wanted to crack his head open like a walnut and read what was inside.

"So many secrets," I whispered.

"You're not in any position to criticize. You and your brother were always so secretive. Always too good to trust anyone else."

It wasn't that we were too good to trust anyone. It was that we couldn't risk people discovering our history. They might tie us to the rumours of two street rats surviving injuries that should've killed them. And then we'd be asked questions we couldn't answer without betraying the queen's orders.

"Paul was your best friend," I said. "You could trust him."

"And yet, he didn't trust me." Ace straightened. "Well, I have secrets worth protecting, too."

"Point taken."

"Come on, Mouse." Ace held open the door.

Music and the low chatter of patrons spilled into the streets along with the smells of beer, cooked meat, and fried food.

My mouth watered.

As I stepped inside Buck's Tavern, dim lighting and musty warmth enveloped me. Despite the smell of stale beer and sweat, I walked forward a bit, drawn to the oddly safe feeling of the room. Ace moved in behind me, letting the door close with a thud.

The main room was small and cozy, lit by low-hanging bulbs illuminated with magic to cast a soft glow. Lining a long wraparound wooden bar, rough-looking men hunched over their drinks, while a few round tables sat empty in the open space behind them.

No one looked up at our entrance. No one approached us. This place offered anonymity and detachment from the outside world. No wonder Ace liked it. I liked it, too.

Tension slipped from my shoulders, and I took a deep breath.

On the far side of the tavern, a lone musician strummed his guitar on a small stage, singing a quiet tune loud enough to enjoy, but not so loud to overpower conversations.

"Go grab us a seat, Mouse," he said, his voice low. He jerked his chin in the direction of the booths flanking the stage. "I'll join you shortly."

I nodded and made my way to the booths with wraparound leather seating, scanning the patrons as subtly as possible. They all looked like they belonged in the same rough gang—long beards, greasy hair, and heavy leather vests over white short-sleeved shirts despite the cold temperatures.

I slipped into the booth, my thighs pressing into the cool leather, and an instant need to curl up and take a nap overcame me. Instead, I pulled off my gloves and placed them on the table.

It had been a long night, and while I was immortal and tended to be a night owl, often hunting into the early hours of the day, I didn't contain boundless energy. I wanted to go home and snuggle with Nala on the couch. She'd still be curled up near our bows in the forest right now, guarding them, and perfectly content to do so, but I wanted to cuddle. I wanted to shove my face in her thick, fluffy fur and inhale her nutty scent while she tried to slather me with her tongue.

I shook away the thoughts—I needed to keep it together around Ace.

He was already making his way to me, holding a pitcher filled with amber ale in one hand and two pint glasses in the other.

Apparently, we weren't eating.

"What's up with you?" Ace slid the pitcher over the table's lacquered surface before setting one of the empty pint glasses in front of me.

"Just missing my wolf."

He slipped into the booth on the opposite side of the table from me and pulled off his own gloves, stacking them on top of mine. He reached for the pitcher and filled my glass before his own.

"It's only been a few hours. You'll be fine." He set the pitcher down with a thud.

I scowled and reached for my drink. The glass was cool to the touch and condensation had already pebbled along the sides. "You don't get it."

"You're right, I don't." He took a long sip of beer. "Why don't you explain it to me?"

I took a sip and sputtered. The sour taste made my skin crawl. I slammed the glass back on the table and glared at Ace. "Did you piss in this?"

He chuckled and took another drink. "No."

"Did the bartender piss in this?"

"I don't believe so, no. I think I'd remember that."

I watched him drink some more and eyed my own glass.

He finally set his pint down. "We can't all have the same refined taste as you, Mouse."

I narrowed my eyes.

"And unless you want to get us thrown out of here, I suggest you keep your voice down, stop insulting the tavern's fine ale, and drink up."

I straightened in the booth and scanned the room. No one had bothered to look over, and since no one sat close by, we didn't have to worry about anyone easily listening in on our conversation.

Despite this, I leaned forward and dropped my voice to a whisper. "This really does taste like piss."

Ace leaned forward, too, mimicking my movement, and whispered, "I wouldn't know. But what I do know, is the more you drink, the less you give a shit about how it tastes."

"Please tell me that's not the line you use to get laid?"

His gaze darkened. "No and phaan you for thinking that."

He paused and leaned back, draping his arm over the top edge of the booth. "When I'm with a woman, I make it my sole mission to shatter her world, ruin all future lovers for her, and ensure she remembers everything I do with her and to her."

I swallowed. "You must have done a lot of practicing while you were away then because all I remember is your impeccable ability to annoy the shit out of everyone."

"Just you."

The tavern suddenly got a lot warmer, but I didn't dare fan myself. Admitting defeat, I plucked the pint from the table and took another drink.

"So?" Ace asked.

"Still tastes like piss."

He glanced at the ceiling as if divine intervention would blast through the ceiling and rescue him from my presence. "So, you were going to tell me about your familiar."

"I think I'd remember that." My lips twitched as I tried to keep a stern expression on my face.

"Funny," Ace said. "But I'm asking you to tell me about your familiar. We're going to be here for a few hours, and as much as I enjoy drinking in tortured silence, I'd genuinely like to know about you and your wolf."

I sank back in the booth. His words were surprisingly honest and without mockery. I narrowed my eyes. What was the catch?

He sighed and held up both hands as if surrendering to the power of my glare.

"Fine." I relented. "What would you like to know?"

He shrugged. "Anything? Everything? Familiars are rare. Almost as rare as any decent information about them. There aren't a lot of bonded galeons."

And now there were two less than before. "Lots of stories, though."

He reached out, grabbed his pint, and lifted it as if to silently toast my statement.

"There's not much to tell," I said. "A little bit after

you left, I started working for the queen as a hunter. I often patrolled the edges of the Danu Forest. When I walked by the woods, I felt this indescribable tug, this pull to enter and head north."

"And you listened? You weren't worried about a someone using their magic on you or the consequences of entering the forest without permission?"

"I didn't consider it," I said. "I'm immortal."

"Yes, but until you found and bonded to your familiar, you were still killable."

"Right." I looked away and drummed my fingers along the smooth surface of the table. "I guess I've always suffered from overconfidence."

I didn't dare look at him.

Paul always said the key to successfully lying was to keep as close to the truth as possible.

"At least you're on the path of self reflection," Ace said.

I barked out a laugh and took a deep drink of the cold ale. Ace was right. The more I drank, the less I cared how it tasted. My whole mouth was numb now.

"So, what happened? You felt a tug, tramped through the woods..."

A smile spread across my face as the memory of meeting Nala for the first time resurfaced. "I remember it like it was yesterday," I said. "I stepped into this small field with a gentle slope and Nala appeared at the top of the hill. The sun had crested the surrounding trees at the same time, so the light hit her in such a way it looked as though she glowed."

"Sounds magical."

I paused, studying his face to detect any sarcasm. Finding none, I continued. "She saw me, yipped in excitement, sped down the hill and barrelled into me."

Ace sat back and crossed his arms over his chest. "She's way too dignified for that kind of behavior."

I shook my head. "She took me right out—knocked my legs from under me. I laid on my back with Nala standing over me, thinking about what a big idiot I was for wandering into the Danu Forest and how I was most likely going to be eaten by a wolf."

Ace leaned forward, beer forgotten. "And?"

"And after our powers merged and my magic unlocked, Nala licked me clean across the face. She had terrible breath." I paused, ruminating over the comment. "She still has terrible breath."

A soft smile tugged at his lips. "She really does."

We sat in companionable silence, drinking the horrible ale.

"Have you ever returned to the clearing?" Ace asked.

"No."

"Why not?" Ace asked.

"Can't find it."

Ace frowned. "I don't believe that. You have always had a great sense of direction."

I shrugged and tried to shake off the sting in his words. I had tried to find the clearing more than once—for Paul's sake—but I'd never succeeded. "It's the truth. I think the clearing shows itself when a familiar is ready to bond to you. We're immortal, so it makes sense that not all of us find our familiars right away. Aside from desperate hunters, I find a lot of galeons wandering the forest trying to find the clearing. Some I find after they've starved to death or met a predator. Some I find before and those ones always demand I tell them the location. When I tell them I can't, they call me a liar."

"I'm sorry. I didn't know," he said.

"It's okay." I took another sip of ale. "What about you?"

"What about me?"

"Why don't you tell me something about yourself now that I've shared my magical moment with Nala."

He grimaced and looked away. "There's not much to tell."

"Oh, I don't know. I think you might have a few things to share that would interest me."

"Like what?"

"Like what made you decide to be a hunter? Or maybe start with when you discovered you had phaaning magic and what you can do with your power." I had so many other questions I wanted to ask. When had he lived in the city? If it was before he lived in Perga, why hadn't we cross paths as children? I was also from the city after all. Or is this where he'd gone after he left us? But if this is where he'd been all this time, why hadn't we crossed paths in Wast more recently? It's not like I hadn't been to the city since he left Perga. And why did he leave without saying anything? Sure, he didn't owe me a thing, but why hadn't he said goodbye to Paul? They had been best friends, inseparable.

Something dark flashed across Ace's gaze. He pressed his lips together, and he sank into his seat.

Maybe I should've started with a lighter question, like his middle name, or whether he preferred cats or dogs, instead of asking why he'd decided to become a hunter. Though I knew the answer to both those questions—he didn't have a middle name and dogs, always dogs.

"My sister," he said, finally breaking the silence between us.

His sister?

When did he have a sister? He'd been an orphan like us—one of the reasons we'd gravitated together. Why had he never mentioned a sister until now? Where had she been all this time?

I waited, dying to blurt out all the questions rampaging in my mind, but something about his expression told me this wasn't a happy story. I had to be patient.

Not my best trait, but Ace needed to tell the story in his own time.

He sighed and took a long drink of beer, finishing off the rest of the pint before placing it on the table.

Instinctively, I reached forward, grabbed the pitcher, and refilled his glass.

"My sister was killed in a forest not unlike your own."

I sat up in the booth. "When?"

"Before we met. I looked up to her and it was just the two of us for so long."

I swallowed, knowing the feeling. It had been Paul and I against the world when we were on the streets, when it was just the two of us. Sometimes, I missed that time when we were so close, I knew what ran through his head without him saying a word. I missed that closeness. Now, I missed him even when he was in the same room.

The rift started when I found my familiar and grew once he started working for the royals. Despite trying to keep him close, we kept growing apart, and I didn't know how to fix it. I didn't even know if there was anything to fix or whether this was just part of growing up. I didn't like it, though. It stung, and I wanted my brother back.

I cleared my throat. "What happened to her?"

"I'm sure I don't need to remind you how feral people have become in their desperation for food and supplies especially during harsh winters and how some are overprotective of what they view as their hunting grounds."

I squeezed my eyes shut and took a deep breath. He didn't need to elaborate. With that short statement, I connected the dots and figured out how he'd lost his sister.

"This all happened when I was a young boy. I vowed that day when I found her with three arrows in her chest that I would become a hunter to make this world a safer place for people like my sister. That's why I moved to Perga."

"You never said anything. At least not to me." How had he kept all that to himself? Sure, he was fourteen when we met, but he'd gone through his teen years grieving alone.

"I didn't want to voice a dream," he said. "It felt as if speaking it out loud would somehow make it even more insurmountable."

"Yet, you're here."

He raised his pint. "I'm here."

I ran through his words again. "What do you mean people like your sister?" Did he mean young, female, both? Something else? I had to know.

"Weak," he said. "I don't mean that in a negative way. Some people are too soft for this hard world."

I nodded, knowing what he meant. I'd seen enough soft individuals on the streets. They never lasted long. "So, you became a hunter to protect the weak?"

"Yes."

"Have you ever thought about using your knowledge and expertise to teach the weak to protect themselves?"

Ace's head snapped up. He narrowed his eyes as he studied my face.

I shrugged and took another sip of ale. "I'm not being flippant. And I'm definitely not trying to give you shit. It's a genuine question. Given your skills with a bow, I think you'd be quite good at it."

"You're also good with a bow. Why have you never tried teaching?"

"Well, that's easy enough to explain."

Ace waved his hand at me to continue while he drank more beer.

"I didn't get into hunting for the same reasons as you."

"And what were your reasons?" Ace asked. "Most galeons like to flock to the city and kiss the king's ass to live in splendor."

"You want to hunt to protect weak humans. I hunt to protect the forest from weak humans."

Ace chuckled, the pinched expression on his face fading away as he relaxed. "You're such an idealist."

"And you're such an asshole."

That earned me a true laugh. His gaze brightened and he leaned forward. "Tell me, Mouse. Do you still hate me?"

"Of course. You're arrogant, rude and over-estimate your significance."

His smile widened. "I'm beginning to think you don't hate those things as much as you want to."

I waved his comment off, but deep down, I worried he was right. "We were born to hate each other. I've made peace with it."

Ace hesitated, his gaze shifting to the side. "I don't hate you as much as you think I do."

"What?"

"I didn't leave by..." Something dark flashed in his gaze and he leaned forward. He opened his mouth to say more when the door to the tavern opened and the room grew quiet.

A woman in a hooded cloak walked into the tavern and let the door slam shut behind her. Along with the heavy winter cloak, she wore riding boots, black leather pants and a woven shirt, but something told me this woman lived a life of luxury. Her boots and the hem of her cloak were too clean, the weave of her shirt too tight.

I sucked in a breath. The hooded cloak drawn up around her face did little to hide her identity from me. Whisps of magic flowed off her like the seductive caress of a late-night lover. I'd recognize the potency of the power anywhere.

"Queen Titania," I whispered.

30

The queen's magic curled around me as I swallowed a number of conflicting emotions along with the piss-tasting beer. Queen Titania always elicited a mixture of feelings. She'd saved me and Paul from a life on the streets, but as I learned over the next few years, she never did anything with purely altruistic motivations. She helped us because it benefitted her in some way. Sure, having an immortal guardian helped her protect the familiars in the forest, but Dita or Shona could've done the job as well. My aim was better, but they could be just as deadly, surely.

To this day, I waited for the reveal—for the queen to finally share why she'd saved us all those years ago.

Ace stiffened in his seat beside me, his grip on his glass tightening. His knuckles were white from the pressure.

I scanned the sparse crowd, but after the initial moment of silence to observe the newcomer, the locals went back to their quiet mutterings and stared down at their near-empty pint glasses.

There was something different about Queen Titania tonight, her usual air of regality was gone, replaced with something else. Not quite urgency, but unease, maybe. Her gaze, a piercing shade of blue, darted around the room, searching for something or someone. Then her gaze locked onto mine, and a shiver crawled down my spine.

Oh no.

"Looks like you get to meet her after all," I said.

"Fantastic," Ace replied, his tone flat and devoid of emotion.

The Queen of Wast approached our table, her steps quick and purposeful. The air grew heavy, as if burdened by her presence. The queen always had a way of making me feel small and insignificant.

Like a mouse.

I grimaced and forced my face and body to relax.

Ace slowly released his grip on his glass. His face was etched with an indecipherable emotion. He certainly didn't look happy.

The queen left her hood drawn up, but long cascades of her moon bright hair had escaped, and the hood couldn't hide her pale and regal features—the same features the musician quietly crooned about no less than ten feet away.

The queen glanced over at the stage and her lips quirked up briefly. "I like this song."

Of course, she did.

"Greetings, my—"

The queen pinned Ace with a fierce glare and her magic wrapped around him as a silent threat.

He snapped his lips closed.

She wanted to keep her identity secret. In addition to using a cloak to cover most of her face, she'd ditched her scandalous dress and entourage from earlier. Had she spent this time searching every pub in Wast or did she come straight here? She'd come here to talk to us, that much was obvious, but how did she know where to find us?

Ace cleared his throat and tried again. "How can we help you?"

"Help?" She sneered. "I don't need help from you, boy."

"Yet, I highly doubt our meeting is a coincidence," he said.

She squinted at him and pressed her lips together. Apparently, I wasn't the only one he annoyed. "May I join you?"

"Of course." I slid over in my seat to make room for her, kicking Ace's leg under the table as a warning. Personally, I tried to antagonize the queen as little as possible. I might give a lot of snark and attitude when I received her orders, but I always watched my words in her presence.

"Where's Odin?" I asked. Her familiar usually went everywhere with her.

"Around."

Huh. Maybe that's how she found us—she'd sent her

raven familiar to keep an eye on our group. I'd even bet my last gale she'd spotted us in the crowd earlier, but instead of calling us out, she sent Odin to follow us. Now that sounded like something the queen would do.

A chill ran along my spine. If she had sent Odin, that meant the familiar had seen us enter and exit the Death House.

Exactly how much did the queen know?

"Nice scratch." The queen nodded at Ace's neck.

"Thank you," Ace replied. He brushed his fingers along the angry red mark I'd left with my blade.

"I'm thirsty." Queen Titania glanced at the pitcher of beer and then at Ace.

"I'll get another glass," he grumbled, sliding from the booth to stalk toward the bar. Tension knotted his shoulders, making his movement stiffer than normal.

"We don't have much time," Queen Titania said. "I assume you know of Dita and Shona's murders?"

"Yes."

"And I'm also assuming from your brother's not so subtle bribes of the guards and a report of a break-in at the Death House, you're aware an immortal is behind these murders."

I grimaced. "Also, yes."

"Do you know what can kill a bonded galeon descendent?"

"Up until a few days ago, I would've said nothing."

The queen nodded, her body stiff, her gaze scanning the crowd. "Do you know what they used to call phaanons?"

I jerked back in my seat. That question had come out of nowhere. What did the phaanons have to do with anything these days besides starring in Sley's fantasies and being used as a swearword?

"No, I don't," I said.

"The curse of immortals."

I froze, not liking where this conversation headed. "Are you suggesting what I think you're suggesting?"

"Phaanons were the only creatures capable of killing galeons."

I sucked in a breath. "But they're gone."

"Because they were too dangerous to let live."

"Exactly, so it can't be a phaanon."

The queen hummed. "Maybe, maybe not. Either someone has found a source of the weapon the phaanons once used on our kind, or the phaanons aren't as dead as they should be. Given my husband's absolute obsession with eradicating phaanons and chasing down any potential sighting, I'm going to assume the former."

"But...how?"

The queen snarled. "I'm not sure and I despise not knowing. All we have are rumours and bedtime stories. The truth has been lost. Or more accurately, destroyed."

"What do you mean?"

"Not only were the phaanons too dangerous to live, but all the information about them and how they killed us was too dangerous to keep too. So like the phaanons, we destroyed it all. I was only young, then. Too young to remember much of anything. But one thing is abundantly clear." She stopped scanning the crowd and turned her ice-blue gaze to me. "You must find who is behind this."

"Why me?"

"You know why. An immortal with impeccable aim who has arrows with magical fletching is responsible for these deaths. If you don't hunt down those responsible, you will become the hunted. You've already been marked."

All the air whooshed out of my lungs and the beer turned sour on my tongue. "Marked?"

Ace had received an empty glass from the grizzly bartender and turned back toward us.

"As the main suspect," the queen said. "It's only a matter of time, now, before my husband comes after you." She leaned forward and dropped her voice. "I can't protect you forever. I know who and what you are. If I can figure it out, so can others."

The queen slipped from the booth, startling Ace. He stopped a few feet away from our booth, glass in hand, and watched the queen approach him with apprehension.

"Turns out I don't need the glass after all." She patted him on the shoulder before she walked past and left the tavern without looking back.

Ace scowled at the tavern's door before joining me at the table. He slid into his seat and placed the extra empty glass on the table. "Are you going to share what that was about?"

"Nothing we didn't already know. I'm the prime suspect for the murders and I don't have a lot of time before the king's men come calling."

"We."

"What?"

"We don't have a lot of time," he said. "You're not in this alone."

I nodded, but my mind still raged, replaying the queen's words over and over again. She knew who and what I was?

"I need you to do something for me," I said, trying to keep my voice even despite the flurry of emotions.

"Okay." He leaned back in the booth and crossed his arms over his chest.

"I need you to stay here while I do something alone. I'll meet you at the gate at sunrise and we'll head back to Perga together."

He narrowed his gaze. "I don't like this idea."

"It's not an idea, it's a plan I'm putting in motion."

"What are you up to?" he asked.

I shook my head, refusing to voice any of the wild thoughts running through my mind. "This is one secret I intend to keep."

31

The fading glow of moonlight and the first hints of the impending sunrise filtered through the cracked windows, casting eerie shadows on the worn-out floor of the old orphanage. Though silence surrounded me, horrible memories of screams echoing down this hall flooded my mind the second I stepped inside. Decay and dampness clung to the air, a musty reminder of the years that had passed since I called this place home.

Ace had reluctantly agreed to let me slip away. We'd meet around the corner from Wast's main gate at sunrise. I had an hour for this side quest, and I couldn't falter, no matter how exhausted I was.

Unease washed over my whole body as I made my way down the creaking halls, my cloak swishing behind me. The doors along the hallway remained shut and locked from the outside, a painful reminder of how I'd spent my time here with my brother—some things really didn't change. Who cowered behind these doors now as I crept past?

At the end of the hall, the door to the headmaster's office was slightly ajar, inviting me to confront the demon from my past. Of course he'd be here. The man never left and tonight, I'd finally demand the answers to my past. In truth, I should've returned a long time ago. With a trembling hand, I pushed open the door.

Headmaster Marcus sat behind his desk, his aging pale face illuminated by a dim lamp flickering beside him. He looked frailer than I remembered, more pathetic. His strong arms had morphed into gnarled sticks covered in leathery skin. His hair had turned white and had thinned into greasy strings. His blue eyes, once piercing, had paled and dulled with time. His weak, watery gaze met mine and widened with surprise.

I stopped short, a few feet inside the doorway. I hadn't expected him to be up, nor sitting behind his desk. I'd hoped to catch him unaware.

"Hello, Marcus," I said. My voice remained cool and calm, a sharp contrast to the shock and raging turmoil inside me. "You're up early."

"Artemis," he said. Though old and withered, his voice still held iron strength. "I've always been an early riser. Have you returned to reminisce?"

Suppressing the anger bubbling within me, I clenched my fists. This man was supposed to be a loving, supportive father figure to us orphans, but instead, he had caused me and my brother endless pain and suffering during our time here. He was the reason we'd left, preferring to survive on the streets than languish under this man's sick interpretation of discipline.

Maybe he was up so early because he couldn't sleep with what he'd done.

"Tell me about me and my brother." I kept my voice steady and strong. "Tell me about the day we were dropped off at your doorstep."

"Or what?" Marcus tilted his head. "You'll kill me? Isn't that why you're here?"

It was.

As soon as I saw his face and the memories slammed into my mind, I'd reached a decision. Marcus wouldn't live another day to hurt anyone else. How many had he already hurt since we left? How many could I have saved if I'd returned sooner?

"Yes," I said.

He sighed and leaned back in his chair, steepling his fingers on the desk in front of him. "Then why have a conversation at all? Why not get on with it?"

"You're dead no matter what," I continued. "You get to choose how you leave this world—will your death be slow and painful, or will it be quick?"

He didn't deserve the mercy, but I'd offer it anyway because I wasn't into torture, and I wanted answers.

Marcus stiffened in his seat, his gaze shifting side to side as if looking for a way out, and his smile slipped away.

"I'm giving you more choice than you ever gave us." I stepped closer. "And no one is going to save you. Even if they wanted to, which I doubt, how could they when you've locked them away?"

Marcus grunted, his mouth turning down in a sneer. "There's no one left. It's just me in this pustule of a building."

"Then why are you here?" I asked.

"Waiting."

"For what? Redemption?" That had fled long ago.

"Closure." He pressed his lips together. "Maybe then I can escape this place."

That made no sense, but I wasn't here to figure out the inner mechanisms of Marcus' mind and at least now I didn't need to figure out what to do with a bunch of children. There was some justice in the world, it seemed. "Then start talking."

"About you and Apollo?" Marcus leaned back in his chair. "There's not much to say. You and your brother were trouble from day one and needed every ounce of the discipline you received."

"We were kids. Children. We needed affection and a father figure, and you gave us stern words, coldness and if we misbehaved in any way, you gave us pain. There's no point in trying to explain why that was so incredibly wrong or damaging. It won't erase the memories or what you did." I took a deep breath. "I don't need to rehash any of that. I want to know more about when and how we arrived at the orphanage."

Marcus studied my face for a moment as if contemplating whether to tell me the truth or not. Maybe I needed to remind him of what awaited him at the end of this conversation.

"We estimated you were a year old when you arrived on our doorstep," Marcus said, finally breaking the silence. "You were both covered in wounds and wrapped in blankets soaked in blood."

My heart thudded painfully at his words. "Wounds?"

"Cuts on your face, arms, legs. Even your ears," Marcus continued. He perked up a little as if he enjoyed sharing this information. Knowing him, he probably did. Maybe I shouldn't have offered him a choice after all. Maybe I should rethink my stance on torture.

"I don't think there was any part of either of you left unscathed." His blunt words hit me like a physical blow, but I refused to let him see how much they hurt.

"What happened to my parents?" I pressed on, needing to know the truth. "Do you know anything about them?"

"Your parents?" He chuckled hollowly. "I never met or saw them. The only evidence they existed besides you and Apollo was a scrap of paper they left with your names on it."

"Scrap of paper?"

He nodded and opened his desk drawer, pulling out a ripped, yellowing piece of paper. He flapped it back and forth over the flickering flame. "Is it worth my life?"

"No." Though the paper had been worth enough for Marcus to keep it readily available after all these years.

The paper was maybe half a hand in length and three fingers wide. Black ink marked our names in the centre—

J. C. MCKENZIE

Artemis & Apollo. Nothing more, nothing less. But the slope of the letters and the style of the & symbol made a tight band of pain squeeze the air from my lungs.

Marcus sighed and dropped the paper on his desk.

"You kept it all these years?"

"I'm not sure I could throw it away if I tried," he said.

"What do you mean?"

"I've tried to destroy it. I've tried to give it away and I've tried to leave it outside the building. Each time, it finds its way back to my desk drawer. I suspect the same magic is what keeps me here."

That...that was not what I expected. "You're stuck here?"

He nodded, face grim. "I can leave for short periods of time, but if I try to stay away, I'm overcome with pain. I have been held prisoner by this building since the day I plucked you and your brother off the steps and touched this cursed note. And that's what this note is—cursed. Like you and your brother."

"I am not cursed."

"Maybe. Maybe not. But you are a curse to others. To me. You weren't normal children. Especially you and the way birds always followed you in the courtyard. No wonder your parents abandoned you here. You should be grateful I took it upon myself to teach you the lessons your so-called parents couldn't. But instead, you ran away, leaving me trapped here."

"You enjoyed hurting us," I whispered through

gritted teeth, while my mind still reeled. I didn't remember the birds following me when I lived in the orphanage. I hadn't noticed them until I was older, and I certainly hadn't realized someone other than my brother had made the connection. And cursed? Why would we be cursed? "Don't act like you did us a favour."

"You deserved it," Marcus spat back. "Little devil children sent to torment me. I knew one of you would be back one day. I knew this note would pull you back."

The note had nothing to do with me returning, but I wanted that piece of paper. Someone had placed enough magic on it to see to its survival. They must've wanted me and Paul to have it.

I gripped the hilt of my dagger and stepped forward. Before I could make a move toward the man who had haunted my nightmares for years, the door swung open and revealed the silhouette of another man.

I sucked in a breath as Ace stepped into the room.

Was he here to stop me?

Without a word, he closed the door behind him and stood beside me, his gaze unwavering and determined. "If you can't do it, I will."

Shock coursed through me at his words. He had heard everything—the truth, the pain, and the anger. For a moment, I hesitated, unsure if I could go through with this on my own. But then, Ace nodded at me, silently offering his support.

One last time, I met Marcus's gaze, feeling a storm of emotions rage within me. He would finally pay for the pain he caused me, my brother, and all the other kids all those years ago. I raised my dagger and took a step forward.

32

The early morning air carried the biting promise of the winter season's impending arrival. Dew pebbled on the orange leaves and moisture clung to the yellow grass. The sun would evaporate everything soon enough, but right now the forest around me glistened with the promise of a new day.

Ace hadn't pressed me for details after we left the orphanage. His gaze kept sliding to me and he opened his mouth more than once to say something, only to shut it again.

We'd left the body of the headmaster to rot in his office, and hopefully, I'd never speak or think of the vile man again. Before we'd left, I'd swiped the paper with my name and my brother's name on it and now it burned in my pocket.

When I'd touched the paper without my gloves on, I felt nothing. My fingers didn't tingle, and I felt no magical curse. When I read the words, however, my stomach twisted in a knot. The writing looked so familiar, but I needed to be sure before I let my mind spiral out of control.

The streets we left behind had been empty from the normal midday riffraff, and only hard-working vendors rushed around to prepare for the market. Merchants arrived and left through the city's main entrance, and we'd slipped out of Wast without causing a scene or drawing attention to ourselves.

"About earlier," Ace said, finally ending his silence.

"I don't want to talk about it."

"No... I know. I just..." Ace shook his head and took a deep breath. "I'm sorry, Mouse."

I paused on the hill and turned to him.

"That's all I wanted to say," he said. "I'm sorry you had to go through that."

I nodded and turned away, my eyes stinging. I refused to shed another tear for my childhood, for that man. Ace took the hint and remained silent as we hiked up the hill toward the forest.

By the time we reached Nala and our bows, the sun had crested the horizon, and the city bustled with noise on the other side of the bridge behind us.

Nala had curled up in a tight ball at the base of the salal bushes, her nose tucked into her hind legs. At our approach, her head popped up, and she let out an excited yip.

I blinked and she was right in front of me with a wide grin, jumping up and knocking me to the ground.

Pinning me in the dirt with both paws on my chest, she licked my face.

"Ugh." I reached up and grabbed her face to ruffle her fur. "I missed you, too, you big baby."

She kept licking, and I thrashed side to side to avoid her tongue in my mouth.

"Nala, stop it." I pushed her away, or at least tried to. She was very persistent. "Ace, help."

He chuckled somewhere off to the side. "You're on your own, Mouse."

I rolled and slowly got up, which was hard to do with a giant wolf insistent on keeping her snout in my face.

"That's enough." I pushed her head away with a laugh.

She whined, but thankfully settled down while I wiped the saliva off my face with my shirt sleeve.

Ace leaned against a tree, arms crossed with his one leg bent to hook his ankle over the other. His lips quirked up at the corners. "Now, I guess I know where that mouth's been."

"You sound jealous." I scratched Nala behind the ears. "Want a kiss?"

He shook his head. "Tempting, but no."

I paused and met his gaze over Nala's fluffy fur. He stood off to the side, his stance radiating quiet danger, relaxed but at the same time ready to launch into battle. He looked tired, and despite being with me, he looked lonely. Almost sad.

Nala whined again and Ace tore his gaze away from

me. Without a word, he retrieved our weapons and held out my bow and quiver.

"Thanks," I said. I ran my hand over the fletching in my quiver. I set out with eight and eight remained. How did the killer or killers gain access to my arrows? Did they steal them from my house? My kills? Or had they expertly copied me? I should've stolen the murder weapon from the Death House to compare the arrow-head and the twine.

"All there?" Ace nodded at my quiver.

"Yeah." I glanced at a bed of spongy moss. "I could take a nap right here."

"In less than an hour, you can be in your own bed." Ace buckled his quiver around his hips and strung his bow across his shoulders. "Let's get back to Perga."

I glanced back at the path that led to the city. Paul could take care of himself, but we hadn't discussed a plan if we'd become separated.

"He's either way ahead of us or he'll follow us when it's a more decent hour," Ace said. "If he's still in the city, he'll see our missing bows when he comes this way. He can take care of himself."

"I know," I said.

"It will be okay, Mouse."

"I know." I reluctantly followed Ace along the path and tried to shake away the heat building inside my chest. Why was he being kind? Caring? Thoughtful? And why did I have to respond this way?

I couldn't possibly like this asshole again. I'd spent way too much time in my youth liking him, obsessing about him, having a giant crush. Just because he was giving me some attention now, didn't mean I had to return those feelings. It certainly didn't mean I should forget all the pain he'd caused me and Paul.

Nala trotted along beside me, her fuzzy face constantly turning up so she could lock those dark eyes on me. She bumped her body into my leg every third step or so as if to reassure herself that I was really there beside her. She still limped a little—her injury likely bothering her after staying put in colder weather overnight. I'd bathe her in heat and feed her some rich meat when we got home to make up for having to sleep outside.

Neither Ace nor I spoke.

We made it back to Perga in record time. The cool morning air clung to the edges of the town as Ace and I walked down the main road. As we passed the warm glow of the bakery, the scent of freshly baked bread beckoning me closer, Maria's voice cut through the morning like a sweet melody. "Emi! Ace! How'd the hunting go?"

She'd opened the window where she sold the baked goods and leaned over the counter, her ample breasts squished and on display just as much as the pastries in the basket beside her.

I looked away from the curiosity in her gaze, unwilling to share any of the details of our trip, and scanned the pastries instead.

Ace mumbled something that sounded like, "Fine."

Maria picked up the end of her braid and coiled it around her finger. "See anything you like, Ace?"

275

"Uh, yeah. I'd like one of those cinnamon rolls, please."

"For you? Anything." She picked one up and placed it in a paper bag before holding it out to Ace. He stepped forward and placed some gales on the counter. "It's for my partner, actually. If she stares at it any harder, I'm worried she'll start moaning."

I reached out and smacked him.

Instead of retaliating, he held out the bag. "Here. You're drooling."

"Thanks." I snatched the bag from his hand and pulled off one of my gloves, tucking it under my arm. Still not sure how to handle Ace playing nice, I turned back to Maria as I pulled a piece of the roll free from the bag. "I was talking to Blake earlier about that red scarf he always used to wear, and he mentioned you had it."

I bit into the soft dough, sugar and spice coating my lips and tongue. "Phaan, this is good."

Maria chuckled and lifted her brows. "Well, I might've borrowed Blake's scarf for a while. A little memento, you know, to keep warm during the chilly nights."

"Where is it now?" I already knew. I'd retrieved it with Sley in the storage house and it was our best clue for tracking down the thieves. I wanted to know who had it last.

"Your brother's place," she replied, a sly grin playing on her lips. "Left it there after a rather enchanting evening."

I paused with a piece of pastry halfway to my mouth. "Gross."

Maria cackled.

I shoved the roll in my mouth, wanting to distract my brain from the disturbing thought of my brother being... well, my brother.

The sugar coated my tongue, and I swallowed another bite. Danu, this was so good. I closed my eyes and licked my lips.

"Maybe getting you that was a mistake." Ace shifted uncomfortably beside me and grimaced.

Maria turned to him, her gaze lingering. "Ace, darling, now that Emi here is taken care of, are you sure I can't help you moan like that?"

I choked on my mouthful of pastry.

"I'm good," Ace said, his gaze still locked on my lips.

"If you're interested," Maria continued. "I could show you how Paul and I used the scarf."

"I'm not interested." He reached out and thumped the flat of his hand on my back as I coughed.

Maria's eyes widened, and her cheeks flushed red.

"Thanks for the cinnamon roll." Ace grabbed my arm and turned us to leave.

I let him lead me away from the bakery as I happily inhaled the rest of the cinnamon roll. After licking my lips clean, I said, "I might need to destroy the scarf. It might be evidence, but it seems to get around and I think setting it on fire is the only viable option at this point."

Ace shook his head, a smile playing at his lips. Before

he could reply, I spotted O'Reilly at the end of the road and stopped in my tracks.

The old man stooped over the gnarled old stick he used as a cane, his weathered face scowling in our direction. Despite his appearance, I half-expected him to chase after us waving his cane and yelling threats. Instead, he shuffled away without a word, disappearing into the darkness.

"It's just O'Reilly," Ace reassured me. "He's harmless."

"You didn't think that when he caught you pissing into his flowerpot," I said, pulling my glove back on. "We were over on the main street and even from there we heard you screaming as you ran away."

"I was like eight," Ace said as he took the path toward my cabin.

"Your memory must be failing you at this old age. You were almost fifteen at the time."

We reached my cabin and walked up the few steps to my door. Ace hesitated and turned to me.

"What now?" I asked.

He leaned against the door frame. He crossed his arms over his chest, and from his smug expression, he was about to say something incredibly infuriating.

"Finally." Orion spoke from the path behind us. "You guys are back."

Ace blanked his expression, shifting his focus to Orion with a detached mask.

I shot Nala a glare. "Where's the warning?"

Nala pinged her ears back and lowered her head.

I reached out and ruffled her fur to let her know I wasn't serious. "You're a good girl, the very best girl." I turned toward the healer. "Hey, Rye."

From the creases in his clothing and the state of his hair, Orion looked like he'd slept in his hunting gear and rolled out of bed before coming here. His hair stuck up and out in all directions. Dark circles lined the undersides of his eyes and lines creased his cheeks as if he'd fallen asleep on an uneven surface.

"Are you okay?" I asked.

"I'm fine." His gaze snagged on Ace, dropping to the wound on his neck. "Did you guys get attacked?"

Ace raised his eyebrows. "In a matter of speaking."

"Did you want me to heal that for you?" Orion asked, biting out the words like it cost him years of his life to make the offer.

Ace raised his hands to gently trace the line of the scratch. "No. I find I quite like this mark."

"Your choice." Orion jerked his chin toward my door. "Let's go inside. I have some news."

33

We shuffled into my small cabin, and I shut the door behind us. Nala limped off to the bedroom, and after hanging my bow, I followed. She'd already hopped onto the bed—our bed—by the time I reached the room. I sat on the edge and reached out to pet her. "Leg's bugging you, huh?"

She chuffed and squirmed over to nuzzle my side with her wet nose. I wrapped my hands around her furry body. "I'm sorry you had to sleep outside with the dampness and cold. You're the bestest."

"Emi?" Orion called from down the hall.

"Coming." I gave Nala a few more pets before leaving her. I shut the door behind me, preventing her from following. She needed to rest. Hopefully, she'd heal some more with time and warmth.

I found Ace and Orion sitting at my small dining table glaring at each other.

"Is everything all right in here?" I asked.

Ace broke the staring match first and let a cocky grin spread across his face. "Of course, Mouse. Onion was just explaining some territorial issues with the forest."

I narrowed my eyes. "Territorial issues?"

"Just where the boundaries are." Orion did not meet my gaze. "And it's Orion."

"Huh." I rocked back on my heels. These two were full of shit, but I had no desire to delve into their issues—too tired and too cold. "Do either of you want something to drink?"

"No," they said in unison.

I pulled out the chair at the end of the table. "Then I guess we better get straight to business. We need to figure out why someone is targeting bonded galeons."

"Not just why, but how," Ace added.

"I might have an answer to the how." Orion licked his lips. "I did a little more testing on the arrow's poison. It's immortal magic."

"We knew that already," Ace said. "Hardly ground-breaking."

Orion scowled at my partner before returning to me. "It's not just that. It's pure."

"Pure?" I asked. "What do you mean?"

"We all thought immortal bloodlines had diluted over generations Growing weaker and weaker from the time when pureblood galeons and phaanons mingled with humans. But this isn't diluted. We're looking for a pureblood galeon."

You've already been marked. The queen's warning

echoed in my head as I stared at Orion with my mouth open.

"A pureblood galeon?" I straightened in my seat. "Like the king and queen?"

Orion nodded.

Ace leaned forward, placing his elbow on the table to prop his head up with his hand. "We could be looking for a phaanon, too, couldn't we? They're also immortal."

"They don't exist," Orion said. "Not anymore, anyway."

"It would explain why galeons are being targeted." Ace shrugged.

"Unlikely. That would mean there's a pureblood phaanon running around, using their magic, recruiting men to kill bonded galeons. Someone would've tattled. We would've heard something."

"Well, we're hearing something now," Ace muttered.

Orion sat back in his chair. "If I was a phaanon, I'd hide. I certainly wouldn't be sticking my neck out and risking discovery. An entire army of galeons would take up arms and hunt me down." Orion shook his head. "There's just no way a phaanon has been involved without being detected."

"Speaking of detection," I said. "How do we detect a pureblood? Galeon or phaanon?"

"Well, phaanons are easy to spot," Orion said.

"Because you've seen so many?" Ace asked.

"No." Orion touched the top of his ears and raised his hands. "Because they have pointy ears. Or at least that's what the history books say."

"So pointy ears and phaanons aside, how do we detect a pureblood galeon?" I asked. "With the exception of self-declaring, like the king and queen, what characteristics set pureblood galeons apart from descendants? Couldn't they just exist among us without anyone noticing?"

"I heard pureblood galeons don't need a familiar to be unkillable," Ace said.

"Rumours," I replied, willing my breath to remain steady.

Ace narrowed his eyes.

"And we can't exactly go around stabbing unbonded galeons to see if they survive," I said.

Orion nodded. "But we need to find one."

"What do you suggest?" Ace asked. "Prick testing the entire legion of hunters?"

"Maybe it's the king," Orion said.

"Why would the king kill his loyal subjects?" I asked. Orion had shared his distaste for the royals before, so I wasn't surprised he suspected them of murder, but this didn't make sense.

"Maybe they weren't so loyal," Orion said.

"I've been loyal," I said. "And I'm being set up."

Orion frowned. "Set up?"

"They're using my arrows."

Orion flinched. He opened his mouth to say more, but Ace interrupted.

"Maybe it's not the king," Ace said.

"And maybe we should figure out the motive first," I

said. "That would help us narrow down a list of suspects."

"The queen is also a pureblood galeon," Orion said.

"We saw her in Wast—twice. She wants the person responsible for these killings as much as we do. I don't think it's her." A shiver ran up my spine, and I snapped my fingers. "We saw the queen yesterday in the Main Square with Paul. He acted weird about it, but what if he's figured out something? What if he knows something about her or the king that we don't?"

"Are you suggesting your own brother is keeping the royals' involvement with the arrows a secret from you?" Ace lifted both eyebrows. "His own twin?"

"What? Of course not. He doesn't even know about the connection between the arrows magic and the bloodlines yet."

"Where is your brother?" Orion asked. "I went by his place before coming here and he wasn't home."

"He had to run interference with the coroner, so we could escape the Death House," I explained. "If he didn't come home last night, he'll be back soon enough. When he returns, I'll confront him with what we discovered and see what he knows."

Orion frowned. "The coroner? You were at the Death House last night?"

"Yeah," I said. "We didn't get anything other than the same magic killed both immortals. That's how we figured out I'm being set up. We saw my arrow."

Orion stared at me. He opened his mouth and then shut it again.

"What?" I asked.

He straightened in his seat and blinked rapidly as if waking himself up. It had been a long night and day. My bed and snuggling with my familiar called to me.

"Carla is dead," Orion said.

"Who?" Ace asked.

"The coroner."

"What?" I pushed back from the table. "Since when?"

"Since last night," Orion said.

"How...how did you find out so fast?" I asked.

"Blake."

That messenger travelled fast. He had to have been ahead of us on the trail, carrying the news with him. But how did he find out so quickly? Was the death public? Had the queen known before she found us in the tavern?

"Originally, I didn't think it was worth noting," Orion continued. "Plenty of people die in Wast and Carla's not immortal, but she is...was...performing autopsies on them."

"And that's why you think she was killed?" I filled in the blank. But where was my brother? He wouldn't have killed the coroner to cover for us. And he certainly wasn't trying to suppress information about the immortals' deaths—that was why we were there in the first place. He was the one who got us in.

He better be okay.

"Was anyone found with her?" I asked. Where was Paul? Was he hurt? Was he hiding? Had something happened when he was with the coroner? Had someone captured him while he was with the coroner and killed the coroner to cover their tracks?

My mind scrambled through the possibilities while my heart raced, and my skin prickled. Images of my brother's face flashed before my eyes.

"She was alone," Orion said. "They found her in the alley behind the lab. The guard said she returned from a late-night date to discover the lab had been broken into. She told the guards to stay behind and went to investigate, but she never returned."

I let out a long breath. My brother wasn't involved. He returned her to the Death House before her death.

"But we were long gone," Ace said. "It wasn't us, and it wasn't Paul. So, who would kill her for investigating our break-in?"

"That might not be the reason for her death." I snapped my fingers. "Maybe they had another motive, and when she stepped outside alone, they finally had their opportunity to act on it."

Ace nodded.

"That sounds most likely, but it still doesn't give us much on the motive."

"But it does raise another problem," Ace said, concern pinching his expression.

"What's that?" I asked.

"Whomever did this had to be watching the Death House. They had to be in a place ready to act when the coroner stepped outside." He looked up and met my gaze, his dark eyes flashing. "They would've seen us enter and exit the Death House."

A chill ran over my skin. If Ace was right, the unknown killer would now suspect or assume we knew whatever Carla knew.

The queen had known we were there. Did she also know who killed Carla?

Or was she the killer?

I shivered and rubbed my hands up and down my arms. The queen seemed an unlikely suspect, but I wouldn't automatically discount her just because it didn't make sense. Nothing about this made sense.

But one thing was certain. I needed to speak to my brother. "I need to sleep for at least five hours or I'm going to fall over. After that, let's go to Paul's place. He should be back from Wast by then."

"I'll sleep on your couch," Ace said.

I opened my mouth to protest.

"Something's going on and I think it's best if we stick together."

"Then I'll stay, too," Orion said. "I'll take the armchair."

Just great. Like I needed these two hovering around while I slept. "Can you two manage your territorial issues over the living room without damaging the place?"

They both scowled at each other, which didn't inspire a lot of confidence.

"Of course," Ace assured me.

Orion nodded.

I didn't believe either of them.

34

I banged my knuckles on the weathered door of Paul's cabin for the third time. The sound echoed through the quiet forest, but there was no response. Ace and Orion stood behind me, silent and tense.

After a fitful four-hour nap, I'd splashed cold water on my face and pulled on leather pants, and a vest to go over my long-sleeved shirt. My hair was a mess, but I managed to wrestle it into a ponytail. With a frustrated sigh, I reached forward and grabbed the handle. It turned easily in my hand, and I pushed open the creaky door. "Paul! If you're there, say something."

Silence greeted us.

A wave of unease prickled my spine and tugged at my scalp. The cabin was unusually cold, with no fire lit recently. Paul hadn't come home last night or this morning.

"Maybe he's still in Wast," Ace suggested. "You know your brother, Mouse. Don't jump to conclusions yet."

But I couldn't stop my mind from running off to the worst-case scenario. My thoughts raced with images of my brother lying dead in some back-alley surrounded by filth and decay while pick pockets looted his belongings, and the rest of the world continued on, oblivious to my loss.

I swallowed hard and nodded. "Let's check the cabin."

The men spread out to search the living room and kitchen while I went straight to the main bedroom. The thick curtains were drawn shut, blocking out the light. The bed had been hastily made, the cotton sheets rumpled and uneven. But Paul wasn't here. He wasn't sprawled across the covers with his usual cheeky grin or asking me about my day in that teasing tone of his.

I squeezed my eyes shut, trying to push the memories away.

A gentle hand rested on my shoulder, and I jumped, opening my eyes. When had Ace walked up behind me?

"What's that?" he pointed at the closet. A piece of fabric had been caught in the door.

With a sigh, I replied. "He's never been known for his housekeeping."

"I'm surprised the bed is made." Ace brushed past me to enter the room and walk over to the closet. As he opened the door, materials spilled out, smacking into his body before falling to the floor.

My heart stopped at the sight of leather pelts and reams of wool.

No.

I rushed over to the closet and peered inside, my nose immediately assaulted by the smell of dust and grain from the storage house. I leaned to the side and sneezed.

"What is it?" Orion appeared beside me, his voice filled with concern.

"Leather, wool and what looks like a barrel of grain," Ace answered for me.

"Leather, wool and grain?" Orion placed his hands on his hips and turned to me.

I looked away, not meeting his gaze. My mind reeled. This didn't make any sense. Why would he do this?

"What am I missing, Mouse?" Ace whispered.

"Leather, wool and grain are the supplies stolen from the storage house," Orion said. "Isn't that right, Emi?"

"A red scarf was also retrieved from the looted storage house and the same scarf was last seen with Paul," Ace added.

"He's not a thief," I said. Not anymore. Why would he do this? Why would he be working with the same men who not only framed me, but tried to kill me?

"Is he a pure blooded galeon?" Orion asked. He hesitated before adding. "Are you?"

"No, of course not," I said. My mind stumbled over the events of the last few days as if frantically trying to solve a complicated puzzle. The thief was connected to the rogue hunters and the rogue hunters were killing galeon descendants somehow with magic of a true blood immortal. It looked like they were trying to frame me for it, but what if it wasn't intentional? What if it was because Paul was involved?

Paul could be the killer.

The killer had to be immortal.

The immortal had to be a pure blood.

The immortal was killing galeon descendants.

The only immortals known to successfully kill bonded galeons were...

No. No. No. No. No.

My mind refused to accept this line of thinking.

Ace's eyebrows furrowed as he gave me a questioning look, clearly perplexed by my behaviour. Meanwhile, Orion stood in the corner of the room with a doubtful expression on his face. Rather than pushing for answers though, he turned and strode out of the bedroom, his footfalls echoing down the quiet hallway. I moved to follow, but Ace stepped in front of me, blocking my escape.

"You never knew your parents," Ace whispered. "It could be possible without you knowing."

"I'm not." I lifted my chin, despite his words touching on something I never wished to discuss.

"When did you say you got hit in the chest with an arrow?" Ace asked.

"I didn't."

He narrowed his eyes at me. "You've only lied to me three times since I returned."

"What?"

"Once when you said you were over me, once when you said you'd killed men for less, and…"

"Are you guys coming?" Orion shouted down the hall.

Ace towered over me. He leaned down to whisper in my ear, "We'll discuss this later."

Yeah, no. That wasn't going to happen. My brother couldn't be involved. He would never hurt me, and I refused to entertain the idea.

"I've been thinking about the Death House. The person or people responsible for killing Carla likely saw us entering and exiting…" Ace started as we headed out of my brother's bedroom.

"What about them?" I asked.

"They're a problem. They might suspect that whatever the coroner knew, we might possess the same information."

"We have an even bigger problem," Orion said.

"And what could that possibly be?" I asked.

"I smell smoke."

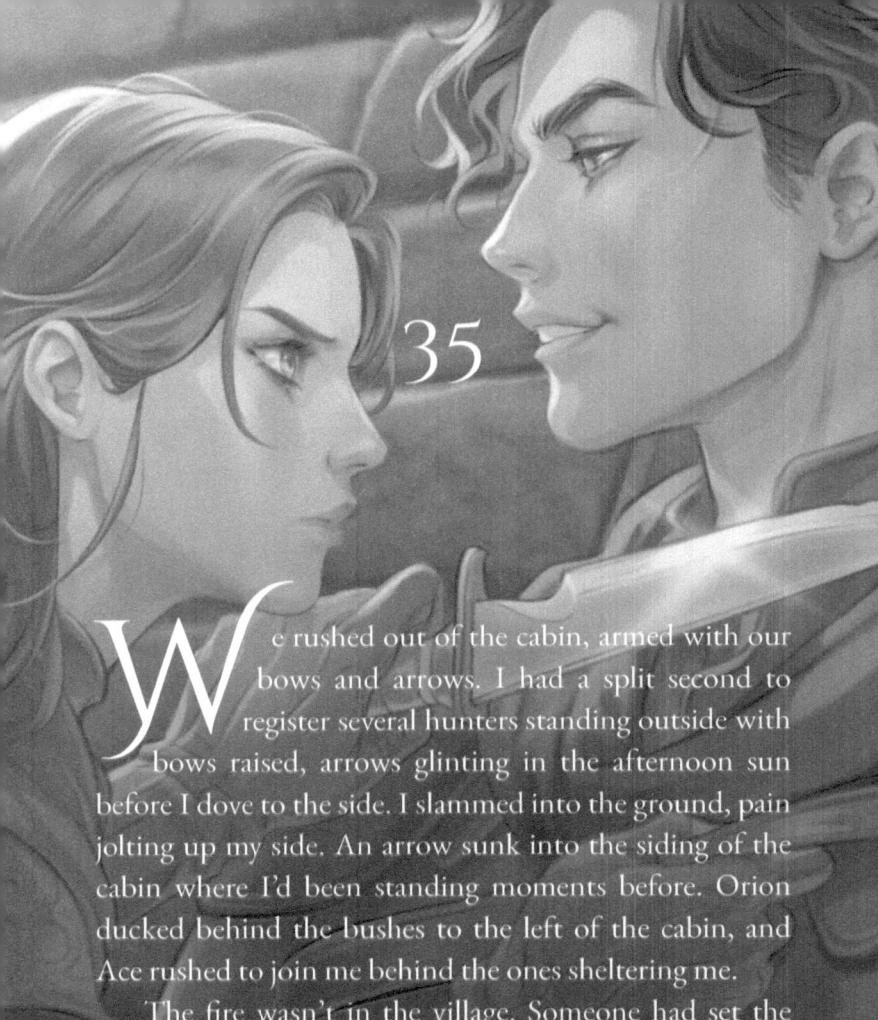

35

We rushed out of the cabin, armed with our bows and arrows. I had a split second to register several hunters standing outside with bows raised, arrows glinting in the afternoon sun before I dove to the side. I slammed into the ground, pain jolting up my side. An arrow sunk into the siding of the cabin where I'd been standing moments before. Orion ducked behind the bushes to the left of the cabin, and Ace rushed to join me behind the ones sheltering me.

The fire wasn't in the village. Someone had set the fire at the back of my brother's cabin to force us out the front. I could see it now as the flames licked up to meet the sky and smoke billowed out.

Were these the king's men or the rogue hunters? Were they here for me or my brother?

Flames rose in the distance. It wasn't just Paul's place on fire.

I scanned the trees. Smoke billowed up in the direction of my own home.

Nala.

Cold covered my entire body. My skin prickled.

My familiar was inside.

I bolted up only to have Ace lock his steely grip on my wrist and haul me to the ground.

"You can't get up, even an immortal has limits with these guys. They might have more poisoned arrows."

"My cabin is on fire," I said.

"Let it go."

"Nala is inside."

Ace hesitated. "She'll get out."

"I closed the bedroom door, Ace. She's trapped. I won't leave her," I said. "I can't leave her."

"I'll go," he said.

"What? No. She's my familiar and I'm immortal. She's my responsibility."

"You're just as vulnerable to these hunters as I am." He loosened his grip on my wrist, and his gaze softened. "You're the better archer between the two of us. Cover me."

Without waiting for a response, he sprung up from where he crouched and sprinted toward the forest.

Men hollered.

I notched my bow and stood to shoot. I kept drawing arrows from my quiver, notching and releasing, notching and releasing. Hitting target after target, their cries of alarm and the sound of their bodies hitting the ground became a highlight note to the crackling fire burning down Paul's cabin behind me.

My magic wound around me, tight and demanding.

More, it whispered. *Kill them all.*

I had three arrows left.

Then two.

Then one.

Orion joined me to shoot at the hunters, taking down enough to keep any of them from shooting at me.

I stepped toward the path leading to my cabin, and sharp pain slammed into me. I looked down to find an arrow protruding from my arm. I snarled, turned, and fired off a shot, killing the last of the hunters. With clenched teeth, I pulled out the arrow and bit back a cry.

Magic from the arrowhead spread through my body. Seeping into my bones. I winced and waited for the poison to take hold.

Nothing happened.

The poison mingled with the magic already inside my body, with the poison that already ran through my veins—a poison that my body had eventually accepted after the initial reaction.

I chucked the arrow to the ground and turned to Orion. "Come on."

We raced to my cabin, the smoke in the air burning my lungs.

Ace barged out of the front entrance of my cabin with Nala in his arms as we exited the path. Steam and smoke rose around him. Nala's eyes were closed, and she lay limp in his arms.

"She's alive," Ace said.

Shouts rose from the centre of the village.

I glanced down the path. "There might be more."

"We need to run." Orion nodded at me. "Get as far away from here as we can before that poison hits you."

"Poison?" Ace stiffened, his gaze raking my body.

"I'm fine," I said.

"But you won't be," Orion said.

"I don't think it was laced," I said.

"Poison?" Ace repeated, his voice dropping low, vibrating with danger.

"She got hit with another arrow," Orion explained.

"I'm fine," I insisted.

Orion's words from what seemed like a millennia ago echoed along my memories. *Her body will acclimatize and absorb it.*

"We're not risking it. Let's go." Ace took off around the side of the cabin toward my workshop and I followed.

"I need arrows." I ducked into the back entrance to my workshop and grabbed an armful of finished arrows. The flames licked the walls and travelled toward me. Billowy smoke gathered along the roof. I coughed as it surrounded me.

"Emi?" Ace called out.

I followed the sound of his voice and stumbled from the building.

"Come on." Orion grabbed my upper arm, careful not to break my grip on the arrows, and hauled me toward the path where Ace waited. They both wore grim expressions as they turned away from the flames.

Without a backward glance at my home going up in flames, I followed Ace into the forest.

I'd lied to both of them. The arrow had been laced, but my body didn't react to the poison—at least not like it had before.

This time my body absorbed it. I only had two explanations. Either my body had developed some sort of immunity to the poison, or I shared the same bloodline used to create this poison. That could only mean...

An immortal killer.

A pure blood.

A...

I shook my head at the possibility and swallowed.

Did he try to kill you with his blood? Sley had asked me. *I heard somewhere that's how phaanons killed galeons.*

Ace and Orion were right. We needed to run, but my reasons were rapidly changing. We needed to run because I'd figured out something they hadn't.

It wasn't that my brother might be the mastermind behind these attacks, though he was involved somehow —I knew he couldn't be responsible for targeting me. He would never harm me.

It wasn't that Paul and I were pure blooded galeons, which is what Ace, Orion and the queen suspected.

Which is what I suspected until tonight.

What I tried to keep hidden and secret all these years.

No.

Cuts on your face, arms, legs. Even your ears...

It took every ounce of self control not to reach up and touch the tips of my ears.

The curse of immortals.

A more dangerous secret lurked beneath the surface of my skin and if anyone ever dared to look, dared to question, my life would be forfeit even though I had nothing to do with the killings.

My life, my familiar and everything I'd built over the last twenty-five years would be gone.

Because I was a pureblood phaanon.

And someone was using my blood or that of my brother to kill immortals.

CHARACTERS & TERMINOLOGY

Actaeon "Ace": Emi's new partner.

Apollo "Paul": Emi's brother.

Artemis "Emi": Guardian of the Forest.

Bonded galeon: a galeon—pureblood or descendant—who has bonded to a familiar. Immortal and cannot be killed by any current day means.

Blake: queen's messenger.

Carla: Wast's coroner.

Danu: referring to the gods.

Danu Forest: forbidden forest where unbonded familiars live.

Danu river: river that runs southwest/northeast through Danu Forest.

Dita: first galeon descendent victim.

Galeon descendant: descendent of pureblood galeons. Immortal, but can be killed if unbonded.

Galeons: immortals who won the war against phaanons. Galeon (sing).

Gales: money. Currency of Wast and Vitor.

Gavin: Perga's woodworker. Graham's best friend.

Graham O'Reilly: Perga's blacksmith and Sley's ex.

King Oberon: pureblood galeon ruler of Wast.

Lesley "Sley": Emi's best friend. Supply coordinator and tailor.

Maria: Perga's baker.

O'Reilly: Graham's uncle. Former blacksmith.

Orion "Rye": Perga's healer.

Perga: town surrounded by forest and borders the

Danu/forbidden forest. Close to Wast and under the control of Wast leaders.

Phaan: referring to the underworld / hell. Also used as a slur/swear word.

Phaanons: immortals who fought the galeons and lost. Only beings capable of killing bonded galeons. Now extinct. Phaanon (sing).

Pureblood galeon: pureblood immortal who is immortal and indestructible, with or without bonding to a familiar.

Queen Titania: pureblood galeon ruler of Wast.

Shona: second galeon descendant victim.

Vitor: next city closest to Wast.

Wast: city closest to Perga.

ACKNOWLEDGMENTS

I'd like to thank Nicole, Wendy and Karen for beta reading, Lara Parker for editing, and Book Nook Nuts for proofreading.

A big thank you to Hannah Sternjakob for the beautiful cover and Koti Komori for the character art.

I'd also like to thank my readers for continuing to support me and enjoy the worlds I create.

I hope you enjoyed the story.

J. C.

...Coming Soon...

About the Author

J. C. McKenzie is a book loving, gumboot-wearing, unapologetic science geek. She predominantly writes urban fantasy and post-apocalyptic dystopian fantasy with strong romantic elements. When she's not spinning tales, she's in the classroom sharing her passion for science and mathematics while secretly warping the young, impressionable minds of our future to carry out her evil plans for world domination. She lives in the Pacific Northwest with her family.

Visit her at jcmckenzie.ca

facebook.com/j.c.mckenzie.author

instagram.com/j.c.mckenzie

tiktok.com/@jcmckenzie0

bookbub.com/authors/j-c-mckenzie

www.ingramcontent.com/pod-product-compliance
Lightning Source LLC
Chambersburg PA
CBHW020536020726
47494CB00006B/1792